- Go to **awmi.net/sg424** to download PDFs of the following resources for each lesson in this study guide:
    - Outlines
    - Discipleship Questions
    - Scriptures
- Share as many copies as you'd like.
- These documents are not for resale.

DISCOVER THE KEYS TO STAYING FULL OF GOD

by
Andrew Wommack

Study Guide

Unless otherwise indicated, all Scripture quotations are taken from the *King James Version* of the Bible.

The author has emphasized some words in Scripture quotations in italicized type.

Discover the Keys to Staying Full of God Study Guide
ISBN: 978-1-59548-115-3

Copyright © 2008 by Andrew Wommack Ministries, Inc.
P.O. Box 3333
Colorado Springs, CO 80934-3333

Contents

Introduction

Growing up in church, I was taught that Christians are leaky vessels. Like a bucket full of holes, we must continually be "refilled," and according to the average believer's experience, this seems true. God touches our lives and we become excited about it, but then—within a short period of time—we're back to being just as empty and needing something special from the Lord as we were before.

This was clearly illustrated to me through a woman who had been listening to my teaching. She told me she had seen the Lord's love for her greater than ever before. In fact, she was overwhelmed with God's unconditional love for her. But then she concluded, "I know this won't last long. It never does. In a month or so I'll be back to where I was—but I'm enjoying it now!"

Although this is what most people experience, it's not what the Lord taught. He told us that we're supposed to go "from glory to glory," not pit to pit (2 Cor. 3:18). We aren't supposed to just struggle all the time, because God's Word promises:

> Every valley shall be exalted, and every mountain and hill shall be made low: and the crooked shall be made straight, and the rough places plain.
>
> Isaiah 40:4

Since this is the case, we ought to be enjoying some consistency in our Christian life. We don't have to have a "yo-yo" experience with God.

Ever since the Lord revealed His love to me on March 23, 1968, I've been one excited and turned-on guy. I've had much opposition and many bad things happen to me, but it's never stolen what God said. Satan has definitely done his best to derail me, but I've never lost the joy of what the Lord did in my heart. In fact, it's actually stronger today than it was back in 1968 when it first happened. My revelation and experience of God's love is even greater now than when I first had that awe-inspiring, life-changing encounter with Him.

Although this isn't the experience of most believers—it can be yours. You can enjoy consistency and stability in your Christian life too!

Who's the Variable?

Romans 11:29 reveals,

> The gifts and calling of God *are* without repentance.

Therefore, the Lord isn't the one who comes and goes in your life. You do perceive His presence, anointing, and joy stronger at times, but it's not God giving and then withdrawing from you. Very few people understand this.

Most Christians bombard heaven, crying, "O God, what's wrong? Please touch my life again. I want a fresh touch from You. Lord, please come and do something new in my life today!"

When you pray that way, you're insulting God. You're assuming that whenever you feel dry and empty, whenever you lose your peace, joy, or whatever, that God is the one who withdrew from you. Not true!

Once you're born again, God never changes toward you—ever! He's always releasing—transmitting—His presence, blessing, anointing, joy, healing, and prosperity into your life. The Lord never changes, but you do. You must understand this as we begin looking into how to stay full of God.

Popular teaching today insinuates that the reason you aren't walking in God's love, peace, and joy is because you've done something to displease Him. Therefore, it mainly centers on what you can do to "please" God and get His power "back" in your life again. This is never the case, because the Lord has never withdrawn from you.

God isn't the variable—you are! Therefore, everything I'm going to share centers on how you can fix yourself. This won't be a lesson on how to bombard the gates of heaven and "make" God do something. He's already done everything through the death, burial, and resurrection of the Lord Jesus Christ. God wants you blessed even more than you do!

As Full as You Want to Be

Right now, you are as full of God as you're believing to be. He doesn't determine how full of love, joy, and peace you are; you do! God is always willing for every single person to be healed, delivered, and prosperous. It's never the Lord who's not moving in your life; it's you who aren't receiving from Him. Therefore, I want to encourage you in how to receive.

Wherever you are right now, there are television signals around you. You may not be able to perceive them, but they're there. If you plugged in, turned on, and tuned in a television set, you could perceive the signal. However, when you turn on the receiver and experience the sight and sound of the picture, this isn't when the broadcast began; it's just when you started receiving it.

That's the way it is with the Lord. God is healing every person who ever needs to be healed. He's giving love, joy, and peace to you constantly. The transmitters of heaven are beaming twenty-four hours a day, every day of the week. God is never the one who's not blessing you; you're the one who has either turned off or are not tuned in!

I'm for revival, but the way most people are seeking it isn't the way it's going to happen. Praying "O God, send revival!" and believing that it's up to Him how much of it we experience, is wrong. It's not God's fault that there isn't more of an outpouring of His power and Spirit in our land. He hasn't stopped pouring out the Holy Spirit upon believers since the Day of Pentecost!

We just aren't very good receivers. We're the ones who are short-circuiting God's power and blessing in our lives. The Lord wants massive worldwide revival. He wants everyone to receive salvation. But since we aren't turned on and tuned in to Him, we aren't receiving as we should.

Fix Your Receiver

Begging for revival and pleading for God to move are common attitudes and practices in Christianity today. "O God, fix Your transmitter! O Lord, why aren't You sending revival? What's wrong with You? Don't You care? If we get thousands of people to fast and pray with us, maybe we can twist Your arm and motivate You to do something." What an ungodly attitude!

"The Lord is ticked off at our country. He's up in heaven with His arms folded, frowning and saying, 'I'm not going to do anything else for you until you repent and grovel in the dirt some more!'" Wrong! People who say things like that don't really believe that God is good.

These truths I'm sharing would get me kicked out of many churches. However, you need to know that God isn't holding anything back; He's transmitting everything Jesus Christ provided through His death, burial, and resurrection.

If you aren't full of God today, it's you who have chosen it. Even though you may strongly desire to stay full of God, you've made choices that have prevented you from receiving and manifesting His love, joy, peace, healing, and prosperity. However, there's good news.

God's Word shows us four things we can do to fix our receivers. That's what these **Lessons** are all about.

How to Use Your Study Guide

Whether you are teaching a class, leading a small group, discipling an individual, or studying *Discover the Keys to Staying Full of God* on your own, you'll find this *Study Guide* a beneficial study tool. Here's how it works:

Each study consists of a **Lesson**, **Lesson Outline**, **Teacher's Guide**, **Discipleship Questions**, an **Answer Key**, and **Scriptures**. Some **Lessons** also have **Additional Information**.

The teacher reads the **Lesson** aloud. While the **Lesson** is being read, each student follows along with their own copy of the **Lesson Outline**.

Once the **Lesson** is read, the teacher then facilitates a group Bible study using the **Teacher's Guide**. Simply read aloud one numbered section at a time, ask the corresponding questions below, and have the group answer them. Then, repeat the process for the next numbered section. For your convenience, answers are provided in parentheses.

Except for the corresponding questions and answers, the information on the **Teacher's Guide** is the same as the **Lesson Outline**. Therefore, the group should use their **Lesson Outlines** to assist them in answering the questions.

Whenever a question mentions a specific scripture, be sure to have the group look it up in their Bibles and read it together before answering the question. Feel free to interact with the group over the scriptures and points from the **Lesson** as time allows. Don't let any individual dominate the discussion, but try to draw out the quieter ones for participation in the group conversation. As much as possible, keep the discussion centered on the scriptures and the **Lesson** points at hand. Remember, the goal is understanding (Matt. 13:19).

Discipleship Questions are provided for further study and meditation. They are designed for use as "homework," but—according to the teacher's discretion—may be helpful during the group study sometimes as well. Each **Lesson** comes with an **Answer Key**. As a brief review before launching into the current **Lesson**, the teacher may wish to go over with the group the **Answer Key** for the previous study's **Discipleship Questions**.

Some **Lessons** also have **Additional Information**. This section is geared toward the teacher. It contains supplementary information, illustrations, and/or resource recommendations for further study.

Scriptures from the *King James Version* of the Bible are included as another tool for reference and meditation.

For personal study, read the **Lesson** and review the **Teacher's Guide**. Then, do the **Discipleship Questions** and check your work with the **Answer Key**. For maximum impact, be sure to utilize the **Additional Information** and **Scriptures**.

Outline for Group Study:
  I. Briefly review previous study by going over the **Answer Key** for the
     Discipleship Questions (homework).
  II. Read the current **Lesson** aloud.
      A. Be sure that each student has a copy of the **Lesson Outline**.
      B. While the **Lesson** is being read, students should use their **Lesson
         Outline** to follow along.
  III. Once the **Lesson** is read, facilitate a group Bible study using the **Teacher's
      Guide**.
      A. Read one entire numbered section (above).
      B. Then ask the corresponding questions (below).
      C. Group looks up and reads aloud each specifically mentioned scripture
         before answering the question.
      D. Discuss the scripture and the answer/point from the **Lesson** as desired.
      E. Then repeat the process by reading the next numbered section (above).
  IV. Distribute copies of the **Discipleship Questions** to be worked on as
      homework.

Materials Needed:
  Study guide, Bible, and enough copies of the **Outline, Discipleship Questions**, and
  Scriptures for each student. (PDFs of the **Outlines, Discipleship Questions**, and
  Scriptures can be downloaded via the URL located on the first page of this study guide.)

Outline for Personal Study:
  I. Read **Lesson**.
      A. Read **Additional Information**, if any.
      B. Meditate on the **Scriptures**, as desired.
  II. Review **Teacher's Guide**.
  III. Do **Discipleship Questions**.
  IV. Check your work with the **Answer Key**.

Materials Needed:
  Study guide, Bible, and something to write with.

Intuitive Revelation
LESSON 1

> For I am not ashamed of the gospel of Christ: for it is the power of God unto salvation to every one that believeth; to the Jew first, and also to the Greek. For therein is the righteousness of God revealed from faith to faith: as it is written, The just shall live by faith.
>
> Romans 1:16-17

This word *Gospel* is a radical term. Prior to and outside of the Bible, we only have two examples of this Greek word *euaggelion*, which was translated "gospel," being used in Greek literature. That's because it's a superlative. It actually means more than just "good news." It means "nearly-too-good-to-be-true news." Since there was virtually no news this good until Jesus came, it was hardly ever used.

But once Jesus came along, people started using "Gospel" to refer to what He was preaching and demonstrating. They were, in effect, saying, "God isn't judging people. He's not even angry anymore!" The Lord extended mercy to the harlot taken in the act of adultery (John 8:10-11), He rebuked His disciples for desiring to call down fire on an unwelcoming village (Luke 9:54-56), and He spoke of living water to the immoral woman at the well (John 4:10). Christ's message and the way He loved people unconditionally were both nearly too good to be true!

The Jews of Jesus' time were very religious. They had been raised under a works-oriented, performance-based, legalistic, judgmental religious system. Therefore, they persecuted anyone who preached the true Gospel. Why? The Gospel—salvation by grace through faith in the Lord Jesus Christ—was nearly too good to be true!

So when Paul said, "It's the Gospel—this nearly-too-good-to-be-true news of the Lord's unconditional love—that is the power of God to change people's lives," the religious folks' immediate response was, "Well, then, what about God's wrath? You need to let people know there's a hell, that God is just, and He's going to send people there. You need to use fear to scare people out of hell!" That was the religious concept of the day.

The Goodness of God

Hell is a real place, and I do tell people about it. Those who don't believe on the Lord Jesus Christ will go there, but that's not the core message of Christianity. It's a truth, but it's not good news, and it's definitely not the Gospel!

God's goodness, not the fear of hell, is what leads people to repentance (Rom. 2:4). However, for so long, the message of the church has been: "Believe on Jesus so you won't go to hell." That's the wrong message! It's a true message, but it's not the Gospel. The good news that truly releases God's power and draws people to Him in droves is the Gospel: "God is good and He loves you. Through Christ's atonement, everything you need for abundant life—both in heaven to come and on earth here and now—has already been provided. All you must do is believe and receive." This is what we should be preaching!

The Homing Device

"But Andrew, what about the wrath of God?" Paul addressed this in Romans 1:18-20.

> For the wrath of God is revealed.
>
> ROMANS 1:18

You could say, "For the wrath of God is already revealed." In other words, the reason why you don't have to preach the wrath of God is because people already know in their hearts that they aren't in right standing with Him. That's why they're afraid of death. In their hearts, they know their eternity is on the line, and they aren't sure how they relate to God.

> For the wrath of God is revealed from heaven against all ungodliness and unrighteousness of men, who hold the truth in unrighteousness; Because that which may be known of God is manifest in them; for God hath [past tense] shewed it unto them.
>
> ROMANS 1:18-19, BRACKETS MINE

This is saying that the Creator placed within His creation a homing device. There is an intuitive revelation of the existence of God on the inside of every human being who has ever breathed on this earth. Some may argue, "Oh, no, that's not so. I don't believe there is a God. I don't feel Him. I have no conviction, no awareness of God at all. He's never touched me. I'm totally godless." They're lying through their teeth! How do I know? I believe God's Word more than what people say.

As an American soldier serving in Vietnam, some of my comrades told me, "I'm an atheist. I don't believe in God." However, once those bombs began dropping and the bullets started to fly, those "atheists" cried out at the top of their lungs for mercy to this God they didn't believe in.

The truth is, every person who has ever breathed has a revelation of the existence of God.

Without Excuse

Romans 1:20 goes on to say,

> For the invisible things of him from the creation of the world are clearly seen [not obscurely or vaguely, but clearly seen], being understood by the things that are made, even his eternal power and Godhead; so that they are without excuse.
>
> BRACKETS MINE

No one will ever stand before God and say, "But I never heard. I never knew You existed!" Even if they haven't heard a preacher preach to them, they've had this inner witness—and they'll be accountable according to the revelation they have. This is true of every person.

When "atheists" tell me they don't believe in God, I just go ahead and talk to them as if they do. They say, "I told you, I don't believe in God," and I answer, "I know what you said, but it's not true. You're lying." I've kept talking like this to many people who have claimed not to believe in God. Somewhere in the conversation, I end up pricking this little part of them that already had this knowledge of God. Then, all of a sudden, they open up and start admitting it.

Psalm 46:10 says,

> Be still, and know that I am God.

When you get still, you can hear this homing device. When you aren't occupied with anything, it'll start drawing you to God. That's the reason why, prior to salvation, people don't like to be still. They call it being "bored," "lonely," or something similar. Although they use many different terms to describe it, this homing device in their hearts is what's speaking to them.

What does it say? "You know this isn't right. You shouldn't be living this way. There has to be more to life than this. Where did I come from? Where am I going? Who created me?" In order to drown this out and ignore it, they have to saturate their eyes and ears with radio, television, and other forms of media. They must constantly keep themselves busy with something, or this homing device will talk to them and convict them regarding their lifestyles.

Progressive Steps

You already have a revelation of God. You were born with it, and it stays with you throughout your entire life.

But the rest of Romans 1, beginning with verse 21, reveals progressive steps you can take that will diminish or stop this intuitive knowledge of God from drawing you home to Him. You can actually reach a place where your heart becomes hardened so much over a period of time that you can't hear this homing device—this revelation of God—anymore. Romans 1:21 and the following verses talk about these progressive steps you must take in order to walk away from this revelation.

Since you are doing this study, you've probably already received the Lord. Therefore, you are not walking away from the intuitive knowledge of God in your heart. However, these principles apply to everything God does in your life. They don't just work before you were saved concerning God's existence. Before you lose the benefit of anything the Lord has done in your life, you must pass through these four steps.

These four keys in Romans 1:21 describe the steps you take both to walk away from and to draw near to God. Take, for instance, the joy of the Lord. Perhaps it's not as strong today as it once was in your life. If you've ever known God's love but you aren't experiencing it today as you did once before, there were steps you took away from Him. These are also the same steps you use to come back to Him.

Let's say the revelation is healing. Perhaps you've been healed, but now it seems like you've lost that healing and you're back to where you were before. God didn't quit transmitting His healing power—you just stopped receiving. You've done at least one of these four things listed in Romans 1:21.

The Four Keys

We could continue right on through the rest of Romans 1, starting in verse 22, and bring out many other important truths. But we're going to limit the scope of this study to the four keys to staying full of God revealed in verse 21.

> Because that, when they knew God, [1] they glorified him not as God, [2] neither were thankful; but [3] became vain in their imaginations, and [4] their foolish heart was darkened.
>
> ROMANS 1:21, BRACKETS MINE

Expressed negatively, as in this verse, the four keys are:
1. "They glorified him not as God"
2. "Neither were thankful"
3. "Became vain in their imaginations"
4. "Their foolish heart was darkened"

These same four keys expressed positively are:
1. Glorify God
2. Be thankful
3. Recognize the power of your imagination
4. Have a good heart

Depending on how you walk out these four progressive steps in your everyday life, you decide whether or not you will stay full of God!

Intuitive Revelation
LESSON 1 – OUTLINE

1. The *Gospel* is more than just "good news"; it's "nearly-too-good-to-be-true news."

> For I am not ashamed of the gospel of Christ: for it is the power of God unto salvation to every one that believeth; to the Jew first, and also to the Greek. For therein is the righteousness of God revealed from faith to faith: as it is written, The just shall live by faith.
>
> ROMANS 1:16-17

   A. Christ's message and the way He loved people unconditionally were both nearly too good to be true! (John 4:10, 8:10-11; and Luke 9:54-56)

   B. God's goodness—not the fear of hell—is what leads people to repentance (Rom. 2:4).

   C. Through Christ's atonement, everything you need for abundant life—both in heaven to come and on earth here and now—has already been provided.

   D. All you must do is believe and receive.

2. "But what about the wrath of God?"

> For the wrath of God is revealed from heaven against all ungodliness and unrighteousness of men, who hold the truth in unrighteousness; Because that which may be known of God is manifest in them; for God hath [past tense] shewed it unto them.
>
> ROMANS 1:18-19, BRACKETS MINE

   A. The reason why you don't have to preach the wrath of God is because people already know in their hearts that they aren't in right standing with Him.

   B. There is a homing device—an intuitive revelation of the existence of God—on the inside of every human being who has ever breathed on this earth.

3. No one will ever stand before God and say, "But I never heard. I never knew You existed!"

> For the invisible things of him from the creation of the world are clearly seen [not obscurely or vaguely, but clearly seen], being understood by the things that are made, even his eternal power and Godhead; so that they are without excuse.
>
> ROMANS 1:20, BRACKETS MINE

A. Even if they haven't heard a preacher preach to them, they've had this inner witness on the inside—and they'll be accountable according to the revelation they have.

B. This is true of every person.

4. When you get still, you can hear this homing device.

> Be still, and know that I am God.
>
> PSALM 46:10

A. Prior to salvation, people don't like to be still.

B. Although they use many different terms to describe it—being "bored," "lonely," or something similar—this homing device in their hearts is what's speaking to them.

C. What does it say?

   i. "You know this isn't right."

   ii. "You shouldn't be living this way."

   iii. "There has to be more to life than this."

   iv. "Where did I come from?"

   v. "Where am I going?"

   vi. "Who created me?"

D. They must constantly keep themselves busy with something, or this homing device will talk to them and convict them regarding their lifestyles.

5. These four keys in Romans 1:21 describe the steps you take both to walk away from and to draw near to God.

> Because that, when they knew God, [1] they glorified him not as God, [2] neither were thankful; but [3] became vain in their imaginations, and [4] their foolish heart was darkened.
>
> ROMANS 1:21, BRACKETS MINE

A. These same four keys expressed positively are:

   i. Glorify God.

   ii. Be thankful.

iii. Recognize the power of your imagination.

iv. Have a good heart.

B. Depending on how you walk out these four progressive steps in your everyday life, you decide whether or not you'll stay full of God!

Intuitive Revelation
LESSON 1 – TEACHER'S GUIDE

1.   The *Gospel* is more than just "good news"; it's "nearly-too-good-to-be-true news" (Rom. 1:16-17). Christ's message and the way He loved people unconditionally were both nearly too good to be true! (John 4:10, 8:10-11; and Luke 9:54-56). God's goodness— not the fear of hell—is what leads people to repentance (Rom. 2:4). Through Christ's atonement, everything we need for abundant life—both in heaven to come and on earth here and now—has already been provided. All we must do is believe and receive.

2.   "But what about the wrath of God?" (Rom. 1:18-19). The reason why we don't have to preach the wrath of God is because people already know in their hearts that they aren't in right standing with Him. There is a homing device—an intuitive revelation of the existence of God—on the inside of every human being who has ever breathed on this earth.

3.   No one will ever stand before God and say, "But I never heard. I never knew You existed!" (Rom. 1:20). Even if they haven't heard a preacher preach to them, they've had this inner witness—and they'll be accountable according to the revelation they have. This is true of every person.

1. A. According to Romans 1:16-17, what is the "nearly-too-good-to-be-true news"? (The Gospel)
   B. Read Romans 2:4. What is it that leads people to repentance? (God's goodness)
   C. What has already been provided through Christ's atonement? (Everything we need for abundant life—both in heaven to come and on earth here and now)
2. A. Read Romans 1:18-19. Why don't we have to preach the wrath of God? (People already know in their hearts that they aren't in right standing with Him)
   B. What is it that's on the inside of every human being who has ever breathed on this earth? (An intuitive revelation of the existence of God)
3. A. According to Romans 1:20, will anyone ever be able to stand before God and say, "But I never heard. I never knew You existed!" (No)
   B. What will they be accountable for? (The revelation they have—this inner witness)

4.   When a person gets still, they can hear this homing device (Ps. 46:10). Prior to salvation, no one likes to be still. Although they use many different terms to describe it—being "bored," "lonely," or something similar—this homing device in their heart is what's speaking to them. What does it say? "You know this isn't right. You shouldn't be living this way. There has to be more to life than this. Where did I come from? Where am I going? Who created me?" They must constantly keep themselves busy with something, or this homing device will talk to them and convict them regarding their lifestyle.

5.   These four keys in Romans 1:21 describe the steps we take both to walk away from and to draw near to God.

>   Because that, when they knew God, [1] they glorified him not as God, [2] neither were thankful; but [3] became vain in their imaginations, and [4] their foolish heart was darkened.
>
>   ROMANS 1:21, BRACKETS MINE

These same four keys expressed positively are: Glorify God, be thankful, recognize the power of our imagination, and have a good heart. Depending on how we walk out these four progressive steps in our everyday life, we decide whether or not we will stay full of God!

4. A. According to Psalm 46:10, when is it that we can hear this homing device? (When we get still)
   B. What does it say? ("You know this isn't right. You shouldn't be living this way. There has to be more to life than this. Where did I come from? Where am I going? Who created me?")
   C. How do people avoid listening to this homing device convict them regarding their lifestyle? (They constantly keep themselves busy with something)
5. A. Read Romans 1:21. What are the four keys to staying full of God expressed positively? (Glorify God, be thankful, recognize the power of our imagination, and have a good heart)
   B. Who decides whether we stay full of God or not? (We do)

For an in-depth study of the Gospel, as revealed through the book of Romans, please refer to my teaching entitled *Grace, the Power of the Gospel.*

Intuitive Revelation
Lesson 1 – Discipleship Questions

1. In Romans 1:16-17, what are we not to be ashamed of?

2. It is the power of God unto _____ to everyone who believes.

3. What is revealed in it from faith to faith?

4. What shall the just live by?
   A. Hope.
   B. Faith.
   C. Fear.
   D. All of the above.
   E. None of the above.

5. Did Jesus show mercy or judgment in John 8:10-11?

6. In Luke 9:54-56, what did the disciples ask Jesus if they could do?

7. Which Old Testament prophet's example were they trying to follow?
   A. Moses.
   B. Elijah.
   C. Elisha.
   D. Daniel.

8. How did Jesus respond to their idea?
   A. He rebuked them.
   B. He commended them.
   C. He ignored them.
   D. He agreed.

9. While speaking to the immoral woman in John 4:10, what did Jesus say He would have given her?

10. According to Romans 2:4, what leads us to repentance?
    A. God's wrath.
    B. God's justice.
    C. God's power.
    D. God's goodness.

11. What does Romans 1:18-19 say about the wrath of God?

12. That which may be known of God is what?

13. What has God done?

14. According to Romans 1:20, how are the invisible things of Him from the creation of the world seen?
    A. Through a glass darkly.
    B. Clearly.
    C. Barely.
    D. Not at all.

15. How does that leave them?

16. What does Psalm 46:10 command us to do?

17. Put the following four keys to staying full of God, expressed negatively as in Romans 1:21, in their biblical order.
    A. "Became vain in their imaginations."
    B. "Neither were thankful."
    C. "Their foolish heart was darkened."
    D. "They glorified him not as God."

18. Put the following four keys to staying full of God, expressed positively, in their proper order.
    A. Have a good heart.
    B. Recognize the power of your imagination.
    C. Glorify God.
    D. Be thankful.

Intuitive Revelation
LESSON 1 – ANSWER KEY

1. The Gospel of Christ.

2. Salvation.

3. The righteousness of God.

4. B. Faith.

5. Mercy.

6. Command fire to come down from heaven and consume this village.

7. B. Elijah.

8. A. He rebuked them.

9. Living water.

10. D. God's goodness.

11. It's already revealed.

12. Manifest in them.

13. He's shown it to them.

14. B. Clearly.

15. Without excuse.

16. Be still and know that He is God.

17. D. "They glorified him not as God."
    B. "Neither were thankful."
    A. "Became vain in their imaginations."
    C. "Their foolish heart was darkened."

18. C. Glorify God
    D. Be thankful
    B. Recognize the power of your imagination
    A. Have a good heart

Intuitive Revelation
LESSON 1 – SCRIPTURES

For I am not ashamed of the gospel of Christ: for it is the power of God unto salvation to every one that believeth; to the Jew first, and also to the Greek. For therein is the righteousness of God revealed from faith to faith: as it is written, The just shall live by faith.

ROMANS 1:16-17

When Jesus had lifted up himself, and saw none but the woman, he said unto her, Woman, where are those thine accusers? hath no man condemned thee? She said, No man, Lord. And Jesus said unto her, Neither do I condemn thee: go, and sin no more.

JOHN 8:10-11

And when his disciples James and John saw this, they said, Lord, wilt thou that we command fire to come down from heaven, and consume them, even as Elias did? But he turned, and rebuked them, and said, Ye know not what manner of spirit ye are of. For the Son of man is not come to destroy men's lives, but to save them. And they went to another village.

LUKE 9:54-56

Jesus answered and said unto her, If thou knewest the gift of God, and who it is that saith to thee, Give me to drink; thou wouldest have asked of him, and he would have given thee living water.

JOHN 4:10

Or despisest thou the riches of his goodness and forbearance and longsuffering; not knowing that the goodness of God leadeth thee to repentance?

ROMANS 2:4

For the wrath of God is revealed from heaven against all ungodliness and unrighteousness of men, who hold the truth in unrighteousness; Because that which may be known of God is manifest in them; for God hath shewed it unto them. For the invisible things of him from the creation of the world are clearly seen, being understood by the things that are made, even his eternal power and Godhead; so that they are without excuse.

ROMANS 1:18-20

Be still, and know that I am God: I will be exalted among the heathen, I will be exalted in the earth.

PSALM 46:10

Because that, when they knew God, they glorified him not as God, neither were thankful; but became vain in their imaginations, and their foolish heart was darkened.

ROMANS 1:21

The Place of Importance
LESSON 2

When God touches your life, Satan immediately comes to steal that touch away (Mark 4:15). He doesn't want you to keep whatever it was the Lord gave you—a revelation, a blessing, or a healing. The Enemy does this by trying to get you to quit glorifying God as God. If you stop glorifying God as God—and glorifying what He's done in your life—then you'll lose the manifestation of that revelation, blessing, healing, or whatever. It'll seem like your joy and peace are diminishing. But if you don't quit glorifying God and what He's done in your life, you'll never lose it—and it'll increase.

So, then, what does it mean to "glorify" God?

When I first ran across this, I looked it up in the *Strong's Concordance*. The Greek word used in Romans 1:21 for *glorify* means "to render or esteem glorious." That didn't help me very much.

So I looked up both *render* and *esteem* in the dictionary. It was when I saw the definition for esteem that God opened my eyes to this truth. *Esteem* means "to value, prize, or reverence."

You Place Value on Everything

When God does something in your life, you place a value upon it, but then Satan immediately comes against that value and competes for it. He tries to steal from you the worth and value you've placed on the things of God. This happens to everyone!

The same thing will happen with this teaching. Some people will receive it—others won't. But one way or another, you are placing a value on what you're learning.

> When ye received the word of God which ye heard of us, ye received it not as the word of men, but as it is in truth, the word of God, which effectually worketh also in you that believe.
>
> 1 THESSALONIANS 2:13

Some people will say, "This is God speaking to me," and others will conclude, "That's just Andrew." Then you'll place a value on these truths and they'll affect your life—or not—accordingly.

You place a value on everything that comes into your life. The devil comes immediately to attack the value you place on God, His Word, and the manifestation of what He's done and is doing in your life.

It's Your Choice

Let's say the Lord speaks to you and reveals His unconditional love. You experience and feel that love, saying, "God loves me. Almighty God loves me!" You receive the peace, joy, and other benefits that revelation and experience brings, but tomorrow the devil will agitate someone at work to come over and dump on you. They'll tell you what an absolute zero you are, criticizing your performance and such. Do you know what's happening? The Enemy is competing for the value you placed on God and His love.

You can go to church and get so blessed and happy. Then you go home and someone jumps all over your case. Satan is trying to steal your joy. Here's what God says about you and here's the opposite. It's like a seesaw, shifting according to the value you place on one side. When one side is up, the other side is down—and vice versa. If you value what God says, then you have to devalue what others say. Like a seesaw, you can't have both sides up at the same time. "God loves me. Not only does He love me, He likes me. He's pleased with me. I'm full of joy unspeakable and full of glory!"

But when the criticism and opposition come, will you hold on to what God has said and done, or will you start honoring, prizing, and valuing the acceptance of those people equal to or above God? If you let their word have power and increase, then the value you place on God's Word and what He's done in your life will decrease. You'll start losing the manifestation of joy, peace, and victory that revelation gave you. It wasn't God who quit transmitting it, but you who quit receiving. You allowed something else to occupy the position in your life that was meant for God.

You place a value on everything that comes against you. No one else can. Nobody else can dictate the worth you place on something in your life. It's your choice.

Love and Hate

Your spouse, child, or boss may have said something that upset you. Let's say it just really ticked you off. However, if they said the exact same words to me, it would have a different effect. Why? I don't value their opinion the way you do.

"But I'm supposed to value my spouse, child, or boss's opinion!" Yes, you should value them more than I do, but in a relative sense. The Lord said:

> If any man come to me, and hate not his father, and mother, and wife, and children, and brethren, and sisters, yea, and his own life also, he cannot be my disciple…He that loveth father or mother more than me is not worthy of me: and he that loveth son or daughter more than me is not worthy of me.
>
> LUKE 14:26 AND MATTHEW 10:37

Your love for even your immediate family ought to pale in comparison to your love for Jesus. The contrast between the worth and value you place on God and others should be as different as love and hate. Of course, you should value certain people who are closer to you more than I do. But in comparison to God and what He's done in your life, you ought to place such a value and worth upon Him that nothing and no one ever competes. However, this isn't the way most Christians operate.

Do you glorify the things of God more than the things of this world? Is the difference so small that I'd have to use a magnifying glass to see which you truly value the most? It ought to be obvious. Compared to how you esteem God, you should disesteem—decrease the worth and value on—everything and everyone else.

Greater Than Your Mate

We've actually become codependent on everyone and everything else except God. If your mate were to leave you, would you fall apart like a two-dollar suitcase? I agree that it's God's best for your marriage to be healed and made whole. Of course the Lord wants to move in that area of your life. But what if your spouse doesn't cooperate? You need to make a commitment and say, "God, You are so much greater than my mate. If things don't work out and my spouse leaves, I won't miss a stride. I'll keep praising, loving, and serving You with all my heart—even if everyone forsakes me. You're awesome!"

Moses' wife left him for a year or two. Zipporah took off when they were on their way down to Egypt, but Moses just kept moving forward with the Lord. The plagues were released, the children of Israel were delivered, and the Red Sea parted. All this happened while he was separated from his wife.

Some people think, *Well, brother, I believe I'm supposed to love and value God, but you can't praise Him while going through a divorce.* Sure you can!

A partner of mine in Charlotte, North Carolina, used to have me in to speak to his employees each year. He'd tell them, "The clock is running. You listen to this guy for as long as he wants to talk." Then I'd just share with them the goodness of God. I did this for many years.

While in the break room after I had spoken once, a certain lady came over to talk to me. She was an alcoholic who had tried to kill herself. She'd slit her wrists and wound up in the hospital. She was going through her third or fourth divorce and was very poor. Everything in her life was depressing and discouraging.

"Who Cares?"

She told me, "Andrew, I'm not a Christian like you, and Chip [my friend, the business owner], but I know that prayer works. I want prayer for my marriage." Then she broke down and started to cry. She told me it was her third or fourth marriage and that her husband had filed for a divorce. But if she got divorced again, she didn't know if she could make it. So she wanted me to pray for her marriage.

I stopped her and asked, "Now, let me make sure I heard you right. You aren't a Christian and you know it."

"That's right."

"If you were to die right now, you would go straight to hell."

"That's correct."

"And you want me to pray for your marriage and not your salvation?"

"Yes."

I said, "Lady, do you realize that after you've burned in hell for a thousand years, you won't give a rip whether you were ever married or not? Who cares about your marriage—you need to be born again!"

She responded, "You know what? You're right!" So I prayed with her and she was born again.

I'm not saying that God isn't concerned about your marriage, but you must look at it in terms of its relative worth. Compared to eternity, marriage is nothing. It's all about the value you place on things.

Jesus Disesteemed

Some people place so much value on their marriage, career, and other people's acceptance that it honestly competes for the worth they've placed on the things of God. If that's you, you need to make a decision and say, "Lord, there is nothing that could even remotely tempt me to ever decrease the value I place on You and what You've done in my life." Then you need to magnify and glorify God, and disesteem everything else.

> Wherefore seeing we also are compassed about with so great a cloud of witnesses, let us lay aside every weight, and the sin which doth so easily beset us, and let us run with patience the race that is set before us, Looking unto Jesus the author and finisher of our faith; who for the joy that was set before him endured the cross, despising the shame, and is set down at the right hand of the throne of God.
>
> HEBREWS 12:1-2

Notice the phrase "despising the shame." The Greek word rendered "despising" literally means "to disesteem." It's the exact opposite of esteeming, glorifying, magnifying, valuing, and prizing. Jesus *disesteemed* the shame associated with what He had to go through.

You cannot truly glorify God and everything else at the same time. It's like that seesaw I mentioned earlier. Both ends can't be up at the same time. You must esteem one and disesteem everything else. Jesus disesteemed the shame associated with His crucifixion. He intentionally minimized and shrunk the cost.

That's not the way most of us function. If you or I had been called on by God to suffer crucifixion, we probably would have immediately looked at the shame, cost, and pain. We would have valued our own lives, peace, and security in such a way that we wouldn't have been able to value what God called us to do.

But Jesus had already disesteemed His own life (Phil. 2:5-8). He viewed everything else as worthless compared to what God had said and done.

Dung!

Paul did the same:

> But what things were gain to me, those I counted loss for Christ. Yea doubtless, and I count all things but loss for the excellency of the knowledge of Christ Jesus my Lord: for whom I have suffered the loss of all things, and do count them but dung, that I may win Christ.
>
> PHILIPPIANS 3:7-8

You place a value on everything in your life. You are the one who esteems what's important to you. Paul said, "I placed a high value on knowing Christ and disesteemed everything else as if it were dung." That's a strong statement!

Most of us can't say that—which is the reason we can't do what Paul did. It's also why we don't have the same joy. Paul wrote the book of Philippians while in prison. Yet it's his happiest book. He used the words "joy," "rejoice," and "rejoicing" a total of seventeen times in just four chapters. Paul was praising God and rejoicing from jail!

If you were thrown in prison this evening, would you be singing and praising the Lord at midnight? Probably not. You've placed too much value and worth on your life, freedom, and possessions. You've put too much value on things that are unimportant. Your life is important compared to others, but compared to God, it's worth nothing. You need to place a relative worth on your life. As long as you're the center of your universe, you're always going to be upset when someone rubs you the wrong way. If you are all wrapped up in yourself, you make a very small package.

Meant for God

Paul had a different value system. He actually struggled with whether to stay here or go to heaven.

> For to me to live is Christ, and to die is gain…For I am in a strait betwixt two, having a desire to depart, and to be with Christ; which is far better: Nevertheless to abide in the flesh is more needful for you.
>
> PHILIPPIANS 1:21 AND 23-24

Paul didn't count his life here as anything. He's the one who placed this value on it.

You're the one who places value on everything that comes into your life. I remember climbing a trail on Pike's Peak with a friend of mine. He started telling me about a mutual friend who had said some very negative things about both of us. I told him I didn't want to hear it. We had discussed this before, and I didn't care to hear the latest thing this guy had criticized me over. My friend became quiet for a while and then asked, "Why doesn't what he says about you bother you the way his criticism of me bothers me?" I answered, "It's because I don't value his opinion of me the way you value his opinion of you." It's all about the value you place on things.

The reason you begin to lose the revelation, blessing, and benefit of what God has said and done is because you've placed value on so many other things instead of Him. These other things that are important to you are sapping your time, energy, and attention. Due to this, what the Lord has done in your life has diminished over time. It's not because God changed His attitude toward you and quit giving; it's because you've let something else occupy that place of importance in your life that was meant for God alone.

The Place of Importance
LESSON 2 – OUTLINE

1. When God touches your life, Satan immediately comes to steal that touch away (Mark 4:15).

   A. The Enemy does this by trying to get you to quit glorifying God as God.

   B. If you stop glorifying God as God—and glorifying what He's done in your life—then you'll lose the manifestation of that revelation, blessing, healing, or whatever.

   C. But if you don't quit glorifying God and what He's done in your life, you'll never lose it—and it'll increase.

2. The Greek word used in Romans 1:21 for *glorify* means "to render or esteem glorious."

   A. *Esteem* means "to value, prize, or reverence."

   B. When God does something in your life, you place a value upon it, but then Satan immediately comes against that value and competes for it.

   C. He tries to steal from you the worth and value you've placed on the things of God.

   D. The same thing will happen with this teaching.

   When ye received the word of God which ye heard of us, ye received it not as the word of men, but as it is in truth, the word of God, which effectually worketh also in you that believe.

   1 THESSALONIANS 2:13

3. You place a value on everything that comes into your life.

   A. The devil comes immediately to attack the value you place on God, His Word, and the manifestation of what He's done and is doing in your life.

   B. If you value what God says, then you have to devalue what others say (like a seesaw).

   C. When criticism and opposition come, will you hold on to what God has said and done, or will you start honoring, prizing, and valuing the acceptance of those people equal to or above God?

   D. Nobody else can dictate the worth you place on something in your life—it's your choice.

4. Your love for even your immediate family ought to pale in comparison to your love for Jesus.

If any man come to me, and hate not his father, and mother, and wife, and children, and brethren, and sisters, yea, and his own life also, he cannot be my disciple…He that loveth father or mother more than me is not worthy of me: and he that loveth son or daughter more than me is not worthy of me.

LUKE 14:26 AND MATTHEW 10:37

A. The contrast between the worth and value you place on God and others should be as different as love and hate.

B. In comparison to God and what He's done in your life, you ought to place such a value and worth upon Him that nothing and no one ever competes.

C. Compared to how you esteem God, you should disesteem—decrease the worth and value on—everything and everyone else.

5. You cannot truly glorify God and everything else at the same time.

A. You must esteem one and disesteem everything else.

B. Jesus disesteemed the shame associated with His crucifixion.

Wherefore seeing we also are compassed about with so great a cloud of witnesses, let us lay aside every weight, and the sin which doth so easily beset us, and let us run with patience the race that is set before us, Looking unto Jesus the author and finisher of our faith; who for the joy that was set before him endured the cross, despising [disesteeming] the shame, and is set down at the right hand of the throne of God.

HEBREWS 12:1-2, BRACKETS MINE

C. Jesus viewed everything else as worthless compared to what God had said and done—even His own life (Phil. 2:5-8).

6. Paul did the same.

But what things were gain to me, those I [despised, disesteemed] counted loss for Christ. Yea doubtless, and I count all things but loss for the excellency of the knowledge of Christ Jesus my Lord: for whom I have suffered the loss of all things, and do count them but dung, that I may win Christ.

PHILIPPIANS 3:7-8, BRACKETS MINE

A. Paul had a different value system.

B. He actually struggled with whether to stay here or go to heaven.

For to me to live is Christ, and to die is gain…For I am in a strait betwixt two, having a desire to depart, and to be with Christ; which is far better: Nevertheless to abide in the flesh is more needful for you.

PHILIPPIANS 1:21 AND 23-24

7. The reason you begin to lose the revelation, blessing, and benefit of what God has said and done is because you've placed value on so many other things instead of Him.

   A. These other things that are important to you are sapping your time, energy, and attention.

   B. Due to this, what the Lord has done in your life has diminished over time.

   C. God hasn't changed His attitude toward you and quit giving—you've let something else occupy the place of importance in your life that was meant for God alone.

The Place of Importance
LESSON 2 – TEACHER'S GUIDE

1.   When God touches our lives, Satan immediately comes to steal that touch away (Mark 4:15). The Enemy does this by trying to get us to quit glorifying God as God. If we stop glorifying God as God—and glorifying what He's done in our lives—then we'll lose the manifestation of that revelation, blessing, healing, or whatever. But if we don't quit glorifying God and what He's done in our lives, we'll never lose it—and it'll increase.

2.   The Greek word used in Romans 1:21 for *glorify* means "to render or esteem glorious." *Esteem* means "to value, prize, or reverence." When God does something in our lives, we place a value upon it, but then Satan immediately comes against that value and competes for it. He tries to steal from us the worth and value we've placed on the things of God. The same thing will happen with this teaching (1 Thess. 2:13).

3.   We place a value on everything that comes into our lives. The devil comes immediately to attack the value we place on God, His Word, and the manifestation of what He's done and is doing in our lives. If we value what God says, then we have to devalue what others say (like a seesaw). When criticism and opposition come, will we hold on to what God has said and done, or will we start honoring, prizing, and valuing the acceptance of those people equal to or above God? Nobody else can dictate the worth we place on something in our lives—it's our choice.

1. A. Read Mark 4:15. When God touches our lives, who comes immediately to steal it away? (Satan)
   B. How does he do this? (He tries to get us to quit glorifying God as God)
   C. What happens if we don't quit glorifying God and what He's done in our lives? (We'll never lose it—and it'll increase)
2. A. Read Romans 1:21. What does the word *esteem* mean? (To value, prize, or reverence)
   B. Read 1 Thessalonians 2:13. What will happen with this teaching? (The same)
3. A. What does the devil come immediately to attack? (The value we place on God, His Word, and the manifestation of what He's done and is doing in our lives)
   B. If we value what God says, what else must we do? (Devalue what others say)
   C. Can anyone else dictate the worth we place on something in our lives? (No)

4.   Our love for even our immediate family ought to pale in comparison to our love for Jesus (Luke 14:26 and Matt. 10:37). The contrast between the worth and value we place on God and others should be as different as love and hate. In comparison to God and what He's done in our lives, we ought to place such a value and worth upon Him that nothing and no one ever competes. Compared to how we esteem God, we should disesteem—decrease the worth and value on—everything and everyone else.

5.   We cannot truly glorify God and everything else at the same time. We must esteem one and disesteem everything else. Jesus disesteemed the shame associated with His crucifixion (Heb. 12:1-2). He viewed everything else as worthless compared to what God had said and done—even His own life (Phil. 2:5-8).

6.   Paul did the same (Phil. 3:7-8). He had a different value system. He actually struggled with whether to stay here or go to heaven (Phil. 1:21 and 23-24).

7.   The reason we begin to lose the revelation, blessing, and benefit of what God has said and done is because we've placed value on so many other things instead of Him. These other things that are important to us are sapping our time, energy, and attention. Due to this, what the Lord has done in our lives has diminished over time. God hasn't changed His attitude toward us and quit giving—we've let something else occupy the place of importance in our lives that was meant for God alone.

4. A. According to Luke 14:26 and Matthew 10:37, our love for even our immediate family ought to what? (Pale in comparison to our love for Jesus)
   B. Compared to how we esteem God, we should what? (Disesteem—decrease the worth and value on—everything and everyone else)
5. A. Can we truly glorify God and everything else at the same time? (No)
   B. Read Hebrews 12:1-2 and Philippians 2:5-8. What did Jesus disesteem? (The shame associated with His crucifixion and everything else as worthless—even His own life—compared to what God had said and done)
6. A. According to Philippians 3:7-8, who also had this value system? (Paul)
   B. What did he struggle with in Philippians 1:21 and 23-24? (Whether to stay here or go to heaven)
7. A. Why is it that we begin to lose the revelation, blessing, and benefit of what God has said and done? (We've placed value on so many other things instead of Him)
   B. When what the Lord has done in our lives diminishes over time, has God changed His attitude toward us and quit giving? (No, we've let something else occupy the place of importance in our lives that was meant for God alone)

The Place of Importance
LESSON 2 – DISCIPLESHIP QUESTIONS

1. According to Mark 4:15, who comes immediately to steal?

2. What does he try to steal?

3. What is the first step away from the knowledge of God, as revealed in Romans 1:21?
    A. "Neither were thankful."
    B. "Became vain in their imaginations."
    C. "They glorified him not as God."
    D. "Their foolish heart was darkened."

4. According to 1 Thessalonians 2:13, is it possible to receive the Word of God that you have heard as the word of men?

5. In what kind of person does the Word of God work effectually?

6. According to Matthew 10:37 and Luke 14:26, a true disciple must love Jesus much more than whom?
    A. Spouse and parents.
    B. Children and siblings.
    C. Extended family and friends.
    D. Their own life.
    E. All of the above.
    F. None of the above.

7. Hebrews 12:1-2 reveals that we are surrounded by what?

8. In light of this truth, what should we do?
    A. Lay aside every weight.
    B. Lay aside the sin, which so easily besets us.
    C. Run with patience the race that is set before us.
    D. All of the above.
    E. None of the above.

9. Who should we keep our eyes focused on?

10. How was Jesus able to endure the cross?

11. What three words best describe the Lord in Philippians 2:5-8?
    A. Jesus humbled Himself.
    B. Jesus exalted Himself.
    C. Jesus considered Himself.
    D. Jesus served Himself.

12. In Philippians 3:7-8, what did Paul count as loss for the excellency of the knowledge of Christ Jesus his Lord?

13. How did he count them—that he may win Christ?

14. In Philippians 1:21, Paul said, "To live is _____, and to die is _____."

15. In Philippians 1:23-24, what did Paul desire?

16. However, what was more needful for the Philippians?

The Place of Importance
LESSON 2 – ANSWER KEY

1. Satan.

2. The Word that was sown in our hearts.

3. C. "They glorified him not as God."

4. Yes.

5. Those who believe.

6. E. All of the above.

7. So great a cloud of witnesses.

8. A. Lay aside every weight.
   B. Lay aside the sin, which so easily besets us.
   C. Run with patience the race that is set before us.
   D. All of the above.

9. Jesus, the author and finisher of our faith.

10. He set joy before Himself and despised—disesteemed, minimized—the shame.

11. A. Jesus humbled Himself.

12. All things.

13. As dung.

14. Christ, gain.

15. To depart and be with Christ.

16. That Paul would continue to abide with them in the flesh.

The Place of Importance

And these are they by the way side, where the word is sown; but when they have heard, Satan cometh immediately, and taketh away the word that was sown in their hearts.

MARK 4:15

Because that, when they knew God, they glorified him not as God, neither were thankful; but became vain in their imaginations, and their foolish heart was darkened.

ROMANS 1:21

For this cause also thank we God without ceasing, because, when ye received the word of God which ye heard of us, ye received it not as the word of men, but as it is in truth, the word of God, which effectually worketh also in you that believe.

1 THESSALONIANS 2:13

If any man come to me, and hate not his father, and mother, and wife, and children, and brethren, and sisters, yea, and his own life also, he cannot be my disciple.

LUKE 14:26

He that loveth father or mother more than me is not worthy of me: and he that loveth son or daughter more than me is not worthy of me.

MATTHEW 10:37

Wherefore seeing we also are compassed about with so great a cloud of witnesses, let us lay aside every weight, and the sin which doth so easily beset us, and let us run with patience the race that is set before us, Looking unto Jesus the author and finisher of our faith; who for the joy that was set before him endured the cross, despising the shame, and is set down at the right hand of the throne of God.

HEBREWS 12:1-2

Let this mind be in you, which was also in Christ Jesus: Who, being in the form of God, thought it not robbery to be equal with God: But made himself of no reputation, and took upon him the form of a servant, and was made in the likeness of men: And being found in fashion as a man, he humbled himself, and became obedient unto death, even the death of the cross.

PHILIPPIANS 2:5-8

But what things were gain to me, those I counted loss for Christ. Yea doubtless, and I count all things but loss for the excellency of the knowledge of Christ Jesus my Lord: for whom I have suffered the loss of all things, and do count them but dung, that I may win Christ.

PHILIPPIANS 3:7-8

For to me to live is Christ, and to die is gain…For I am in a strait betwixt two, having a desire to depart, and to be with Christ; which is far better: Nevertheless to abide in the flesh is more needful for you.

PHILIPPIANS 1:21 AND 23-24

"God Loves Me!"
LESSON 3

God supernaturally revealed His love to me in a Saturday night prayer meeting. It was March 23, 1968, and I was eighteen years old. All of a sudden, I knew that God passionately loved me. I understood that He carried my picture in His wallet and had an 8x10 of me on His mantle. God's unconditional love was no longer an abstract concept to me—it was real! For the next four-and-a-half months, I literally experienced God's supernatural love transforming my life.

I was so excited that the very next morning, I stood up in front of my conservative denominational church and told them, "God loves me! He doesn't just love me from a distance, but God passionately loves me. He's pleased with me, and even likes me!" It would have been better if I had cussed. They would've been more merciful on me if I had gone out and committed adultery. At least that could be forgiven. But they equated my testimony of God loving me passionately as me claiming to have some great virtue. Since they didn't understand grace, they thought God's love was based on performance. They interpreted what I was sharing as me thinking I was better than them. So, the criticism came immediately.

Someone walked up to me and asked, "Who do you think you are? You said you're filled with the Spirit."

"God did fill me with His Spirit. That's what it felt like to me. In Ephesians 5:18, Paul told us to be filled with the Spirit."

"Yeah, but that was Paul. Who do you think you are? Are you putting yourself in the same category as Paul?"

"I'm just telling you what happened!"

Satan was using this seminary professor and all these educated people who did this for a living to criticize me. He was trying to get me—an eighteen-year-old boy—to value man's opinion more than what God had revealed to me.

"I Don't Care What You Say!"

I was so overwhelmed with God's love that I hardly slept at night. I'd sleep a few minutes, and then I'd be awake thinking about how much God loves me. Then I'd read the Word until I passed out again. I didn't sleep for more than an hour at a time for four-and-a- half months! I don't remember ever sitting down to a meal that entire time either. Who could eat or sleep knowing that God loves them? I was excited!

There I was, valuing the fact that God loved me. When another voice came, would I value it the same? If I had begun placing value on that, then my value, worth, and reverence for what

God had said would have started coming down, and I would have begun losing the revelation of it. This wasn't because of some great strength of my own. I didn't even know how hungry I was before God touched my life. But once I experienced His awesome love and acceptance, I knew that nothing would ever excite me more. I immediately put God above everything and disesteemed anything else.

When these people—whom I respected, had tried to please, and had tried to gain their acceptance—started ragging on me, I just turned away. I said, "Look, I don't care what you say!" I maintained the same relative worth and value on the things of God. Because of this, God's supernatural, unconditional love that He had given me didn't diminish.

I was a freshman math major in college at the time, but once I fell head over heels in love with God, I lost all interest in both math and college. In fact, I got to where I hated it! I went to school every day for about three months, but never made it to a single class. Somewhere along the way, I'd start talking to somebody about the Lord. That's what I loved to do—tell others how God loved me and how He loved them also. I wanted them to know that God could change their lives too. Although the bell would ring, I couldn't let the person I was talking to go to hell just so I could be in class. So I'd just keep right on sharing with them and miss class. Then I'd talk to somebody else and another bell would ring. This went on for nearly three months!

After a while, I thought, *Why am I paying money to go to school if I don't like it and never make it to class?* So I prayed about it, and the Lord told me to quit. Now, that's not for everybody. You might need an education to do what God is calling you to do. But I didn't need to be a math major to do what I'm doing today.

Relative Worth

Things got really bad once I announced this to everyone. Quitting school meant I was giving up $350 a month in Social Security payments from my father's death. Since this was during the height of the Vietnam War, I had a deferment for as long as I stayed in school, but if I quit, I instantly had an all-expenses-paid trip to Vietnam. Everyone kept telling me, "This isn't smart. It's not what you're supposed to do!"

My mother didn't understand it. She wasn't mean or against me, but she couldn't believe that this was God. (My dad died when I was twelve, so Mom and I had a special bond—and we still do to this day.) Satan tried to get me to value my relationship with my mother more than I valued God, but for me, nothing in my life competes with God. My mother didn't die for me. She didn't go to hell and rise from the dead for the forgiveness of my sin. I love my mother, but I love God infinitely more!

"But, Andrew, I could never make a distinction. I love God and my mother (spouse, children, whomever) the same!" No, you can't do that. Your love for God ought to make your love for your parents, spouse, children, and friends look like hate in comparison (Luke 14:26). I'm not saying to actually hate them. You should love them, but your love and intimacy with the Lord should far surpass it.

You'll run into problems when your relative worth for these things, such as relationships, the recognition of others, and your career is too close to your worth for God. These things are okay in their proper place, but what if loving, following, and speaking for God costs you relationships, career, or acceptance? Would you do whatever the Lord asked you, or would your relative worth be too close?

There is nothing of relative worth to me that even comes close to God. My wife knows I love the Lord far more than I love her. I also know that she loves Him much more than she loves me. Instead of this detracting from our relationship, it's a plus! If Jamie only loved me according to how I treated her, she would have left me a long time ago.

Misunderstood

I've put my wife through the wringer backwards! It's been tough being a minister's wife and going through some of the things we've been through.

I was visiting with this minister once who had committed adultery, spent time in a mental hospital, was an alcoholic, and used drugs before he was born again. Although he'd been through some really terrible things, the Lord changed his life and turned him around. After telling me about his background, he asked me to give my testimony. So I told him about some of the poverty, hardship, and pain we'd gone through. I shared how my wife went two weeks without a stitch of food—a forced fast—while eight months pregnant. This guy stood up and declared, "My God, you were more ungodly than I ever thought about being. That's the worst testimony I've ever heard!" In many ways, that's true.

If Jamie just loved me for who I was, she would have left me a long time ago. It's her commitment to God that keeps her loving me, and it's my commitment to the Lord that keeps me loving her. Loving God doesn't distract from our relationship—it improves it!

Most people are codependent upon their little world they've created. If something were to happen and it looked like they'd lose their marriage, kids, wealth, home, respect, or fame, they'd come crashing down emotionally. Why? They place such value and importance on these things.

When I first received the revelation of God's love, my mother didn't understand. The Enemy was tempting me to look at what this experience was costing me. I lost the recognition of my church. The people I looked up to were criticizing and rejecting me. My own mother went two weeks without talking to me. It wasn't that she hated me; she just flat didn't know what to say!

Finally, I took her out to eat and forced her to say something. Mom broke down crying and said, "I'm just so ashamed by what you're doing!" What she said wasn't positive, but negative. Satan was trying to get me to value that relationship above what the Lord had said. But by His grace, I always believed my relationship with my mother would work out, and it did. Things turned around after the Lord appeared to her in a dream. She worked for me twenty-one years until she finally retired for the last time at age eighty-eight. Mom is a real blessing! But whether "But, Andrew, I'm not sure I'd do something if it meant I'd be drafted and required to go to war!" Well, I placed such a value on the truth that God loved me that I was willing to die for it.

The cost didn't matter to me. I didn't care. I'd rather die and be with the Lord than live my life separated from Him. I didn't give a rip about going to Vietnam. That's why I can truthfully say that since 1968, I've never lost the joy of what God did in my life. My very worst day since then has been better than my best prior to it. God is good!

Home Base

I've had terrible things happen in my life, but they've just been momentary flashes. Any discouragement or depression I've felt has never lasted more than an hour or so. Since 1968, there hasn't been a full day that I haven't had peace and joy. Why? I place value and worth on the fact that God loves me.

As a kid in Arlington, Texas, we often played a game called "Wolf and Sheep." The "wolf" had to capture the "sheep" and put them in jail. While the wolf was away, other sheep could come and set the prisoners free. The sheep had a "home base." Often, home base was a tree. But whenever the sheep were touching home base, they were safe. The wolf couldn't do anything to them and had to leave.

God is my home base! Whenever something bad happens, I just retreat and say, "Lord, You love me. Father, You value me. You're pleased with me." I start thinking about how much God loves me, and it makes every problem I have just melt away in comparison. Satan can't touch me when I'm valuing God's love for me.

I've spent a huge amount of time glorifying—esteeming, placing value and worth on—what God has done in my life. Because of that, it's only grown stronger and gotten better.

The reason you're a leaky vessel is because you aren't valuing what God has done in your life above all else. You're esteeming other things equal to, close to, or greater than the Lord and His opinion of you. You need to get to a place where you can honestly say, "God, You're more important to me than anyone or anything else. Nothing will compete with You!" Intentionally glorify God and disesteem everything else.

Focus on the Joy

Jesus disesteemed the shame that accompanied His crucifixion.

> For the joy that was set before him endured the cross, despising the shame.
>
> HEBREWS 12:2

Jesus chose to focus on the joy. Most of us would have had such short-term thinking in that situation that we wouldn't have seen any joy in it. But Jesus looked ahead to the resurrection. He knew the cross wasn't going to be the end. He knew that He would triumph over Satan and liberate the human race. The Lord looked down through eternity and saw you and me. He saw our bondages, hurts, pains, sicknesses, diseases, and poverty. He said in His heart, "I'm going to die to redeem them. I'm going to bring them joy." He chose to magnify and glorify that and to disesteem the shame, rejection, and physical suffering. He chose to disesteem the fact that He was going to be stripped naked, mocked, and insulted. He chose to minimize those things and maximize the other. He's the one who placed that value on it.

You are the one who determines the value of everything in your life. You choose how you esteem or disesteem anything and everything. Once that lady in North Carolina put a relative value on her divorce, she decided that receiving the Lord was much more important. Then she began to magnify and glorify that. You're the one who determines that you can't live with or without all these things—but you can always change your determination!

"God Loves Me!"
LESSON 3 – OUTLINE

1. God supernaturally revealed His love to me in a Saturday night prayer meeting.

   A. It was March 23, 1968, and I was eighteen years old.

   B. God's unconditional love was no longer an abstract concept to me—it was real!

   C. For the next four-and-a-half months, I literally experienced God's supernatural love transforming my life.

2. Satan tried to get me to value man's opinion more than what God had revealed to me.

   A. If I had begun placing value on that, then my value, worth, and reverence for what God had said would have started coming down, and I would have begun losing the revelation of it.

   B. When these people—whom I respected, had tried to please, and had tried to gain their acceptance—started ragging on me, I just turned away.

   C. I maintained the same relative worth and value on the things of God, and because of this, God's supernatural, unconditional love that He had given me didn't diminish.

3. Your love for God ought to make your love for your parents, spouse, children, and friends look like hate in comparison (Luke 14:26).

   A. You should love them, but your love and intimacy with the Lord should far surpass it.

   B. You'll run into problems when your relative worth for these things, such as relationships, the recognition of others, and your career is too close to your worth for God.

   C. These things are okay in their proper place, but what if loving, following, and speaking for God costs you relationships, career, or acceptance?

   D. Would you do whatever the Lord asked you, or would your relative worth be too close?

4. At one time or another, the Lord has touched you in a significant way.

   A. Then Satan came at you in a myriad of ways in order to get you to place value on something other than God.

B. He attacked that Word and the worth you placed on it in an attempt to get your identity off of what God said.

C. If you've lost the manifestation of your joy, peace, healing, or revelation, it's because somewhere along the way you quit glorifying God.

5. I've had terrible things happen in my life, but they've just been momentary flashes.

   A. Any discouragement or depression I've felt has never lasted more than an hour or so.

   B. Since 1968, there hasn't been a full day that I haven't had peace and joy.

   C. I place value and worth on the fact that God loves me.

   D. I've spent a huge amount of time glorifying—esteeming, placing value and worth on—what God has done in my life, and because of that, it's only grown stronger and gotten better.

6. The reason you're a leaky vessel is because you aren't valuing what God has done in your life above all else.

   A. You're esteeming other things equal to, close to, or greater than the Lord and His opinion of you.

   B. You need to intentionally glorify God and disesteem everything else.

   For the joy that was set before him endured the cross, despising the shame.

   HEBREWS 12:2

   C. You are the one who determines the value of everything in your life.

   D. You're the one who determines that you can't live with or without all these things— but you can always change your determination!

"God Loves Me!"
LESSON 3 – TEACHER'S GUIDE

1.   God supernaturally revealed His love to me in a Saturday night prayer meeting. It was March 23, 1968, and I was eighteen years old. God's unconditional love was no longer an abstract concept to me—it was real! For the next four-and-a-half months, I literally experienced God's supernatural love transforming my life.

2.   Satan tried to get me to value man's opinion more than what God had revealed to me. If I had begun placing value on that, then my value, worth, and reverence for what God had said would have started coming down, and I would have begun losing the revelation of it. When these people—whom I respected, had tried to please, and had tried to gain their acceptance—started ragging on me, I just turned away. I maintained the same relative worth and value on the things of God, and because of this, God's supernatural, unconditional love that He had given me didn't diminish.

3.   Our love for God ought to make our love for our parents, our spouses, our children, and friends look like hate in comparison (Luke 14:26). We should love them, but our love and intimacy with the Lord should far surpass it. We run into problems when our relative worth for these things—relationships, the recognition of others, our careers—and God are too close. These things are okay in their proper place, but what if loving, following, and speaking for God costs us relationships, our careers, or acceptance? Would we do whatever the Lord asked us, or would our relative worth be too close?

1. A. When was it that God supernaturally revealed His love to Andrew? (At a Saturday night prayer meeting on March 23, 1968)
   B. What happened during those next four-and-a-half months? (Andrew literally experienced God's supernatural love transforming his life)
2. A. What did Satan do? (He tried to get Andrew to value man's opinion more than what God had revealed to him)
   B. When Andrew maintained the same relative worth and value on the things of God, what happened? (God's supernatural, unconditional love that He had given him didn't diminish)
3. A. According to Luke 14:26, our love for God ought to make our love for our parents, our spouses, our children, and our friends look like what in comparison? (Hatred)
   B. We should love them, but our love and intimacy with the Lord should what? (Far surpass it)
   C. When is it that we run into problems? (When our relative worth for these things—relationships, the recognition of others, our careers—and God are too close)

4. At one time or another, the Lord has touched us in a significant way. Then Satan came at us in a myriad of ways in order to get us to place value on something other than God. He attacked that Word and the worth we placed on it in an attempt to get our identity off of what God said. If we've lost the manifestation of our joy, peace, healing, or revelation, it's because somewhere along the way we quit glorifying God.

5. I've had terrible things happen in my life, but they've just been momentary flashes. Any discouragement or depression I've felt has never lasted more than an hour or so. Since 1968, there hasn't been a full day that I haven't had peace and joy. I place value and worth on the fact that God loves me. I've spent a huge amount of time glorifying—esteeming, placing value and worth on—what God has done in my life, and because of that, it's only grown stronger and gotten better.

6. The reason we're leaky vessels is because we aren't valuing what God has done in our life above all else. We're esteeming other things equal to, close to, or greater than the Lord and His opinion of us. We need to intentionally glorify God and disesteem everything else (Heb. 12:2). We are the ones who determine the value of everything in our lives. We're the ones who determine that we can't live with or without all these things—but we can always change our determination!

4. A. When the Lord touches us in a significant way, what happens next? (Satan comes at us in a myriad of ways in order to get us to place value on something other than God)
   B. Why do we lose the manifestation of our joy, peace, healing, or revelation? (Somewhere along the way, we quit glorifying God)
5. A. Andrew has spent a huge amount of time doing what? (Glorifying—esteeming, placing value and worth on—what God has done in his life)
   B. What has that done? (Caused it to grow stronger and get better)
6. A. Why are we leaky vessels? (We aren't valuing what God has done in our lives above all else)
   B. According to Jesus' example in Hebrews 12:2, what must we do to correct this? (We need to intentionally glorify God and disesteem everything else)

"God Loves Me!"
LESSON 3 – DISCIPLESHIP QUESTIONS

1. According to Luke 14:26, what should your love for God make your love for your parents, spouse, children, and friends look like in comparison?

2. Which of these people compete with your love for God the most?
   A. Parents.
   B. Spouse.
   C. Children.
   D. Friends.

3. In this Lesson, Andrew shared how the devil tried to use certain people in his life to steal away the Word. Describe a time in your life when you experienced this too. What did you do? How did things turn out?

4. What did Jesus set before Himself in Hebrews 12:2?

5. What did this enable Him to do?

6. How did Jesus handle the shame?

7. What is it that you need to despise (disesteem) today?

8. What joy should you set before yourself today?

"God Loves Me!"
LESSON 3 – ANSWER KEY

1. Hatred.

2. Answers will vary.

3. Answers will vary.

4. Joy.

5. Endure the cross.

6. He despised it.

7. Answers will vary.

8. Answers will vary.

"God Loves Me!"
LESSON 3 – SCRIPTURES

And be not drunk with wine, wherein is excess; but be filled with the Spirit.

EPHESIANS 5:18

If any man come to me, and hate not his father, and mother, and wife, and children, and brethren, and sisters, yea, and his own life also, he cannot be my disciple.

LUKE 14:26

Looking unto Jesus the author and finisher of our faith; who for the joy that was set before him endured the cross, despising the shame, and is set down at the right hand of the throne of God.

HEBREWS 12:2

What Do You Value?
LESSON 4

For I speak to you Gentiles, inasmuch as I am the apostle of the Gentiles, I magnify mine office.

ROMANS 11:13

This Greek word rendered "magnify" here is the same one translated "glorified" in Romans 1:21. Therefore, *magnify* and *glorify* can be used interchangeably. They're the same thing. To glorify God is to magnify Him. *Magnify* means "to make bigger."

Did you know that you can make God bigger? Technically speaking, you can't affect His actual size and greatness. God is who He is, regardless of what you think. However, as far as your perception and experience of Him goes, you can make God bigger or smaller in your life. It all depends on how you think.

When you look through the small end of a set of binoculars, everything becomes bigger. But if you turned it around and looked through the big end, everything would become smaller. Although it's the same binoculars, your view enlarges or shrinks according to how you use it.

Our minds are like a pair of binoculars. Depending on the choices we make and the things we focus on, we can either magnify God and diminish our problems—or vice versa. The sad truth is that most of us have become masters at making the smallest, most insignificant things bigger, minimizing God and His Word. In our negativity, we focus on and magnify the tiny little toothpick the devil puts in our path. By the time we're finished thinking about what could happen, it's become a huge baseball bat that Satan uses to beat our brains out. But we're the ones who magnified it and made it so big!

What's Bothering You?

One of our Bible college students wanted to see me. He came into my office and began to cry. Since something always seemed to bother him, I asked, "What's wrong now?" It was a Monday and he had attended church the day before. He said, "I was so hungry to hear God's Word, but the two women who were sitting in front of me talked and laughed throughout the entire service. They distracted me!" Then he broke down weeping about how the devil had used this to steal away the Word.

I had just gotten off the phone with a friend of mine. He'd just lost his wife of nearly fifty years. I'd called to minister to him, but he was glorifying and magnifying the Lord, saying, "God is so great! God is so good! I love Him so much!" His mate of almost half a century had just died, yet he was praising and thanking God.

Yet, here was this other guy sitting in my office crying because he missed hearing a message. Two women talked, and he was ready to give up. That's stupid! Why didn't he just get up and move or ask them to be quiet? This wasn't a big deal until he magnified it.

What's bothering you today? A year from now, you probably won't even remember it. Even if the Lord doesn't intervene and fix this situation you're so upset about, in twelve months you'll forget it. Why? It's insignificant. It's not really a problem. You're just magnifying it.

When people come up to me in prayer lines and tell me their problem, sometimes I literally have to bite my lip to keep from laughing. I want to say, "This is it? This is the big problem that's derailed you? I've had worse things happen on my good days!"

Honestly, some of the things people get so upset over are nothing. I'd like to buy them a one-way ticket to some third-world country I've been to where they can see firsthand what true hardship and suffering is really like. They'd return with a whole new perspective—and they'd magnify things very differently!

Misplaced Values

We talk about how kids have it so hard today. They whine if they don't have the newest electronic device. Life isn't difficult on children today. This is the easiest generation that has ever been!

Thomas A. Crapper was born in England in 1836. When he was eleven years old, his parents gave him a sack with some clothes and one day's food supply in it. They told him they loved him, patted him on the back, and sent him on his way. He walked 165 miles to London. He had no relatives or anyone else to look out for him. He was on his own—live or die, sink or swim. He didn't have a government-sponsored social system like we have today. He couldn't exist on welfare. He could have died. Thomas was on his own at eleven years of age!

I couldn't imagine one my kids being out on their own and trying to make their way in life at eleven years old. *This had to be unusual!* The next paragraph said this was very unusual. Most kids didn't leave home until they were twelve. If you were a typical twelve-year-old in England in the 1840s, you were on your own to make your way in life as an adult—live or die, sink or swim. Now that's pressure!

Not having designer jeans, the newest video game, or being able to watch MTV isn't pressure. Not being able to drive a car, stay out past eleven, or do everything their friends do isn't pressure.

The reason we consider that pressure is because we've magnified it. We've said that peer acceptance is so important, that kids need to feel good about themselves and have positive self-esteem. One hundred and fifty years ago, people were just trying to survive and live another day. They didn't have time to think about their self-esteem. The reason so many people are so messed up emotionally today is because we have misplaced values.

"But we live in a high-stress society. Nobody has lived under the pressure we have today!" Have you ever been a soldier in a combat zone? That's pressure. Wives and children during World War II had to see their husbands and fathers go off to war and never come back. That's pressure. Sitting in a traffic jam is only pressure because you make it pressure. It's because of the way you think. You needed five minutes to get from A to B, but you only gave yourself three. You've put pressure on yourself and magnified these things.

This isn't a high-pressure society; it's the most privileged, luxurious, easy generation that's ever lived on the face of the earth! If you're feeling pressure, worn out, and burned out, it's because you have misplaced values. You're pressing yourself. It's not our society. You chose to get on the treadmill. You're the one who magnifies or minimizes everything that comes into your life.

What's Bigger to You?

What do you value? What's big to you? Is your problem bigger to you than God? You can magnify the Lord and make Him bigger. The way you do so is by glorifying, praising, and thanking Him. Find someone in the Word who had a similar situation and overcame it. Meditate on it and make these things more real to you than what your bank account, relatives, friends, or even what your own mind says. You need to get to a place where God's Word is true and the Lord is far bigger than the situation.

Consider Jehoshaphat going out and fighting the mighty armies arrayed against him (2 Chr. 20:20-22). He put the singers out in front praising the Lord, and He defeated the enemy without them even drawing a sword or firing an arrow. Just say, "God, that's how big You are! You destroyed hundreds of thousands of enemy troops through singers praising. You're awesome!" That makes God bigger. Then you intentionally disesteem your problems and say, "This is of no value. It's of no worth to me!"

I'm not in the ministry to have you like me; I'm doing it because God has placed a call on my life. When He called me, I was an introvert. I was shy, embarrassed, and could hardly talk to anyone. Standing in front of people was the last thing I wanted to do, and for the first two years, it was terrible. I struggled with fear and all kinds of things. But the Lord has shared some truths with me that have changed both my life and the lives of many others. I minister out of love for God and to help people. However, I don't prefer that you dislike me.

It doesn't bless me when someone comes up after a service and tells me they didn't like the message. But do you know what? It doesn't keep me up at night either. I don't lose one bit of sleep over it. Why? When it comes right down to it, I don't give a rip! I minister because I value God so much and He's leading me to do it—whether anyone likes what I have to say or not.

If you're afraid to witness, it's because you value the opinion and acceptance of others more than God's in your life. You don't want to expose yourself to the possibility of someone ridiculing, criticizing, or otherwise rejecting you. You haven't placed a proper value on God.

Refreshed and Restored

All Satan has to do after the Lord moves in your life is to put you in a situation where you compromise in some way or another. You have all these other things that are so important to you that you have to maintain, so you walk away from the revelation of God. But the Lord never quits transmitting.

God's love, joy, peace, healing, anointing, presence—or anything else—is there for you the same now as the moment you experienced Him. God loves you the same now as He did then. In fact, He loves you more than you've ever yet perceived—ever! God isn't the variable; you disesteemed God when you started esteeming someone or something else.

However, you can go back and refresh those things in your life by glorifying God. Say, "Father, forgive me for placing such value on other things. Forgive me for letting what other people thought be more important than what You've said and done. Forgive me for being more interested in the Super Bowl and the World Series than You. Forgive me for magnifying my business, family, and other things above You. I put them ahead of You and forgot You."

The way you glorify God is by talking about Him. Remember what He's said and done. Be thankful, and as you magnify the Lord, what He's done in your life will be refreshed and restored.

I constantly go back and remember the things that God has done in my life. They're actually more real to me now than when they first happened. They're bigger in my life today than they were almost forty years ago. I've never had to return to my first love, because I've never left (Rev. 2:4).

If you have to return to your first love, don't be condemned. Just return to Him. But don't ask God for a "fresh outpouring" of His love. That's like saying, "Lord, what You did wasn't good enough." God never quit transmitting; it was you who stopped receiving. Come back to Him and say, "Father, forgive me for ever walking away from what You said and did in my life. I valued, prized, and esteemed other things more highly than You." You can go right back to wherever you left God and start putting the proper worth, value, and esteem on Him. You can recover anything that you've "lost."

Encourage Yourself

The truth is—you never lost it! If you were ever healed, His healing virtue is still in you. It never leaves (Rom. 11:29). God never stopped releasing, but you quit receiving. Go back and build yourself up in that area. Receive by faith what the Lord has already provided by grace.

David encouraged himself in the LORD his God.

1 SAMUEL 30:6

In the midst of David's darkest moment, he magnified God. His troops spoke of stoning him. All their beloved wives and children were gone—not to mention their possessions. But instead of becoming discouraged and thinking, *Poor old me*, David encouraged himself in the Lord. He began to glorify and magnify God in the midst of a bad situation.

You can do that too! You can choose to get down, bawl and squall, gripe and complain. Or you can choose to magnify and glorify God.

I haven't been discouraged and depressed since 1968. "But, Andrew, you must not have any problems." I have problems just like anybody! In fact, ministers have more problems than others because they have invisible targets on them in the spirit realm. However, I've made some conscious decisions, that I like being full of joy and peace more than I like being discouraged and depressed. Therefore, I just encourage myself in the Lord.

Sometimes I have to literally shut out what's going on in my life and force myself to focus on God. I have to turn away from looking at the natural circumstances and choose to magnify and glorify God. At times, I've had to start doing it through gritted teeth. I didn't feel like it. I didn't have a rush of positive emotion. But through gritted teeth, I said, "God, I glorify You. You are awesome!" It wasn't very long before the joy and peace started flowing.

Raised from the Dead

Jamie and I received a call at 4:15 in the morning on March 4, 2001. It was our oldest son (Joshua), who told us that our youngest son (Peter) was dead. He'd been dead for over four hours. We had negative emotions just like you would've had, but—like I've been teaching in this study—I refused to let grief and sorrow occupy a higher place than my praise of God. We took authority over the situation, released our faith, and jumped in the car.

As Jamie and I drove that hour into town, I just started praising God. I thanked Him for His faithfulness and let Him know that I would continue serving and loving Him with all my heart regardless of what happened with our son.

As I began to magnify God, faith rose up in my heart, and I knew that I knew Peter would live. When we arrived into Colorado Springs, we found out that five or ten minutes after we had received the call and prayed, Peter just sat up and started talking. He'd been stripped naked and put in a cooler with a toe tag on him, but God raised him from the dead after nearly five hours. Thank You, Jesus! And there was no brain damage—or as Peter himself says—"No more brain damage than before."

All of this happened because I refused to let anything else occupy God's rightful place.

You're the one who can choose to do these things. You can edify yourself!

Give Glory

Abraham was...

Strong in faith, [How?] giving glory to God.

ROMANS 4:20, BRACKETS MINE

Magnify God! Give Him glory! Put worth and value on Him. Say, "Lord, You're bigger than this financial problem, marriage issue, relationship challenge, health crisis, or job. God, You're bigger than anything! You are awesome!" When you start magnifying God, your faith just grows.

The reason some of us don't operate in more faith is because we haven't spent any time magnifying God and verbally acknowledging that He's bigger than our problems.

You need to say things like, "God, You are bigger than my problem. You're bigger than these situations I'm facing!" When you magnify and glorify Him, your faith rises and anything is possible.

All things are possible to him that believeth.

MARK 9:23

But it's up to you to glorify God!

God Matters Most

Most of us aren't doing this very well today. We magnify our problems. Our society is geared toward magnifying insignificant things. Therefore, we need to put the right value on things.

One night, someone broke into a department store and didn't steal anything. However, they did change all the price tags. The next day, a $200 vacuum cleaner sold for $8, and an $8 item sold for $200. That store did business until noon before they figured out what had happened. This caused great havoc!

That's what Satan has done in our society. He's come in and changed the value on us. We think we need certain things. We put so much attention on physical, material things, but they don't really matter in light of eternity. When it's all over, God is who will matter most.

Your relationship with the Lord is really the only thing that matters in your life. Therefore, you need to place the appropriate value and worth upon it. Do so consistently and you'll stay full of healing, joy, peace, deliverance, anointing, power—whatever you need. You are the one who determines how full you are. God isn't the one who decides. True revival is simply you becoming so full of God that you overflow onto someone else. This isn't up to God—it's up to you!

What Do You Value?
LESSON 4 – OUTLINE

1. The Greek word rendered "magnify" in Romans 11:13 is the same one translated "glorified" in Romans 1:21.

>   For I speak to you Gentiles, inasmuch as I am the apostle of the Gentiles, I magnify mine office.
>
>   ROMANS 11:13

   A. Therefore, *magnify* and *glorify* can be used interchangeably.

   B. To glorify God is to magnify Him.

2. *Magnify* means "to make bigger."

   A. Technically speaking, you can't affect God's actual size and greatness.

   B. However, as far as your perception and experience of Him goes, you can make God bigger or smaller in your life.

   C. It all depends on how you think.

3. Depending on the choices you make and the things you focus on, you can either magnify God and diminish your problems—or vice versa.

   A. The sad truth is that most of us have become masters at making the smallest, most insignificant things bigger while minimizing God and His Word.

   B. What's bothering you today?

   C. Even if the Lord doesn't intervene and fix this situation you're so upset about, in twelve months you'll forget it.

   D. The reason so many people are so messed up emotionally today is because they have misplaced values.

   E. You're the one who magnifies or minimizes everything that comes into your life.

4. The way you magnify the Lord and make Him bigger is by glorifying, praising, and thanking Him.

   A. Find someone in the Word who had a similar situation and overcame it.

B. Meditate on it and make these things more real to you than what your bank account, relatives, friends, or even what your own mind says.

C. You need to get to a place where God's Word is true, and the Lord is far bigger than the situation (2 Chr. 20:20-22).

5. All Satan has to do after the Lord moves in your life is to put you in a situation where you compromise in some way or another.

A. You have all these other things that are so important to you that you have to maintain, so you walk away from the revelation of God.

B. God's love, joy, peace, healing, anointing, presence—or anything else—is there for you now the same as the moment you experienced Him.

C. You can go back and refresh those things in your life by glorifying God.

D. God never stopped releasing (transmitting), but you quit receiving (Rom. 11:29).

6. Receive by faith what the Lord has already provided by grace.

A. In the midst of David's darkest moment, he magnified God.

David encouraged himself in the LORD his God

1 SAMUEL 30:6

B. You can choose to get down, bawl and squall, gripe and complain—or you can choose to magnify and glorify God.

C. Sometimes I have to literally shut out what's going on in my life and force myself to focus on God.

7. The reason some of us don't operate in more faith is because we haven't spent any time magnifying God and verbally acknowledging that He's bigger than our problems.

A. Abraham was…

Strong in faith, [How?] giving glory to God.

ROMANS 4:20, BRACKETS MINE

B. When you magnify and glorify Him, your faith rises and anything is possible.

All things are possible to him that believeth.

MARK 9:23

8. Your relationship with the Lord is really the only thing that matters in your life.

   A. As you consistently place the appropriate value and worth upon it, you'll stay full of healing, joy, peace, deliverance, anointing, power—whatever you need.

   B. You are the one who determines how full you are; God isn't the one who decides.

   C. True revival is simply you becoming so full of God that you overflow onto someone else.

What Do You Value?
LESSON 4 – TEACHER'S GUIDE

1.   The Greek word rendered "magnify" in Romans 11:13 is the same one translated "glorified" in Romans 1:21. Therefore, "magnify" and "glorify" can be used interchangeably. To glorify God is to magnify Him.

2.   *Magnify* means "to make bigger." Technically speaking, we can't affect God's actual size and greatness. However, as far as our perception and experience of Him goes, we can make God bigger or smaller in our lives. It all depends on how we think.

3.   Depending on the choices we make and the things we focus on, we can either magnify God and diminish our problems—or vice versa. The sad truth is that most of us have become masters at making the smallest, most insignificant things bigger and minimizing God and His Word. What's bothering us today? Even if the Lord doesn't intervene and fix this situation we're so upset about, in twelve months we'll forget it. The reason so many of us are so messed up emotionally today is because we have misplaced values. We're the ones who magnify or minimize everything that comes into our lives.

4.   The way we magnify the Lord and make Him bigger is by glorifying, praising, and thanking Him. Find someone in the Word who had a similar situation and overcame it. We need to meditate on it and make these things more real to us than what our bank accounts, relatives, friends, or even what our own minds say. Let's get to the place where God's Word is true and the Lord is far bigger than the situation (2 Chr. 20:20-22).

1. A. Which word in Romans 1:21 is translated from the same Greek word rendered "magnify" in Romans 11:13? ("Glorified")
   B. Complete this phrase: To glorify God is to _____ Him. (Magnify)
2. A. What does magnify mean? (To make bigger)
   B. What does our perception and experience of God depend on? (How we think)
3. A. Why are so many of us so messed up emotionally today? (We have misplaced values)
   B. Who is it that magnifies or minimizes everything that comes into our lives? (We do)
4. A. Read 2 Chronicles 20:20-22. How is it that we magnify the Lord and make Him bigger in our lives? (By glorifying, praising, and thanking Him)
   B. What should we meditate on until it becomes more real to us than what our bank accounts, relatives, friends, or even what our own minds say? (God's Word)

5.   All Satan has to do after the Lord moves in our lives is to put us in a situation where we compromise in some way or another. We have all these other things that are so important to us that we have to maintain, so we walk away from the revelation of God. God's love, joy, peace, healing, anointing, presence—or anything else—is there for us the same as the moment we experienced Him. We can go back and refresh those things in our lives by glorifying God. God never stopped releasing (transmitting), but we quit receiving (Rom. 11:29).

6.   Receive by faith what the Lord has already provided by grace. In the midst of David's darkest moment, he magnified God (1 Sam. 30:6). We can choose to get down, bawl and squall, gripe and complain—or we can choose to magnify and glorify God. Sometimes we have to literally shut out what's going on in our lives and force ourselves to focus on God.

7.   The reason some of us don't operate in more faith is because we haven't spent any time magnifying God and verbally acknowledging that He's bigger than our problems. Abraham was "strong in faith, [How?] giving glory to God" (Rom. 4:20, brackets mine). When we magnify and glorify Him, our faith rises and anything is possible (Mark 9:23).

8.   Our relationship with the Lord is really the only thing that matters in our lives. As we consistently place the appropriate value and worth upon it, we'll stay full of healing, joy, peace, deliverance, anointing, power—whatever we need. We are the ones who determine how full we are; God isn't the one who decides. True revival is simply us becoming so full of God that we overflow onto someone else.

5. A.   How can we go back and refresh God's love, joy, peace, healing, anointing, presence—or anything else? (By glorifying God)
   B.   Read Romans 11:29. If God never stopped releasing (transmitting), then what happened? (We quit receiving)
6. A.   What did David do in 1 Samuel 30:6? (In the midst of his darkest moment, he magnified God)
   B.   What must we do sometimes? (Literally shut out what's going on in our lives and force ourselves to focus on God)
7. A.   According to Romans 4:20, how was Abraham strong in faith? (He gave glory to God—magnifying Him and verbally acknowledging that God was bigger than his problem)
   B.   Read Mark 9:23. What happens when we magnify and glorify God? (Our faith rises and anything is possible)
8. A.   What is the only thing that really matters in our lives? (Our relationship with the Lord)
   B.   How do we stay full of healing, joy, peace, deliverance, anointing, power—or anything else we need? (By consistently placing the appropriate value and worth upon our relationship with God)
   C.   What is true revival? (Us becoming so full of God that we overflow onto someone else)

What Do You Value?
LESSON 4 – ADDITIONAL INFORMATION

A young minister and his wife were recently married. She told everyone that she wanted a dozen children. While they were out itinerating, she became pregnant. She called back and told everyone about it. They rejoiced with her. But when she returned and went to the doctor, they said it was a cancer and they needed to do an immediate hysterectomy. The doctor told her she only had a 50 percent chance of living and that she couldn't live more than two weeks without the surgery. This woman was just devastated.

After a Thursday night service, I was laughing, joking, and cutting up with someone. This woman came over and tapped me on the shoulder. When I turned around, she was crying and asked, "Andrew, have you heard what they said?" I don't always respond this way, but I believe God had me do so. I just started laughing and declared, "Cancer's no problem with God. You act like all the lights in heaven would dim from the power drain if the Lord were to heal you, but it's not hard for God to heal cancer. No problem!"

It seemed as if I had slapped this woman in the face! She immediately stopped crying and asked, "Would you come over to our house and tell my husband and me about this?" So Jamie and I went over and talked to her. She said, "Well, what should I do?"

"It's your choice. You can let them do the hysterectomy. You can go that route if you want to, but you'll never have children again."

"What other option do I have?"

"You can just believe God. It's not any harder to be healed of cancer than it is a cold."

She asked, "Do you really believe that?" So I started magnifying and glorifying God. I made the Lord bigger and diminished cancer. The only thing that makes cancer hard is the value you place on it.

She decided to believe God. The doctors came and made her sign a ton of paperwork to absolve them of liability and responsibility "when" she died. They intimidated her and told her she was foolish. They tried to make her put more value on their diagnosis than God's Word.

Now, I'm not against doctors. I have one on my board of directors. Praise God for doctors. If it weren't for them, many Christians would have died prematurely. However, medical professionals are limited to the natural realm, and they don't often value God, His Word, or His power.

These doctors tried to get her to change the value she had placed on God's ability. By His grace, she stood her ground. It's now been almost twenty years since she refused that operation—and she has a whole slew of children. Since no doctor would ever deliver her kids after seeing her records, she just had them all at home. It was that simple!

What Do You Value?
LESSON 4 – DISCIPLESHIP QUESTIONS

1. According to Romans 11:13, what was Paul's office?

2. What did he do with this office?

3. Which word in Romans 1:21 is translated from the same Greek word as "magnify" in Romans 11:13?

4. In 2 Chronicles 20:20-22, what did Jehoshaphat admonish the people to do?

5. If they did, what did he say would happen?

6. What did the appointed singers do?

7. What did the Lord do when His people began to sing and praise?

8. What did the Lord have against His people in Revelation 2:4?

9. According to Romans 11:29, what are without repentance?
   A. The wrath of God.
   B. The gifts of God.
   C. The judgment of God.
   D. The calling of God.

10. In light of this truth, will God ever change His mind and take away from you something He's given?

11. According to 1 Samuel 30:6, who encouraged David in the darkest moment of his life?

12. According to Romans 4:20, how was Abraham strong in faith?

13. In Mark 9:23, what is possible?

14. To whom?

What Do You Value?

1. Apostle of the Gentiles.

2. He magnified it.

3. Glorified.

4. Believe in the Lord your God and His prophets.

5. They would be established and prosper.

6. They went out before the army and said, "Praise the Lord, for His mercy endures forever."

7. He set up ambushes against their enemies, and their enemies were smitten.

8. They had left their first love—they stopped glorifying and magnifying how much the Lord had loved them first.

9. B. The gifts of God.
   D. The calling of God.

10. No.

11. David encouraged himself in the Lord his God.

12. He gave glory to God—magnified and glorified Him.

13. All things.

14. Those who believe.

What Do You Value?
LESSON 4 – SCRIPTURES

For I speak to you Gentiles, inasmuch as I am the apostle of the Gentiles, I magnify mine office.

ROMANS 11:13

Because that, when they knew God, they glorified him not as God, neither were thankful; but became vain in their imaginations, and their foolish heart was darkened.

ROMANS 1:21

As they went forth, Jehoshaphat stood and said…Believe in the LORD your God, so shall ye be established; believe his prophets, so shall ye prosper. And when he had consulted with the people, he appointed singers unto the LORD, and that should praise the beauty of holiness, as they went out before the army, and to say, Praise the LORD; for his mercy endureth for ever. And when they began to sing and to praise, the LORD set ambushments against the children of Ammon, Moab, and mount Seir, which were come against Judah; and they were smitten.

2 CHRONICLES 20:20-22

Nevertheless I have somewhat against thee, because thou hast left thy first love.

REVELATION 2:4

For the gifts and calling of God are without repentance.

ROMANS 11:29

And David was greatly distressed; for the people spake of stoning him, because the soul of all the people was grieved, every man for his sons and for his daughters: but David encouraged himself in the LORD his God.

1 SAMUEL 30:6

He staggered not at the promise of God through unbelief; but was strong in faith, giving glory to God.

ROMANS 4:20

Jesus said unto him, If thou canst believe, all things are possible to him that believeth.

MARK 9:23

Set Joy Before You
LESSON 5

Most Christians don't know how to maintain what God has done in their lives. He touches them and they get turned on, but six months later it's as if they lost it. This isn't the way God intended for it to be.

Romans 1:21 shows us how people walk away from a revelation of God's existence, His hatred for sin, and our accountability to Him. It reveals four things we do to harden and desensitize ourselves to what God has done in our lives.

First, we don't glorify God. We don't put value and worth on Him. We don't esteem or prize the revelation He gives us. The word *glorify* speaks of the value we place on what God has said and done.

Most people don't value the things of God properly. When we begin valuing the opinions and experiences of others more than what God says in His Word and what He's done in our lives, we turn insensitive. The blessing, benefit, and joy from what God has done in our lives starts wearing off when we quit placing the proper value on it.

Look Past the Heartache

Not only do you need to put a positive value on what God has said and done in your life, but you also need to devalue anything else that comes against you. It's a two-edged sword!

You can't just say, "Father, I value what You've done. I glorify You and magnify what You've done in my life"; you also have to make a conscious effort to disesteem and devalue everything else in a comparative sense.

Jesus faced the cross, but focused on the joy that was "set before" Him (Heb. 12:2). Mentally, He captured His thoughts. It wasn't natural. As He headed to the cross, Jesus didn't have a rush of natural feelings, like excitement and happiness. It took effort, but He looked beyond the cross and saw the joy there. He saw the fact that this would please His Father, appease His wrath, and that He would resurrect from the dead and one day be seated at His Father's right hand. He also saw you and me. The Lord's heart beat with such love for the world that it enabled Him to look past the heartache.

Minimize the Negative

This is such an important key to victory! If you ever do anything that amounts to anything, if you ever touch someone else's life, if you ever succeed in any endeavor, there will be problems between you and that success. The person who succeeds is the one who can look past those problems, hurts, and pains and actually glorify, magnify, and esteem the solution. It's a person that can see beyond the cost and value the answer above it. That's what separates losers from victors.

Every millionaire I've ever read about has gone bust more than once, but they had something on the inside that just kept them moving forward anyway. They knew that they knew that they knew that there was a way to succeed. So they kept this goal—this prize—in front of them. Because of it, they were able to endure things that destroyed other people.

I've also seen just the opposite. Even though everything seems to work for some people, they just have a defeated mentality and expect something to fail. Then they fall apart like a two-dollar suitcase when the first little problem comes their way. The issue isn't the challenging situation on the outside, but the failure on the inside.

The Lord set the joy in front of Him and despised—disesteemed—the shame (Heb. 12:2). Your thoughts either magnify or shrink everything. It's not what happens to you that's important, but how you perceive and process it.

When you magnify negative things, they become insurmountable. But you can also take huge things and disesteem or shrink them. If Jesus could take the cross and the shame associated with it and disesteem it, then you can despise anything. You can reduce anything that comes against you to nothing.

All Times

> I will bless the LORD at all times: his praise shall continually be in my mouth.
> PSALM 34:1

Most Christians know this scripture, but don't really believe it works. They say, "Well, you can praise God up to a point, but beyond that you can't expect me to praise the Lord in this situation!" In other words, the Word doesn't really mean "all times"; it means all times except "these times."

If you put the proper value and worth on God and spiritual things, nothing in this life can compare. You can disesteem and devalue anything in this life so that nothing can bother you or steal your joy.

But what if you're going through a divorce? What if your spouse cheated on you? It's terrible! How can you rejoice through that? Psychology would say that you're in denial if you do.

You could focus on the Lord and say, "Thank You, Jesus, that Your Word says that in heaven, we won't marry or be given in marriage. This is temporary. I'm so glad I get to live forever with You and not this other person." Now, that's something to rejoice about! "Thank You, Jesus, that You'll never divorce me. You'll never leave me nor forsake me." You can rejoice even if you're going through a divorce.

Change Your World

Who cares if you're going to die? You're going to die someday anyway. Life is a terminal experience. We're all in different stages of dying—even you younger folks. You don't have as many years left as you used to. "Oh, that's terrible!" Paul didn't think so. He wrestled between his strong desire to be with the Lord and staying on earth to minister.

If you value things properly, you can get to a place where dying isn't a problem. When the doctor tells you you're going to die, you could just reach up and kiss him, saying, "That's awesome! I believe in healing, so I believe God will heal me. But if I'm not healed, it'll be awesome just to sit in the presence of the Lord. What a deal!"

If you can't do that, it's because you have misplaced values. You still glorify this physical life—carnal things—more than eternal things.

Marriage is wonderful. Praise God for marriage. But if your marriage is so important that you couldn't make it without your mate, you have misplaced values. If your marriage went south all of a sudden and you couldn't survive, you have wrong values.

John Wesley, the great revivalist, had a horrible marriage. I've been to his house in London. His wife used to kick him and hit him while he was praying. She hated both God and him, yet he lived with her for twenty years. Even though she beat him, Wesley just went on and changed the world for God.

Responsive to God

"But my spouse doesn't love and appreciate me. It's stunting my growth." Pull your thumb out of your mouth and grow up! Recognize that there's something bigger than that. Just go on and follow the Lord.

Jesus faced the cross and counted it as nothing compared to the joy He focused on. He was stripped naked, spit on, His beard was plucked out, a crown of thorns was put on His head, His back was shredded, and He was ridiculed, but He disesteemed all that. It didn't matter. He was thinking on the joy to come.

Most of what we worry about is so insignificant. Some people say, "When I get to heaven, I'm going to ask God about this and that." No, you won't! Once you get there and know all things as you are known, you'll see everything in its right perspective. In view of God's awesomeness and splendor, you'll say, "I'm sure glad I didn't ask that stupid question and air out my little gripe." When you find yourself standing before Almighty God, you won't be holding Him to account, saying, "Why didn't You do this, and why didn't You do that?" Once you get God's perspective, it'll change your life.

The reason things are so big to us is because God is so small. If we would exalt, magnify, and value the Lord properly, He would become so big to us that all this other stuff wouldn't even matter. It wouldn't even be important. Once we get that attitude, we'll find that everything else in the natural will work better for us. We'll receive our healings easier. Our finances will work better. Our marriages will improve because we aren't codependent upon a person anymore. If they do something wrong, it won't affect our walk. We'll just keep right on walking with God, which is the best thing we can do for our mates anyhow.

My wife knows that I love God more than her—and vice versa. That would hurt and bother some people, but it's a blessing to me. Why? There are times when I do things wrong and disappoint my wife. If she gave me what I deserved, then I'd be in trouble. But Jamie has a commitment to the Lord, and I know He's never wrong. God is always the same. He's the one who brought us together in the first place, and He's the one who wants our marriage to stay together. I take great pleasure in the fact that my wife is more responsive to God than she is to me!

Perspective

Jesus set this joy before Himself, and that allowed Him to endure the cross. If you aren't enduring, it's probably because you don't have any joy set before you that you're focusing on. You're like a fly on a painting. Flies have compound eyes and see a thousand images of everything. Right now, you see 2,000 blobs of this ugly red color. But if you backed up and viewed the picture in perspective, you'd see how that little blob of paint fits perfectly and helps make it a masterpiece.

You can get so close to your problem that you can't see anything else, and you think the whole world is falling apart because of it. You need to get focused on something other than what's going on right now. Look beyond it. Lift up your eyes and look somewhere other than just down at your feet and what's going on.

Jesus overlooked His problem. That's what enabled Him to endure it. He disesteemed the shame and focused on the joy—and you can too!

Set Joy Before You
LESSON 5 – OUTLINE

1. Most people don't value the things of God properly.

   A. When we begin valuing the opinions and experiences of others more than what God says in His Word and what He's done in our lives, we turn insensitive.

   B. The blessing, benefit, and joy from what God has done in our lives starts wearing off when we quit placing the proper value on it.

2. Not only do you need to put a positive value on what God has said and done in your life, but you also need to devalue anything else that comes against you.

   A. It's a two-edged sword.

   B. Just like Jesus despised the shame of the cross and kept joy in front of Himself, you need to disesteem your situation and keep joy in front of yourself.

3. If you ever do anything that amounts to anything, if you ever touch someone else's life, if you ever succeed in any endeavor, there will be problems between you and that success.

   A. The person who succeeds is the one who can look past those problems, hurts, and pains and actually glorify, magnify, and esteem the solution.

   B. They can see beyond the cost and value the answer above it.

4. Your thoughts either magnify or shrink everything.

   A. It's not what happens to you that's important, but how you perceive and process it.

   B. When you magnify negative things, they become insurmountable.

   C. But you can also take huge things and disesteem or shrink them.

   D. If Jesus could take the cross and the shame associated with it and disesteem it, then you can despise and reduce anything that comes against you to nothing (Heb. 12:2).

5. If you put the proper value and worth on God and spiritual things, nothing in this life can compare.

   I will bless the LORD at all times: his praise shall continually be in my mouth.

   PSALM 34:1

A. You can disesteem and devalue anything in this life so that nothing can bother you or steal your joy.

B. Most of what we worry about is so insignificant.

C. The reason things are so big to us is because God is so small.

D. If you would exalt, magnify, and value the Lord properly, He would become so big to you that all this other stuff wouldn't even matter.

E. Once you get that attitude, you'll find that everything else in the natural will work better for you.

6. Jesus set this joy before Himself, and that allowed Him to endure the cross.

A. If you aren't enduring, it's probably because you don't have any joy set before you that you're focusing on.

B. You can get so close to your problem that you can't see anything else, and you think the whole world is falling apart because of it.

C. You need to focus on something other than what's going on right now.

D. Lift up your eyes and look somewhere other than just down at your feet and what's going on.

E. Jesus overlooked His problem, which is what enabled Him to endure it.

F. He disesteemed the shame and focused on the joy—and you can too!

Set Joy Before You
LESSON 5 – TEACHER'S GUIDE

1. Most of us don't value the things of God properly. When we begin valuing the opinions and experiences of others more than what God says in His Word and what He's done in our lives, we turn insensitive. The blessing, benefit, and joy from what God has done in our lives starts wearing off when we quit placing the proper value on it.

2. Not only do we need to put a positive value on what God has said and done in our lives, but we also need to devalue anything else that comes against us. It's a two-edged sword. Just like Jesus despised the shame of the cross and kept joy in front of Himself, we need to disesteem our situation and keep joy in front of ourselves.

3. If we ever do anything that amounts to anything, if we ever touch someone else's life, if we ever succeed in any endeavor, there will be problems between us and that success. The person who succeeds is the one who can look past those problems, hurts, and pains and actually glorify, magnify, and esteem the solution. They can see beyond the cost and value the answer above it.

1. A. When do we begin to be insensitive to God? (When we begin valuing the opinions and experiences of others more than what God says in His Word and what He's done in our lives)
   B. What happens to the blessing, benefit, and joy from what God has done in our lives when we quit placing the proper value on it? (They start wearing off)
2. A. In addition to placing a proper positive value on what God has said and done in our lives, what else must we do? (We need to devalue anything else that comes against us)
   B. How did Jesus exemplify this to us? (He despised—disesteemed—the shame of the cross and kept joy in front of Himself)
3. A. If we ever do anything that amounts to anything, what will be between us and that success? (Problems)
   B. Who is the person who will succeed? (The one who can look past those problems, hurt, and pains and actually glorify, magnify, and esteem the solution)

4.   Our thoughts either magnify or shrink everything. It's not what happens to us that's important, but how we perceive and process it. When we magnify negative things, they become insurmountable. But we can also take huge things and disesteem or shrink them. If Jesus could take the cross and the shame associated with it and disesteem it, then we can despise and reduce anything that comes against us to nothing (Heb. 12:2).

5.   If we put the proper value and worth on God and spiritual things, nothing in this life can compare (Ps. 34:1). We can disesteem and devalue anything in this life so that nothing can bother us or steal our joy. Most of what we worry about is so insignificant. The reason things are so big to us is because God is so small. If we would exalt, magnify, and value the Lord properly, He would become so big to us that all this other stuff wouldn't even matter. Once we get that attitude, we'll find that everything else in the natural will work better for us.

6.   Jesus set this joy before Himself, and that allowed Him to endure the cross. If we aren't enduring, it's probably because we don't have any joy set before us that we're focusing on instead. We can get so close to our problems that we can't see anything else, and we think the whole world is falling apart because of it. We need to focus on something other than what's going on right now. Let's lift up our eyes and look somewhere other than just down at our feet and what's going on. Jesus overlooked His problem, which is what enabled Him to endure it. He disesteemed the shame and focused on the joy—and we can too!

4. A. What do our thoughts do? (They either magnify or shrink everything)
   B. Read Hebrews 12:2. If Jesus can take the cross and the shame associated with it and disesteem it, what can we do? (We can despise and reduce anything that comes against us to nothing)
5. A. Read Psalm 34:1. What happens when we exalt, magnify, and value the Lord properly? (He becomes so big to us that all this other stuff doesn't even matter)
   B. Once we get that attitude, what will we find? (That everything else in the natural will work better for us)
6. Why is it we aren't enduring? (We don't have any joy set before us that we're focusing on)

Set Joy Before You
LESSON 5 – DISCIPLESHIP QUESTIONS

1. According to Romans 1:21, put the four progressive steps in their biblical order of how people walk away from a revelation of God's existence, His hatred for sin, and how we're accountable to Him:

   A. "Became vain in their imaginations."
   B. "They glorified him not as God."
   C. "Their foolish heart was darkened."
   D. "Neither were thankful."

2. According to Hebrews 12:2, what did Jesus focus His attention on?

3. What did He despise?

4. Where is He now?

5. According to Psalm 34:1, when should we bless the Lord?

6. When should His praise be in our mouths?

7. Is there any situation, scenario, or circumstance where we can't praise and bless the Lord?

Set Joy Before You
LESSON 5 – ANSWER KEY

1. B. "They glorified him not as God."
   D. "Neither were thankful."
   A. "Became vain in their imaginations."
   C. "Their foolish heart was darkened."

2. The joy that was set before Him.

3. The shame.

4. At the right hand of the throne of God.

5. At all times.

6. Continually.

7. No.

Set Joy Before You
LESSON 5 – SCRIPTURES

Because that, when they knew God, they glorified him not as God, neither were thankful; but became vain in their imaginations, and their foolish heart was darkened.

ROMANS 1:21

Looking unto Jesus the author and finisher of our faith; who for the joy that was set before him endured the cross, despising the shame, and is set down at the right hand of the throne of God.

HEBREWS 12:2

I will bless the LORD at all times: his praise shall continually be in my mouth.

PSALM 34:1

It's Always Better to Choose God!
LESSON 6

By faith Moses, when he was come to years, refused to be called the son of Pharaoh's daughter; Choosing rather to suffer affliction with the people of God, than to enjoy the pleasures of sin for a season; Esteeming the reproach of Christ greater riches than the treasures in Egypt: for he had respect unto the recompence of the reward.

HEBREWS 11:24-26

Moses esteemed suffering, rejection, and persecution as being more valuable than all the treasures of Egypt. This was no small deal! He was second in command of the world superpower of his day. Secular history records that Moses went out and defeated the Ethiopians. He was a general who held a great position of authority, but he esteemed God's will above all this wealth and power.

What Do You Respect?

If you were put in that position, it'd be a struggle for you to identify with the slaves. If God said, "These Egyptians you grew up with aren't really your people," you'd probably struggle. Why? Because you'd say, "O Lord, look what I'd be giving up!" The reason you sometimes struggle to do God's will is because of the value you place on other things.

Moses was able to do it because he determined in his heart that doing God's will meant much more to him than losing the throne. Suffering with Christ and giving up this power and wealth paled in comparison to his reward. Even if he had to go out into the wilderness for forty years, God was worth more. Fulfilling his God-given destiny was more valuable to him than all Egypt could offer. That's the reason he could do it.

Sometimes we look at people who have made great sacrifices and wonder, *How could they do it?* Well, they couldn't with *our* values! We will do what we value, prize, and respect the most. Therefore, the problem is not that we don't know the right thing to do. The problem is that our values are so skewed that we can't make the right decisions, because we feel we're losing so much.

It appeared as if Moses was losing everything, but he looked beyond that. He had "respect" unto his reward (Heb. 11:26). Respect means "to look away from everything but." Moses looked away from everything but his reward. In other words, he refused to sit down, count, and dwell on all the different things he was giving up. He turned away from everything and became single minded on what God had promised him. If he hadn't, you probably never would have heard of Moses.

Choosing God will always, always, always work out to your best interests! It looked like Moses was giving up a lot, but he chose God and changed the course of the entire world. There isn't a Christian on the planet today who hasn't heard the name of Moses. Most secular, Jewish, and Muslim people have heard his name too. Everybody has heard of Moses! But no one would have heard of him in this day and age if he had chosen the riches of Egypt instead. Moses made the better choice. When you choose God's way, it'll always work out better for you in the end. But if you say "Lord, if I do what You're asking me to do, I'll have to give up this and that!" that's the problem.

"No Way!"

After returning home from Vietnam, I started working in a film department in the public school system. Even though I was a college dropout, I gave that job everything I had. I developed and edited films and delivered them to the schools. That's what I did, but I did it as unto the Lord. I prayed over my work and gave it my best effort.

Within a few months, the head of the entire department came to me and said, "I really like you and the work you do, so I'm going to offer you a job. You could work here for thirty-five years and retire. This job includes guaranteed retirement. The catch is you have to have a minimum of five years commitment." He wanted to put me into a management position when I was just twenty years old!

This was a great opportunity, especially for a college dropout. However, it was right at the time when the Lord had told me I was supposed to go into the ministry. Therefore, I decided, "No way!" Even though I didn't know much of God's plan for my life yet, I valued it more. At the time, this was a real temptation for me. But I look back now and say, "Thank You, Jesus, that I didn't choose that film editing job!"

What God has done in my life is so much greater than that. It's so much more awesome. I never would have gotten out of town had I done that. But I get to travel the world and minister to all kinds of different people. What a privilege!

It's always better to choose God. You just need to change your value system and disesteem everything else. Get to a place where you look away from anything except the Lord. Say, "Father, You are all I want. Your will is all I need in my life."

Paul Counted

Paul considered everything he had as worthless compared to knowing God. He wasn't talking about all of his failures and the things he did wrong. Paul was referring to all of his education, degrees, and accomplishments. Paul was probably one of the most educated men of his day. He was the up-and-coming Rabbi in the nation of Israel. He had all these things going for him in the natural.

> But what things were gain to me, those I counted loss for Christ. Yea
> doubtless, and I count all things but loss for the excellency of the knowledge of

Christ Jesus my Lord: for whom I have suffered the loss of all things, and do count them but dung, that I may win Christ.

PHILIPPIANS 3:7-8

The Greek word for "count" is used in Hebrews 11:26 where the Bible says that Moses esteemed the persecution that came with serving God as greater riches than all of Egypt's treasures.

Paul valued God and disesteemed everything else. The worth he placed on all of his education and accomplishments was equal to dung. But do you know what we do with things in our lives that should be considered dung? We frame them and put them on the wall.

"Jesus, You're It!"

If you truly counted everything except the knowledge of Christ as dung, then you'd be like Paul when persecutors come and say, "We're going to kill you!"

He answered, "Wonderful! Kill me. I'll go be with God."

However, very few of us would react that way. Why? We haven't yet counted everything but the intimate, experiential knowledge of Christ as dung.

I'm not saying you shouldn't value your reputation and the material possessions you have at all. But comparatively, their relative worth ought to pale in light of the high value you place on the Lord and His power in your life. If someone pointed a gun at your head and said, "Choose between your life and God right now," it'd be no choice. Say, "Jesus, You're it! I'd die for You in a heartbeat." You might think you can't do that, but you can.

Every person in the Bible who ever did anything important glorified God. They put more value and worth on what God said and His plan for their life than anything else. They simply loved God more than they loved themselves. That's the key.

You'll Love It!

You need to get to the place where you value the things of God more than you value your things. When the Lord is worth more to you than even your own life, the Christian life becomes easy.

Most people believe that God will make them do something they don't want to do. They think the Lord might send them to the deepest corners of Africa, for example. God isn't going to do something to hurt them. That's not how He works at all!

Delight thyself also in the LORD; and he shall give thee the desires of thine heart.

PSALM 37:4

This doesn't mean He'll just give you anything you want. It means He'll put His desires in your heart. When you're delighting yourself in the Lord—valuing and esteeming Him more than anything else—you can do what you want to do. Why? Because your desires will change! If the Lord wants to send you to the uttermost parts of the earth—and you've been delighting yourself in Him—you won't be happy anywhere else but the uttermost parts of the earth. You'll love it!

I have friends who are missionaries to Mexico. They've lived there for over twenty years now. They can't even conceive moving back to the States. They love it there because that's where God has called them to be.

It's Always Better to Choose God!
LESSON 6 – OUTLINE

1. Moses esteemed suffering, rejection, and persecution as being more valuable than all the treasures of Egypt.

    By faith Moses, when he was come to years, refused to be called the son of Pharaoh's daughter; Choosing rather to suffer affliction with the people of God, than to enjoy the pleasures of sin for a season; Esteeming the reproach of Christ greater riches than the treasures in Egypt: for he had respect unto the recompence of the reward.

    HEBREWS 11:24-26

    A. Moses was second in command of the world superpower of his day.

    B. He was a general who held a great position of authority, but he esteemed God's will above all this wealth and power.

2. The reason you sometimes struggle to do God's will is because of the value you place on other things.

    A. You will do what you value, prize, and respect the most.

    B. Therefore, the problem isn't knowing the right thing to do.

    C. Our values are so skewed that we can't make the right decisions, because we feel we're losing so much.

3. *Respect* means "to look away from everything but."

    A. Moses looked away from everything but his reward.

    B. He refused to sit down, count, and dwell on all the different things he was giving up.

    C. He turned away from everything and became single minded on what God had promised him.

4. Choosing God will always, always, always work out to your best interests!

    A. When you choose God's way, it'll always work out better for you in the end.

    B. But if you say "Lord, if I do what You're asking me to do, I'll have to give up this and that!" that's the problem.

    C. You just need to change your value system and disesteem everything else.

5. Paul considered everything he had—all of his education, degrees, and accomplishments—as worthless compared to knowing God.

> But what things were gain to me, those I counted loss for Christ. Yea doubtless, and I count all things but loss for the excellency of the knowledge of Christ Jesus my Lord: for whom I have suffered the loss of all things, and do count them but dung, that I may win Christ.
>
> PHILIPPIANS 3:7-8

    A. The Greek word for "count" is used in Hebrews 11:26 where the Bible says that Moses esteemed the persecution that came with serving God as greater riches than all of Egypt's treasures.

    B. Paul valued God and disesteemed everything else.

    C. The worth he placed on all of his education and accomplishments was equal to dung.

6. Every person in the Bible who ever did anything important glorified God.

    A. They put more value and worth on what God said and His plan for their life than anything else.

    B. They simply loved God more than they loved themselves.

    C. You need to get to the place where you value the things of God more than you value your things.

    D. When the Lord is worth more to you than even your own life, the Christian life becomes easy.

7. Most people believe that God will make them do something they don't want to do.

    A. That's not how He works at all!

    B. God will put His desires in your heart.

> Delight thyself also in the LORD; and he shall give thee the desires of thine heart.
>
> PSALM 37:4

    C. When you're delighting yourself in the Lord—valuing and esteeming Him more than anything else—you can do what you want to do because your desires will change.

    D. If the Lord wants to send you to the uttermost parts of the earth—and you've been delighting yourself in Him—you won't be happy anywhere else but the uttermost parts of the earth.

It's Always Better to Choose God!
LESSON 6 – TEACHER'S GUIDE

1. Moses esteemed suffering, rejection, and persecution as being more valuable than all the treasures of Egypt (Heb. 11:24-26). He was second in command of the world superpower of his day. Moses was a general who held a great position of authority, but he esteemed God's will above all this wealth and power.

2. The reason we sometimes struggle to do God's will is because of the value we place on other things. We will do what we value, prize, and respect the most. Therefore, the problem isn't knowing the right thing to do. The problem is that our values are so skewed that we can't make the right decisions, because we feel we're losing so much.

3. *Respect* means "to look away from everything but." Moses looked away from everything but his reward. He refused to sit down, count, and dwell on all the different things he was giving up. He turned away from everything and became single minded on what God had promised him.

4. Choosing God will always, always, always work out to our best interests! When we choose God's way, it'll always work out better for us in the end. But the problem is that we say, "Lord, if I do what You're asking me to do, I'll have to give up this and that!" We just need to change our value system and disesteem everything else.

1. A. According to Hebrews 11:24-26, what did Moses esteem the suffering, rejection, and persecution as being more valuable than? (All the treasures of Egypt)
   B. What did he esteem above all this wealth and power? (God's will)
2. A. Why do we sometimes struggle to do God's will? (It's because of the value we place on other things)
   B. What will we do? (What we value, prize, and respect the most)
3. A. What does respect mean? (To look away from everything but)
   B. What did Moses refuse to sit down, count, and dwell on? (All the different things he was giving up)
4. When we choose God's way, what happens? (It always works out better for us in the end)

5. Paul considered everything he had—all of his education, degrees, and accomplishments—as worthless compared to knowing God. The Greek word for "count" is used in Hebrews 11:26 where the Bible says that Moses esteemed the persecution that came with serving God as greater riches than all of Egypt's treasures. Paul valued God and disesteemed everything else. The worth he placed on all of his education and accomplishments was equal to dung.

6. Every person in the Bible who ever did anything important glorified God. They put more value and worth on what God said and His plan for their life than anything else. They simply loved God more than they loved themselves.

    We need to get to the place where we value the things of God more than we value our things. When the Lord is worth more to us than even our own lives, the Christian life becomes easy.

7. Most people believe that God will make them do something they don't want to do. That's not how He works at all! God will put His desires in their hearts (Ps. 37:4).

    When we're delighting ourselves in the Lord—valuing and esteeming Him more than anything else—we can do what we want to do because our desires will change. If the Lord wants to send us to the uttermost parts of the earth—and we've been delighting ourselves in Him—we won't be happy anywhere else but the uttermost parts of the earth.

5. A. Read Philippians 3:7-8. How did Paul consider everything he had—all of his education, degrees, and accomplishments? (As worthless compared to knowing God)
   B. The worth he placed on all these things was equal to what? (Dung)
6. A. Every person in the Bible who ever did anything loved God more than what? (More than they loved themselves)
   B. When does the Christian life become easy? (When the Lord is worth more to us than even our own lives)
7. A. Read Psalm 37:4. What does God put in our hearts? (His desires)
   B. If God wants to send us to the uttermost parts of the earth—and we've been delighting ourselves in Him—will we be happy anywhere else? (No)

It's Always Better to Choose God!

1. According to Hebrews 11:24-26, what did Moses refuse?

2. What did he choose instead?

3. What did he give up?

4. What did Moses esteem as greater riches than the treasures in Egypt?

5. Why?

6. How did Moses do all of this?

7. According to Philippians 3:7-8, what did Paul count as loss for Christ?

8. For what did he count all things but loss?

9. He counted them as dung that he might what?

10. What does Psalm 37:4 command us to do?

11. As we do, what does God promise?

It's Always Better to Choose God!

1. To be called the son of Pharaoh's daughter.

2. To suffer affliction with the people of God.

3. Enjoying the pleasures of sin for a season.

4. The reproach of Christ.

5. He had respect unto the recompense of the reward.

6. By faith.

7. Those things that were gain to him.

8. The excellency of the knowledge of Christ Jesus his Lord.

9. Win Christ.

10. Delight ourselves in the Lord.

11. To give us the desires of our hearts.

It's Always Better to Choose God!
LESSON 6 – SCRIPTURES

By faith Moses, when he was come to years, refused to be called the son of Pharaoh's daughter; Choosing rather to suffer affliction with the people of God, than to enjoy the pleasures of sin for a season; Esteeming the reproach of Christ greater riches than the treasures in Egypt: for he had respect unto the recompence of the reward.

HEBREWS 11:24-26

But what things were gain to me, those I counted loss for Christ. Yea doubtless, and I count all things but loss for the excellency of the knowledge of Christ Jesus my Lord: for whom I have suffered the loss of all things, and do count them but dung, that I may win Christ.

PHILIPPIANS 3:7-8

Delight thyself also in the LORD; and he shall give thee the desires of thine heart.

PSALM 37:4

Thankfulness Glorifies God
LESSON 7

The second key to staying full of God is:

> Neither were thankful.
>
> Romans 1:21

In **Lesson 4**, we saw that to magnify God is to glorify Him. In light of this truth, consider this verse in Psalm 69.

> I will praise the name of God with a song, and will magnify him with thanksgiving.
>
> Psalm 69:30

Glorifying, magnifying, and thanking God are all interrelated and intertwined. In order to glorify God, you need to be thankful. As you are thanking Him, you're reminding yourself of what He has said and done, which magnifies Him. As you think on the Lord in this way, He becomes bigger and more powerful in your life. In order to truly magnify and glorify God, you must be thankful for what He's done.

Memory and Humility

Un-thankfulness is one of the blights of our generation.

> In the last days perilous times shall come. For men shall be lovers of their own selves, covetous, boasters, proud, blasphemers, disobedient to parents, **unthankful**, unholy…lovers of pleasures more than lovers of God.
>
> 2 Timothy 3:1-2 and 4, emphasis mine

Being unthankful is listed right there next to being unholy. It's mentioned in the same list as blasphemers and lovers of pleasure more than lovers of God. Does that describe our society or what! Huge amounts of the population today are unthankful. They simply don't remember or acknowledge the goodness of God.

Being thankful involves memory and humility. You can't be thankful without remembering the good things that have been done for you. A proud person doesn't believe anyone else has helped them do anything. They've accomplished everything "on their own." They don't acknowledge the contribution and help of anyone or anything else. This attitude of "I'm a self-made man (or woman)" is just rampant today. Very few people remember.

> Bless the LORD, O my soul, and forget not all his benefits.
>
> Psalm 103:2

God commanded you not to forget, because He knows that you will if you don't make a decision to remember. That's why the Lord instituted the different observances in the Bible like communion, Passover, and other special feasts. This was also why memorial markers and piles of stones were erected. It was to stir the people up through memory.

You Can't Function without Memory

Your memory is one of the most powerful faculties you have.

A couple of weeks after their wedding, a man and his wife were in a car wreck. The woman was driving, and the man was asleep in the backseat. He survived relatively unhurt, but she almost died. Although she pulled through and recovered, she lost the last twelve months of her memory. She remembered her parents, her name, and everything about herself up to a year before the accident, but everything after that was gone.

Those previous twelve months had been when she met, fell in love with, and married this man. Although she didn't remember him, everyone told her that this guy was her husband. She went home with him but didn't remember him. They tried to have a physical relationship, but she just couldn't handle it. Finally, they had to break up, move out, and start courting again because she couldn't maintain the relationship without her memory.

If you couldn't remember, just think what it would do to your life. What would it do to your marriage, children, work, and church situation? You can't function without memory, and yet, very few people remember the goodness of God.

Never Forget!

In order to maintain the things God does in your life, you're going to have to be a thankful person. You need to constantly go back and rehearse your victories and the encounters you've had with Him.

For some Christians, every day is a brand-new day with no history. When they get up in the morning, they aren't sure whether or not they'll still be serving God by that night. It just depends on how things go during the day. They don't want to disown God; they desire to remain faithful, but they can't guarantee that they will. God forbid they get into a compromising situation, because they just don't know for sure what they're going to do.

My life is the exact opposite. I can truthfully say that nearly every day since March 23, 1968, I've remembered what God has done in my life. I'm one thankful guy! I thank the Lord constantly. I stir myself up to remember when God touched my life, and I've never forgotten it.

Remember the Pit

Hearken to me, ye that follow after righteousness, ye that seek the LORD: look unto the rock whence ye are hewn, and to the hole of the pit whence ye are digged.

Isaiah 51:1

At the same time that you're looking at the Lord and seeing your position in Him, you must also remember the pit you crawled out of. If you did, it would change the way you act. If I woke up one morning and Satan put pressure on me to renounce God, I couldn't do it. Why? I have a history! I have nearly five decades worth of being born again and forty years of wholeheartedly seeking God interwoven into my thoughts and life. If someone came up to me and tried to get me to deny the Lord, I couldn't. He's been such an important part of my life for so long now. But there are some folks who wake up each morning having forgotten everything the Lord has done for them.

I remember where I was when God touched my life. It was so dramatic and so important that nothing compares to it. There's nothing that could tempt me to ever turn away from God. I recognize that I'm capable of doing anything that anybody else is capable of, but not today. My heart is fixed on God and I'm rehearsing my victories. I'm glorifying and thanking God.

I don't know how long it would take me—six months, a year, two years, three years of denying God—to let these memories and this passion for the Lord fade. I could eventually do something, but not today. You can't make me turn on God and commit adultery today, because I love Him and I'm remembering what He has done.

Are you glorifying, remembering, and being thankful for what God has already done in your life? Or are you just driving down the street hoping that the devil doesn't put a temptation in your path, because you don't know if you'll make it? There's something powerful about going back, rehearsing your victories, and being thankful!

Thankfulness Glorifies God
LESSON 7 – OUTLINE

1. The second key to staying full of God is to be thankful.

   Neither were thankful.

   ROMANS 1:21

   A. Glorifying, magnifying, and thanking God are all interrelated and intertwined.

   I will praise the name of God with a song, and will magnify him with thanksgiving.

   PSALM 69:30

   B. In order to glorify God, you need to be thankful.

   C. As you are thanking Him, you're reminding yourself of what He has said and done, which magnifies Him.

   D. As you think on the Lord this way, He becomes bigger and more powerful in your life.

2. Un-thankfulness is one of the blights of our generation.

   In the last days perilous times shall come. For men shall be lovers of their own selves, covetous, boasters, proud, blasphemers, disobedient to parents, unthankful, unholy...lovers of pleasures more than lovers of God.

   2 TIMOTHY 3:1-2 AND 4

   A. Being unthankful is listed right there next to being unholy.

   B. They simply don't remember or acknowledge the goodness of God.

3. Being thankful involves memory and humility.

   A. You can't be thankful without remembering the good things that have been done for you.

   Bless the LORD, O my soul, and forget not all his benefits.

   PSALM 103:2

   B. God commanded you not to forget, because He knows that you will if you don't make a decision to remember.

4. Your memory is one of the most powerful faculties you have.

    A. If you couldn't remember, just think what it would do to your life.

    B. What would it do to your marriage, children, work, and church situation?

    C. You can't function without memory, and yet, very few people remember the goodness of God.

5. In order to maintain the things that God does in your life, you're going to have to be a thankful person.

    A. You need to constantly go back and rehearse your victories and the encounters you've had with Him.

    B. I stir myself up to remember when God touched my life, and I've never forgotten it.

    C. At the same time that you're looking at the Lord and seeing your position in Him, you must also remember the pit you crawled out of.

    Hearken to me, ye that follow after righteousness, ye that seek the LORD: look unto the rock whence ye are hewn, and to the hole of the pit whence ye are digged.

    ISAIAH 51:1

    D. Are you glorifying, remembering, and being thankful for what God has already done in your life?

    E. There's something powerful about going back, rehearsing your victories, and being thankful!

Thankfulness Glorifies God
LESSON 7 – TEACHER'S GUIDE

1.   The second key to staying full of God is to be thankful (Rom. 1:21). Glorifying, magnifying, and thanking God are all interrelated and intertwined (Ps. 69:30). In order to glorify God, we need to be thankful. As we are thanking Him, we're reminding ourselves of what He has said and done, which magnifies Him. As we think on the Lord this way, He becomes bigger and more powerful in our lives.

2.   Un-thankfulness is one of the blights of our generation (2 Tim. 3:1-2 and 4). Being unthankful is listed right there next to being unholy. Most people simply don't remember or acknowledge the goodness of God.

3.   Being thankful involves memory and humility. We can't be thankful without remembering the good things that have been done for us (Ps. 103:2). God commanded us not to forget, because He knows that we will if we don't make a decision to remember.

4.   Our memory is one of the most powerful faculties we have. If we couldn't remember, just think what it would do to our lives. What would it do to our marriage, children, work, and church situation? We can't function without memory, and yet, very few people remember the goodness of God.

5.   In order to maintain the things that God does in our lives, we're going to have to be very thankful people. We need to constantly go back and rehearse our victories and the encounters we've had with Him. It's important to stir ourselves up to remember when God touched our lives so that we'll never forget it. At the same time that we're looking at the Lord and seeing our position in Him, we must also remember the pit we crawled out of (Is. 51:1). Are we glorifying, remembering, and being thankful for what God has already done in our lives? There's something powerful about going back, rehearsing our victories, and being thankful!

1. A. According to Romans 1:21, what is the second key to staying full of God? (Be thankful)
   B. Read Psalm 69:30. What three things are all interrelated and intertwined? (Glorifying, magnifying, and thanking God)
2. Read 2 Timothy 3:1-2 and 4. Un-thankfulness is what? (One of the blights of our generation)
3. A. Being thankful involves what two things? (Memory and humility)
   B. Read Psalm 103:2. Why did God command us not to forget? (He knows that we will forget if we don't make a decision to remember)
4. A. What is one of the most powerful faculties we have? (Our memory)
   B. Can we function without memory? (No)
5. A. What do we need to constantly go back and rehearse? (Our victories and the encounters we've had with God)
   B. According to Isaiah 51:1, what else must we remember as we're looking at the Lord and seeing our position in Him? (The pit we crawled out of)

Thankfulness Glorifies God
LESSON 7 – DISCIPLESHIP QUESTIONS

1. How does Romans 1:21 express the second key to staying full of God?

2. How does Psalm 69:30 say we should praise the name of God?

3. How should we magnify Him?

4. How is this second key to staying full of God expressed negatively in 2 Timothy 3:1-2?

5. In these last days, what kind of times shall come?
   A. Peaceful.
   B. Perilous.
   C. Pleasant.
   D. Easy.

6. Psalm 103:2 admonishes us to bless the Lord with what part of our being?
   A. Spirit.
   B. Soul.
   C. Body.

7. What are we not to forget?

8. Who is God talking to in Isaiah 51:1?
   A. Those who follow after righteousness.
   B. Those who sin.
   C. Those who seek the Lord.
   D. Those who serve themselves.

9. What are they to look to and remember?
   A. The tree from which they are picked.
   B. The rock whence they are hewn.
   C. The vine from which they are plucked.
   D. The hole of the pit whence they are digged.

Thankfulness Glorifies God

1. Neither were thankful.

2. With a song.

3. With thanksgiving.

4. Unthankful.

5. B. Perilous.

6. B. Soul.

7. All His benefits.

8. A. Those who follow after righteousness.
    C. Those who seek the Lord.

9. B. The rock whence they are hewn.
    D. The hole of the pit whence they are digged.

Thankfulness Glorifies God
LESSON 7 – SCRIPTURES

Because that, when they knew God, they glorified him not as God, neither were thankful; but became vain in their imaginations, and their foolish heart was darkened.

ROMANS 1:21

I will praise the name of God with a song, and will magnify him with thanksgiving.

PSALM 69:30

This know also, that in the last days perilous times shall come. For men shall be lovers of their own selves, covetous, boasters, proud, blasphemers, disobedient to parents, unthankful, unholy…lovers of pleasures more than lovers of God.

2 TIMOTHY 3:1-2 AND 4

Bless the LORD, O my soul, and forget not all his benefits.

PSALM 103:2

Hearken to me, ye that follow after righteousness, ye that seek the LORD: look unto the rock whence ye are hewn, and to the hole of the pit whence ye are digged.

ISAIAH 51:1

Stirred Up by Memory
LESSON 8

Memory is such a powerful force, Peter referred to it three times in his second letter:

Wherefore I will not be negligent ***to put you always in remembrance of these things***, though ye know them, and be established in the present truth. Yea, I think it meet, as long as I am in this tabernacle, ***to stir you up by putting you in remembrance***.

2 PETER 1:12-13, EMPHASIS MINE

Moreover I will endeavour that ye may be able after my decease ***to have these things always in remembrance***.

2 PETER 1:15, EMPHASIS MINE

This second epistle, beloved, I now write unto you; in both which I ***stir up your pure minds by way of remembrance***.

2 PETER 3:1, EMPHASIS MINE

If you don't stir yourself up, you'll settle to the bottom. Therefore, go back and remember! I bet God has saved your bacon more than once. If you would just sit down and spend some time thinking about how the Lord has been good to you, your entire outlook would change for the better. If you're wondering *God, where are You? Do You love me?* just think about the awesome things the Lord has done for you.

He Preserves the Simple

Some pastors and I were joking and sharing experiences with each other in Florida. I told them about the time I rode in a tiny little airplane with this one guy. The plane was so small, his shoulder touched the window, my shoulder touched the window, and our two other shoulders touched in between. That plane was going up and down like a roller coaster, dropping a thousand feet at a time, and flying nearly sideways. It was a mess!

This "pilot" finally threw his hands up over his eyes and screamed, "My God, we're going to die! We're going to die!" Then he just rolled up into a ball—and there I was with him in this airplane. So I flew it with one hand and shook him with the other, saying, "God didn't let me live through Vietnam to die in your plane!" I had to fly that thing for over an hour.

We flew over Alamogordo Rifle Range. They came on the radio and said they were going to shoot us down. I told them, "Hey, the pilot has freaked! Have mercy on me! I'm getting out of here just as fast as I can." I never heard from the tower again. They were probably laughing too hard to speak.

On another occasion, a three-foot-tall boulder weighing close to a ton rolled over my arm and head. I immediately jumped up, started shouting the name of Jesus and screaming, "I'm healed! I'm healed!" About thirty seconds later, I stopped, looked, and everything on my body worked. Praise God! So I erected a monument there that says, "August 25th, 1999. Jesus saved my life when this rock rolled over my hand, arm, and head. Psalm 116:6." That verse says:

The LORD preserveth the simple: I was brought low, and he helped me.

Every time I walk by that spot on our property, I see it and thank God.

Escapes from Death

As these pastors and I were sharing our stories, I recounted over thirty different times where I should have been dead. I remembered when my brother picked me off the bottom of a hotel swimming pool at eleven o'clock at night. I'd been knocked out when I hit my head on the diving board while trying to do a flip. My brother saw what happened and saved my life. On another occasion, I fell off a thousand-foot cliff, and my brother caught me in midair. As I remembered these things, I was deeply moved.

I told the Lord, "Father, You have a purpose for my life, and You aren't through with me yet. There's a reason for me being alive today—praise Your awesome name!" Even though it's been more than a year since these pastors and I had this conversation, I've been overwhelmed thinking about God's goodness and grace in my life ever since.

He that is our God is the God of salvation; and unto GOD the Lord belong the issues [escapes] from death.

PSALM 68:20, BRACKETS MINE

I bet God has saved your life many times, but you have forgotten. Now that I've jogged your memory, it's coming back to you. If you would just rehearse those victories and think about God's goodness, you wouldn't get halfway through them before someone would have to scrape you off the ceiling. Discouragement would just leave.

If you're depressed, you haven't been thinking about what God has done for you. Instead, you're thinking on what the devil is doing to you. You aren't focusing on the joy that is set before you. You aren't saying, "If I die, I'll go to be with the Lord. If I'm poor, I have a mansion in heaven on streets of gold." You're just looking at your present situation. You can't be depressed without first getting your eyes off Jesus and what He's done, forgetting His goodness in the past, and forgetting the goodness of the future He's promised you. You just forget everything!

If you want to be depressed, there are plenty of depressing things you can think on. But if you look at things properly, are thankful, and choose to remember, you have no reason to be discouraged. You'll get an attitude that says, "It doesn't matter what's happening on the outside, God in me is bigger and stronger!"

The Vacuum Within

I remember a science experiment my sixth-grade teacher did. He put a little one-gallon metal gas can on a Bunsen burner and heated it. Then as soon as it became hot, he put the cap back on tight. He set that can on his desk and kept on teaching. As the air cooled, it formed a vacuum on the inside of the can. Since I was sitting in the front row, I can vividly remember watching that can. It started crackling and popping without anyone touching it. Then—all of a sudden—it crushed. It looked like someone had taken a sledgehammer to it. The can fell to the ground and continued being crushed. I watched the entire scenario. Nobody touched it. This was just natural atmospheric pressure acting on a can with nothing inside.

It's the vacuum within—not the pressure without—that's causing people to be crushed today. Under normal circumstances, the pressure within would have enabled the can to have no problem withstanding the pressures without. However, the absence of pressure within caused normal atmospheric pressure to crush it. Some people just can't handle the pressure in their marriages. They love talking about how bad it is, putting great value on these pressures, and saying, "Nobody knows the trouble I feel. Nobody knows my sorrow!" Then they sing songs about how "Nobody has as much trouble as I do," and it makes them feel justified.

As long as the devil can make you feel like nobody else has ever had your situation, it doesn't matter. I could preach my heart out and tell you everything I know, but you'd still say, "That's true, but it won't work for me."

> There hath no temptation taken you but such as is common to man.
>
> 1 Corinthians 10:13

The temptations you face are common to everyone. We all have the same problems. It may be packaged in a different wrapper, but it's the same contents. The devil doesn't have a bunch of different tricks; he just has a few that he rewraps and uses on all of us. But the moment you say "I'm the only one," you've fallen for a lie and exempted yourself from the answer.

You don't have any pressure that's beyond God's ability. It's your vacuum within that's the problem. It's the fact that you aren't glorifying God, rehearsing your victories, or being thankful. You aren't using your mind to remember what God has said and done.

Be Thankful

If you remembered God, your situation wouldn't seem so bad. Remember when you were born again. What was it the Lord saved you and led you out of? Remember the joy and peace that flooded your entire being. What vision has He placed in your heart? What words has He spoken to you? Remind yourself, then…

> Enter into his gates with thanksgiving, and into his courts with praise: be thankful unto him, and bless his name. For the LORD is good; his mercy is everlasting; and his truth endureth to all generations.
>
> Psalm 100:4-5

Even if you think your situation is so bad that you need to gripe and complain, enter into His gates with thanksgiving and His courts with praise. For every five minutes you spend whining, spend another ten minutes thanking God for His goodness. If you do that, you'll find that your gripe will have shrunk really small by the time you get around to it. Then you'll look at that thing and say, "It's no big deal!"

I've seen people who were miraculously healed of incurable diseases come down with a cold. The cold dragged on, and they've had trouble getting their faith to work. They've come to me and said, "If God can't heal me of this cold, I'm going to quit!" That's when the spirit of slap comes all over me. I just want to whack them upside the head and say, "Don't you remember what God did? You've already been healed, but you forgot. Now you have everything way out of perspective!"

No one has a right to gripe and complain. Nobody will stand before the Lord and say, "God, You let me down." Don't grow weary and faint. Maintain your faith and enthusiasm. Be a good receiver!

Light Affliction

> For which cause we faint not; but though our outward man perish, yet the inward man is renewed day by day.
>
> 2 CORINTHIANS 4:16

Paul wasn't saying that he didn't have problems; he said, "Outwardly I perish. All of these circumstances and situations keep happening to me all the time. But my inward man is renewed day by day."

> For our light affliction, which is but for a moment.
>
> 2 CORINTHIANS 4:17

Many people think, *Well, Paul's affliction was light. Mine is heavy. Therefore, I can't relate to or accept what you're saying.*

Paul experienced some extremely harsh situations. Let's take a look at some of Paul's "light" afflictions:

> In labours more abundant, in stripes above measure, in prisons more frequent, in deaths oft. Of the Jews five times received I forty stripes save one. Thrice was I beaten with rods, once was I stoned, thrice I suffered shipwreck, a night and a day I have been in the deep; In journeyings often, in perils of waters, in perils of robbers, in perils by mine own countrymen, in perils by the heathen, in perils in the city, in perils in the wilderness, in perils in the sea, in perils among false brethren; In weariness and painfulness, in watchings often, in hunger and thirst, in fastings often, in cold and nakedness. Beside those things that are without, that which cometh upon me daily, the care of all the churches.
>
> 2 CORINTHIANS 11:23-28

No Right to Complain

Also, Paul was stoned in Lystra:

> And there came thither certain Jews from Antioch and Iconium, who persuaded the people, and, having stoned Paul, drew him out of the city, supposing he had been dead. Howbeit, as the disciples stood round about him, he rose up, and came into the city: and the next day he departed with Barnabas to Derbe.
>
> ACTS 14:19-20

When the Jews stoned someone, they didn't stop until they were sure the person was dead. Therefore, it's very likely that Paul was raised from the dead. These were just some of his "light" afflictions.

Paul's afflictions were much more in quantity and intensity than anything you've experienced. If he could say, "My afflictions were light," then you don't have any right to gripe or complain. Your problems don't even come close to what Paul went through!

Praise the Lord!

After Hebrews 12:2 reveals that Jesus despised—disesteemed—the cross' shame, God's Word continues, saying:

> Consider him that endured…lest ye be wearied and faint in your minds. Ye have not yet resisted unto blood, striving against sin.
>
> HEBREWS 12:3-4

Consider what Jesus suffered for you. Until you've suffered to the point that it costs you your life, you have no right to complain.

If you're alive, you ought to be praising God!

> Let every thing that hath breath praise the LORD.
>
> PSALM 150:6

You should be thanking God instead of griping and complaining.

"But, Andrew, you don't know my situation!" Wrong. You value things differently than God does. You really do value your problems, hurts, and pains. However, the truth is you don't have a right to complain. God's supply is far bigger than your need!

> For our light affliction, which is but for a moment.
>
> 2 CORINTHIANS 4:17

Your affliction is light because it's temporary. It's "but for a moment." If you think everything in your life is bleak, you don't have a very good reference point. You're comparing yourself with your neighbors, or you're looking at the totally unrealistic picture of reality that's painted on television. If you're using those things as your standard, it'll create dissatisfaction on the inside of you. You need the proper perspective. Stir yourself up to remember what God has done!

Stirred Up by Memory
LESSON 8 – OUTLINE

1. Memory is such a powerful force, Peter referred to it three times in his second letter.

> Wherefore I will not be negligent *to put you always in remembrance of these things*, though ye know them, and be established in the present truth. Yea, I think it meet, as long as I am in this tabernacle, *to stir you up by putting you in remembrance*.
>
> 2 PETER 1:12-13, EMPHASIS MINE

> Moreover I will endeavour that ye may be able after my decease *to have these things always in remembrance*.
>
> 2 PETER 1:15, EMPHASIS MINE

> This second epistle, beloved, I now write unto you; in both which I *stir up your pure minds by way of remembrance*.
>
> 2 PETER 3:1, EMPHASIS MINE

   A. If you don't stir yourself up, you'll settle to the bottom.

   B. If you would just sit down and spend some time thinking about how the Lord has been good to you, your entire outlook would change for the better.

2. Just think about the awesome things the Lord has done for you.

> The LORD preserveth the simple: I was brought low, and he helped me.
>
> PSALM 116:6

   A. I bet God has saved your life many times, but you have forgotten.

> He that is our God is the God of salvation; and unto GOD the Lord belong the issues [escapes] from death.
>
> PSALM 68:20, BRACKETS MINE

   B. If you would just rehearse those victories and think about God's goodness, you wouldn't get halfway through them before someone would have to scrape you off the ceiling.

3. If you're depressed, you haven't been thinking about what God has done for you.

   A. You can't be depressed without first getting your eyes off Jesus and what He's done, forgetting His goodness in the past, and forgetting the goodness of the future He's promised you.

B. If you want to be depressed, there are plenty of depressing things you can think on.

C. But if you look at things properly, are thankful, and choose to remember, you have no reason to be discouraged.

D. You'll get an attitude that says, "It doesn't matter what's happening on the outside, God in me is bigger and stronger!"

4. The temptations you face are common to everyone.

> There hath no temptation taken you but such as is common to man.
>
> 1 CORINTHIANS 10:13

A. It may be packaged in a different wrapper, but it's the same contents.

B. The moment you say "I'm the only one," you've fallen for a lie and exempted yourself from the answer.

5. You don't have any pressure that's beyond God's ability.

A. Even if you think your situation is so bad that you need to gripe and complain, enter into His gates with thanksgiving and His courts with praise.

> Enter into his gates with thanksgiving, and into his courts with praise: be thankful unto him, and bless his name. For the LORD is good; his mercy is everlasting; and his truth endureth to all generations.
>
> PSALM 100:4-5

B. No one has a right to gripe and complain.

C. Maintain your faith and enthusiasm, and be a good receiver!

6. Paul spoke of his afflictions as being "light."

> For which cause we faint not; but though our outward man perish, yet the inward man is renewed day by day. For our light affliction, which is but for a moment.
>
> 2 CORINTHIANS 4:16-17

A. Let's take a look at some of Paul's "light" afflictions.

> In labours more abundant, in stripes above measure, in prisons more frequent, in deaths oft. Of the Jews five times received I forty stripes save one. Thrice was I beaten with rods, once was I stoned, thrice I suffered shipwreck, a night and a day I have been in the deep; In journeyings often, in perils of waters, in perils of robbers, in perils by mine own countrymen, in perils by the heathen, in perils in the city, in perils in the wilderness, in perils in the sea, in perils among false

brethren; In weariness and painfulness, in watchings often, in hunger and thirst, in fastings often, in cold and nakedness. Beside those things that are without, that which cometh upon me daily, the care of all the churches.

2 Corinthians 11:23-28

B. When the Jews stoned someone, they didn't stop until they were sure the person was dead.

And there came thither certain Jews from Antioch and Iconium, who persuaded the people, and, having stoned Paul, drew him out of the city, supposing he had been dead. Howbeit, as the disciples stood round about him, he rose up, and came into the city: and the next day he departed with Barnabas to Derbe.

Acts 14:19-20

C. Therefore, it's very likely Paul was raised from the dead.

D. Paul's afflictions were much more in quantity and intensity than anything you've experienced.

E. If he could say, "My afflictions were light," then you don't have any right to gripe or complain.

7. After Hebrews 12:2 reveals that Jesus despised—disesteemed—the cross' shame, God's Word continues, saying:

Consider him that endured…lest ye be wearied and faint in your minds. Ye have not yet resisted unto blood, striving against sin.

Hebrews 12:3-4

A. If you're alive, you ought to be praising God!

Let every thing that hath breath praise the LORD.

Psalm 150:6

B. God's supply is far bigger than your need.

C. Your affliction is light because it's temporary.

For our light affliction, which is but for a moment.

2 Corinthians 4:17

D. You need the proper perspective.

E. Stir yourself up to remember what God has done.

Stirred Up by Memory
LESSON 8 – TEACHER'S GUIDE

1.   Memory is such a powerful force, Peter referred to it three times in his second letter (2 Pet. 1:12-13, 15; and 3:1). If we don't stir ourselves up, we'll settle to the bottom. If we would just sit down and spend some time thinking about how the Lord has been good to us, our entire outlook would change for the better.

2.   Just think about the awesome things the Lord has done (Ps. 116:6). God has saved our lives many times, but we have forgotten (Ps. 68:20). If we would just rehearse those victories and think about God's goodness, we wouldn't get halfway through them before someone would have to scrape us off the ceiling.

3.   If we're depressed, we haven't been thinking about what God has done for us. We can't be depressed without first getting our eyes off Jesus and what He's done, forgetting His goodness in the past, and forgetting the goodness of the future He's promised us. If we want to be depressed, there are plenty of depressing things we can think on. But if we look at things properly, are thankful, and choose to remember, we have no reason to be discouraged. We'll get an attitude that says, "It doesn't matter what's happening on the outside, God in me is bigger and stronger!"

4.   The temptations we face are common to everyone (1 Cor. 10:13). It may be packaged in a different wrapper, but it's the same contents. The moment we say "I'm the only one," we've fallen for a lie and exempted ourselves from the answer.

1. A. Read 2 Peter 1:12-13, 15; and 3:1. What happens when we don't stir ourselves up? (We settle to the bottom)
   B. How can we change our entire outlook for the better? (By sitting down and spending some time thinking about how the Lord has been good to us)
2. Read Psalm 116:6 and 68:20. How many times and in what ways has the Lord saved your life?
3. A. If we're depressed, what haven't we been thinking about? (What God has done for us)
   B. If we look at things properly, are thankful, and choose to remember, what attitude will we have? (That it doesn't matter what's happening on the outside; God in me is bigger and stronger!)
4. A. According to 1 Corinthians 10:13, the temptations we face are what? (Common to everyone)
   B. What happens when we say, "I'm the only one"? (We fall for a lie and exempt ourselves from the answer)

5.   We don't have any pressure that's beyond God's ability. Even if we think our situation is so bad that we need to gripe and complain, enter into His gates with thanksgiving and His courts with praise (Ps. 100:4-5). No one has a right to gripe and complain. Let's maintain our faith and enthusiasm and be good receivers!

6.   Paul spoke of his afflictions as being "light" (2 Cor. 4:16-17). These "light" afflictions are listed in 2 Corinthians 11:23-28. When the Jews stoned someone, they didn't stop until they were sure the person was dead (Acts 14:19-20). Therefore, it's very likely Paul was raised from the dead. Paul's afflictions were much more in quantity and intensity than anything we've experienced. If he could say, "My afflictions were light," then we don't have any right to gripe or complain.

7.   After Hebrews 12:2 reveals that Jesus despised—disesteemed—the cross' shame, God's Word continues, saying, "Consider him that endured…lest ye be wearied and faint in your minds. Ye have not yet resisted unto blood, striving against sin" (Heb. 12:3-4). If we're alive, we ought to be praising God (Ps. 150:6). God's supply is far bigger than our needs. Our afflictions are light because they're temporary (2 Cor. 4:17). We need the proper perspective. Let's stir ourselves up to remember what God has done.

5. A. Do we have any pressure that is beyond God's ability? (No)
   B. Read Psalm 100:4-5. What should we do instead of griping and complaining? (Enter His gates with thanksgiving and His courts with praise)
6. A. Read 2 Corinthians 4:16-17, 11:23-28; and Acts 14:19-20. How did Paul speak of his afflictions as being? (Light)
   B. In light of this, do we have any right to gripe or complain? (No)
7. A. According to Hebrews 12:2-4, where is it that we're tempted to faint? (In our minds)
   B. According to Psalm 150:6, if we're alive we ought to be doing what? (Praising God)

Stirred Up by Memory
LESSON 8 – DISCIPLESHIP QUESTIONS

1. According to 2 Peter 1:12-13, what did Peter not want to be negligent to do?

2. Do we already know them?

3. What are we to be established in?

4. How long did he purpose to do this?

5. How are we stirred up?

6. According to 2 Peter 1:15, what was Peter's endeavor?

7. According to 2 Peter 3:1, what was Peter's purpose in writing this letter?

8. Who does Psalm 116:6 say preserves the simple?

9. What does God want to do when we're brought low?

10. According to Psalm 68:20, our God is _____?

11. What belongs to Him?

12. According to 1 Corinthians 10:13, is there any uncommon temptation?

13. When we are tempted, God is _____?
    A. Angry.
    B. Sleeping.
    C. Faithful.
    D. Indifferent.

14. Will God allow us to be tempted beyond what we can bear?

15. With the temptation, what does He do?

16. According to Psalm 100:4-5, how should we come into God's presence?

17. Why?
    A. Because the Lord is good.
    B. Because His mercy is everlasting.
    C. Because His truth endures to all generations.
    D. All of the above.

18. According to 2 Corinthians 4:16-17, what part of us is perishing?

19. What part of us is being renewed day by day?

20. How long does our light affliction last?
    A. But for a moment.
    B. But for a day.
    C. But for a month.
    D. But for a year.

21. What is it working for us?

22. Read 2 Corinthians 11:23-28 and Acts 14:19-20. Are any of your problems heavier than Paul's light afflictions?

23. According to Hebrews 12:3-4, whom should we consider?

24. Why?

25. Psalm 150:6 instructs everything that has breath to do what?

Stirred Up by Memory
LESSON 8 – ANSWER KEY

1. To put you always in remembrance of these things.

2. Yes.

3. This present truth.

4. For as long as he was in this tabernacle.

5. By being put in remembrance.

6. That we would—after his decease—have these things always in our remembrance.

7. To stir up our pure minds by way of remembrance.

8. The Lord.

9. Help us.

10. The God of salvation.

11. The issues [escapes] from death.

12. No.

13. C. Faithful.

14. No.

15. He makes a way to escape that we may be able to bear it.

16. With thanksgiving and praise, blessing His name.

17. A. Because the Lord is good.
    B. Because His mercy is everlasting.
    C. Because His truth endures to all generations.
    D. All of the above.

18. Our outward man.

19. Our inward man.

20. A. But for a moment.

21. A far more exceeding and eternal weight of glory.

22. No.

23. Jesus.

24. Lest we be wearied and faint in our minds.

25. Praise the Lord.

Stirred Up by Memory
LESSON 8 – SCRIPTURES

Wherefore I will not be negligent to put you always in remembrance of these things, though ye know them, and be established in the present truth. Yea, I think it meet, as long as I am in this tabernacle, to stir you up by putting you in remembrance.

2 PETER 1:12-13

Moreover I will endeavour that ye may be able after my decease to have these things always in remembrance.

2 PETER 1:15

This second epistle, beloved, I now write unto you; in both which I stir up your pure minds by way of remembrance.

2 PETER 3:1

The LORD preserveth the simple: I was brought low, and he helped me.

PSALM 116:6

He that is our God is the God of salvation; and unto GOD the Lord belong the issues from death.

PSALM 68:20

There hath no temptation taken you but such as is common to man: but God is faithful, who will not suffer you to be tempted above that ye are able; but will with the temptation also make a way to escape, that ye may be able to bear it.

1 CORINTHIANS 10:13

Enter into his gates with thanksgiving, and into his courts with praise: be thankful unto him, and bless his name. For the LORD is good; his mercy is everlasting; and his truth endureth to all generations.

PSALM 100:4-5

For which cause we faint not; but though our outward man perish, yet the inward man is renewed day by day. For our light affliction, which is but for a moment, worketh for us a far more exceeding and eternal weight of glory.

2 CORINTHIANS 4:16-17

Are they ministers of Christ? (I speak as a fool) I am more; in labours more abundant, in stripes above measure, in prisons more frequent, in deaths oft. Of the Jews five times received I forty stripes save one. Thrice was I beaten with rods, once was I stoned, thrice I suffered shipwreck, a night and a day I have been in the deep; In journeyings often, in perils of waters, in perils of robbers, in perils by mine own countrymen, in perils by the heathen, in perils in the city, in perils in the wilderness, in perils in the sea, in perils among false brethren; In weariness and painfulness, in watchings often, in hunger and thirst, in fastings often, in cold and nakedness. Beside those things that are without, that which cometh upon me daily, the care of all the churches.

2 CORINTHIANS 11:23-28

And there came thither certain Jews from Antioch and Iconium, who persuaded the people, and, having stoned Paul, drew him out of the city, supposing he had been dead. Howbeit, as the disciples stood round about him, he rose up, and came into the city: and the next day he departed with Barnabas to Derbe.

ACTS 14:19-20

For consider him that endured such contradiction of sinners against himself, lest ye be wearied and faint in your minds. Ye have not yet resisted unto blood, striving against sin.

HEBREWS 12:3-4

Let every thing that hath breath praise the LORD. Praise ye the LORD.

PSALM 150:6

Remember His Goodness
LESSON 9

Everyone has a reason to praise God. But if you think your situation really is that pitiful, put it in its proper perspective and say, "Praise God, this is temporary!" Whether you are suffering physically, financially, emotionally, relationally—whatever it is—it's just temporary. After you've been in eternity for a billion years, you'll look back on this and think, *That wasn't so bad.* When you look at your circumstances in light of eternity, it changes your perspective.

> While we look not at the things which are seen, but at the things which are not seen: for the things which are seen are temporal; but the things which are not seen are eternal.
>
> 2 CORINTHIANS 4:18

If you're depressed, discouraged, and losing your joy, you aren't looking at the Lord and His Word. If the things of God aren't fresh in your life, then you aren't esteeming eternal reality. You're placing a higher value on the natural realm and magnifying physical things instead. That's where your discontent comes from.

Depression isn't caused by genes or hormones. It's not a chemical imbalance either. Chemical imbalances do happen, but it's a byproduct of wrong thinking.

One of our Bible college students is manic-depressive. He went off his medication and flipped out. This guy is headed to Mexico with us, and he's believing God he's healed. I told him, "Brother, I believe you're healed, too, but we aren't going to let you run off and try to hurt someone in a foreign culture. You don't want to live in a Mexican prison! So we're going to believe God with you for your healing to manifest, and as long as you're fine, we're with you. But if you start flipping out, you're going to have to take your medicine. Because we love you, we'll dope you up to the point where you settle down and we can drag you back here to the States."

This fellow's chemical imbalance isn't causing his depression. It's his negativism and tendency to focus on the wrong things.

Fix Your Mind

Your emotions affect your body. They'll cause wrinkles on your face and your hair to turn gray. Mary, the Queen of Scots, was a redhead. Some say that fear caused her hair to become snow white. Doctors try to find out what's happening in your physical body and give you some way around it. But your body is responding to you!

> For to be carnally minded is death.
>
> ROMANS 8:6

Carnal-mindedness affects your body.

> But to be spiritually minded is life and peace.
>
> ROMANS 8:6

If you aren't experiencing life and peace, it's because of your carnal mind.

The Lord…

> Wilt keep him in perfect peace, whose mind is stayed on thee: because he trusteth in thee.
>
> ISAIAH 26:3

Peace is related to your thoughts. Your emotions are related to your thoughts, not your hormones. If it were just your circumstances that dictated how you feel, then everyone who is in bad circumstances would always feel bad. But that's not so. Some folks are in much worse situations than you, but they're rejoicing and praising the Lord.

All of our problems are small in comparison to God and His eternal point of view. He isn't up in heaven wringing His hands and saying, "Oh no! I don't know what to do!" He's not upset or worried. Our "problems" don't overwhelm God. They're nothing compared to what He's already done for us through His Son. We need to adopt God's attitude and start seeing things from His perspective through the Word.

Just be thankful and remember His goodness. Study God's dealings with the children of Israel, especially when they came out of Egypt and were on their way into the Promised Land. Psalm 106 recounts three different times how they forgot His mighty works and ended up falling into problems (verses 7, 13, and 21).

If you keep your mind fixed on the goodness of God, you can't fail. Remember, the Lord is powerful! If you constantly keep God on your mind, it'll change your entire life.

Guard Your Heart and Mind

This is so simple that we have to have somebody help us to misunderstand it. God didn't make it complicated. It's our lifestyle, society, and value system. We've elevated the things God despises. We give great honor to movie stars and musicians who glorify and magnify sin. Reporters delve into their lives and tell us everything they can about these "wonderful" people. God isn't impressed when they win Oscars and Academy Awards for portraying adultery, murder, lying, and stealing in their movies and music. He doesn't value things the way we do.

Heaven doesn't shut down on Super Bowl Sunday so that everyone can watch the game. It's really no big deal! Now, there's nothing wrong with you catching the Super Bowl. But if watching people run a little pigskin ball up and down a field, kicking and throwing it, and hurting other people is more important to you than attending church and learning about the things of

God, then something is wrong with your thinking. If watching "your team" every week is of higher value to you than God, then you have some serious problems.

You can't react differently than your dominant thoughts. You are what you think, and if you're thinking of all these other things, it'll draw you in that direction. You have to go out of your way to guard your heart and mind. When everyone else is falling at these people's feet saying "They're so awesome. Look at their wealth. And, oh, they're so beautiful!" it'll take effort for you to say, "Father, I know that's not the way You view things. This isn't important to You." God sees wealth and beauty differently than we do.

This is especially important in ministry. I know people who would be dead today if I hadn't prayed for them. Others would be in hell right now if I hadn't shared the Gospel with them. A mother recently wrote to me how one of her sons had received my materials in prison. He became born again, and God totally turned his life around through my tapes. Although he's since died, this grateful woman told me how her son was finally happy for the first time in his entire life. When you hear good reports like that on a regular basis, it's tempting to change values and think, *God, I really did something. I'm somebody special!*

That's when it's important to remember. When I was in high school, I was the flunky of everything. I was so bashful and intimidated that I couldn't even look a person in the face and talk to them. I was terribly introverted and had nothing going for me. I was heading nowhere in a hurry!

"I Can't Handle it Anymore!"

Memory will help you keep your feet on the ground. It'll prevent you from reading your own press releases or fainting in the middle of the fight.

Don Francisco told me that he block stuttered as a child. His teacher made him stand up in front of the whole class once to read a poem. He spent forty-five minutes and only got two sentences out! Now he sings powerfully anointed songs, words just flow out of him, and he gets great acclaim and praise. But Don remembers that it's God, and not him.

Bob Nichols is another good friend of mine. His daughter has been in a coma for many years. She wasn't supposed to live. I was there when the doctors came in and said, "Brother Nichols, you know that she's dead. Take the tubes out." They did a tracheotomy, and I went in and saw her. Normally 130 pounds, she was down to sixty. She didn't look like a person. I'd never seen anybody look that bad and still be alive. It took all the faith I had not to confess my unbelief in front of Bob and Joy.

When the doctors pressed Bob, he didn't get mad and blast them. He didn't stand up and yell. He just said, "No, that's not what we're believing for," and continued on. She's back home now and can stand up and walk with a walker. They say she's still in a coma. She doesn't talk, but she'll squeeze your hand. The lights are on—praise God! Although they're seeing progress, the Nichols' have struggled under this longer than most people could endure.

While I was preaching this message at a ministers' conference and emphasizing how God is good and nobody has a right to gripe, Bob stood up on the front row and declared, "I've taken all I can take. I can't handle it anymore!" Then he took off running, jumping, and yelling, "O God, You're so good! I love You!" He just went wild praising God. He ruined the whole sermon! I lost the whole group! A man who has suffered much more than we have probably ever thought about was so thankful that he just couldn't handle it. He wound up falling on the floor praising, thanking, and worshiping God for His goodness. And some of us gripe and complain over the piddling little problems we have.

No Reason to Complain

We need to repent. We need to say, "Father, forgive me for my hard heart. Forgive me for looking at others and taking the average of the way everyone else is and trying to be just a little bit better. God, You are a good God! You have blessed me so much. Thank You!" If you're born again, you have no reason to gripe or complain.

If you're lost, you have no reason either, because God Almighty has died to save you. If you were the only person alive on the face of the earth, He still would have come and died just for you. That's how much He loves you, and if you remember this, nothing could ever make you gripe or complain.

I believe in the full Gospel—salvation, healing, deliverance, and prosperity. But if God never healed, delivered, or prospered me ever again, the fact that He loves me is enough to keep me shouting and praising His name. If nothing ever worked out for me again in this life, the truth that God redeemed me from hell and I'm heaven bound is more than enough to praise Him. He's building a mansion just for me, and I get to spend eternity with Him. No more sorrow, pain, or shame. Hallelujah! I have no reason to gripe or complain. I'm blessed!

Whether you know it or not, you're blessed too! Every believer is blessed. The question is: What have you been valuing? What have you magnified? Where is your attention? Turn your thoughts away from the negative things of this world, and put them on the goodness of God. The Lord has been good to you!

Firm in the Face of Contrary

A woman recently told me how someone she had prayed for died. She said, "Without consciously thinking about it, I know this circumstance has devalued my revelation of God. I've been confused and it's hindered my faith."

I've been through that too. I prayed for four people who died before I saw the first one rise from the dead. There was once a girl I had thought about marrying, although I'd never proposed to her. Her parents told the Red Cross we were engaged, and I received an emergency leave from Vietnam to come home and see her. She had leukemia and ended up strangling to death on her own blood. I was with her when she died. We prayed over her for more than two hours after she died, but she didn't come back.

That affected me and every other person associated with this. They all said, "It must not be God's will to heal, because if anyone was going to be healed, it would have been Debbie." Although I was just as confused and hurt as anyone else, I declared, "God, Your Word says that by Your stripes, we were healed (1 Pet. 2:24)."

The Lord had even given her a special promise:

> I shall not die, but live, and declare the works of the LORD.
>
> PSALM 118:17

I walked out saying, "I don't understand it, but this wasn't God's will." And to this day, those people who were associated with that think I've gone off the deep end. Although I had no answers and didn't know what was going on, I maintained this attitude. For three and a half years I had to look at something that was contrary to what God's Word said. But I stood firm, saying, "God, Your Word says it, and I won't back off. It's true whether I see it or not." I just had to shelve it and go on with God.

"Lord, Your Word Says…"

Three and a half years later, the Lord showed me why it happened. Once I received the revelation, I went over to my neighbor's house. She had leukemia just like Debbie. I prayed for her and she was healed. Praise God! And to this day, I've seen that truth set many, many people free.

I've been through things, but I've done what I'm sharing with you. Even through gritted teeth at times, I just kept saying, "Lord, Your Word says…" and because of it, I'm still happy in Jesus, walking in victory, and seeing people healed today.

Regardless of what your problems, pressures, and pains are, you can believe God. It's just as simple as glorifying Him. Place value and worth on what He's said and done. Magnify Him, be thankful, and remember His goodness. That's how you stay full of God!

Remember His Goodness
LESSON 9 – OUTLINE

1. When you look at your circumstances in light of eternity, it changes your perspective.

> While we look not at the things which are seen, but at the things which are not seen: for the things which are seen are temporal; but the things which are not seen are eternal.
>
> 2 CORINTHIANS 4:18

   A. If you're depressed, discouraged, and losing your joy, you aren't looking at the Lord and His Word.

   B. If the things of God aren't fresh in your life, then you aren't esteeming eternal reality.

   C. You're placing a higher value on the natural realm and magnifying physical things instead.

2. Your emotions affect your body.

> For to be carnally minded is death, but to be spiritually minded is life and peace.
>
> ROMANS 8:6

   A. If you aren't experiencing life and peace, it's because of your carnal mind.

> [The Lord] wilt keep him in perfect peace, whose mind is stayed on thee: because he trusteth in thee.
>
> ISAIAH 26:3, BRACKETS MINE

   B. Your emotions are related to your thoughts, not your hormones.

   C. If you keep your mind fixed on the goodness of God, you can't fail (Ps. 106:7, 13, and 21).

3. You can't react differently than your dominant thoughts.

   A. You are what you think, and if you're thinking of all these other things, it'll draw you in that direction.

   B. You have to go out of your way to guard your heart and mind.

4. Memory will help you keep your feet on the ground.

   A. It'll prevent you from reading your own press releases or fainting in the middle of the fight.

   B. If you're born again, you have no reason to gripe or complain.

   C. If nothing ever worked out for you again in this life, the truth that God redeemed you from hell and that you're heaven bound is more than enough reason to praise Him.

   D. Turn your thoughts away from the negative things of this world and put them on the goodness of God.

   E. The Lord has been good to you!

5. I've been through things, but I've done what I'm sharing with you.

   A. Even through gritted teeth at times, I just kept saying, "Lord, Your Word says..." (1 Pet. 2:24 and Ps. 118:17).

   B. Because of it, I'm still happy in Jesus, walking in victory, and seeing people healed today.

6. Regardless of what your problems, pressures, and pains are, you can believe God.

   A. Place value and worth on what He's said and done.

   B. Magnify Him, be thankful, and remember His goodness.

   C. That's how you stay full of God!

Remember His Goodness
LESSON 9 – TEACHER'S GUIDE

1.   When we look at our circumstances in light of eternity, it changes our perspective (2 Cor. 4:18). If we're depressed, discouraged, and losing our joy, we aren't looking at the Lord and His Word. If the things of God aren't fresh in our lives, then we aren't esteeming eternal reality. We're placing a higher value on the natural realm and magnifying physical things instead.

2.   Our emotions affect our bodies (Rom. 8:6). If we aren't experiencing life and peace, it's because of our carnal minds (Is. 26:3). Our emotions are related to our thoughts, not our hormones. If we keep our minds fixed on the goodness of God, we can't fail (Ps. 106:7, 13, and 21).

3.   We can't react differently than our dominant thoughts. We are what we think, and if we're thinking of all these other things, it'll draw us in that direction. We have to go out of our way to guard our hearts and minds.

1. A. Read 2 Corinthians 4:18. What happens when we look at our circumstances in light of eternity? (Our perspective changes)
   B. If the things of God aren't fresh in our lives, then we aren't esteeming what? (Eternal reality—the Lord and His Word)
2. A. Read Romans 8:6 and Isaiah 26:3. Why aren't we experiencing life and peace? (Because of our carnal minds)
   B. Read Psalm 106:7, 13, and 21. We can't fail how? (By keeping our minds fixed on the goodness of God)
3. A. We can't react differently than what? (Our dominant thoughts)
   B. What must we go out of our way to guard? (Our hearts and minds)

4.   Memory will help us keep our feet on the ground. It'll prevent us from reading our own press releases or fainting in the middle of the fight. If we're born again, we have no reason to gripe or complain. If nothing ever worked out for us again in this life, the truth that God redeemed us from hell and we're heaven bound is more than enough to praise Him. Let's turn our thoughts away from the negative things of this world and put them on the goodness of God. The Lord has been good to us!

5.   I've been through things, but I've done what I'm sharing with you. Even through gritted teeth at times, I just kept saying, "Lord, Your Word says…" (1 Pet. 2:24 and Ps. 118:17). Because of it, I'm still happy in Jesus, walking in victory, and seeing people healed today.

6.   Regardless of what our problems, pressures, and pains are, we can believe God. We need to place value and worth on what He's said and done. When we magnify Him, are thankful, and remember His goodness, that's how we stay full of God!

4. A. How does memory help us keep our feet on the ground? (It prevents us from reading our own press releases or fainting in the middle of the fight)
   B. What should we turn our thoughts away from? (The negative things of this world)
   C. What should we put them on instead? (The goodness of God)
5. Read 1 Peter 2:24 and Psalm 118:17. What has Andrew had to say, even through gritted teeth, at times? ("Lord, Your Word says…")
6. A. What can we do regardless of our problems, pressures, and pains? (Believe God)
   B. How do we stay full of God? (Magnify Him, be thankful, and remember His goodness)

Remember His Goodness
LESSON 9 – DISCIPLESHIP QUESTIONS

1. According to 2 Corinthians 4:18, we look not at what?

2. What do we look at?

3. What things are temporal?

4. What things are eternal?

5. According to Romans 8:6, carnal-mindedness produces what?

6. But what does spiritual-mindedness produce?

7. According to Isaiah 26:3, when our minds are stayed on God, how will He keep us?

8. What does Psalm 106; verses 7, 13, and 21; all have in common?

9. According to 1 Peter 2:24, who bore our sins in His body on the tree?

10. Now that we are dead to sins, how should we live?

11. What did the stripes Jesus endured produce for us?

12. By whose stripes, ye _____ healed.
    A. Will be (future tense).
    B. Are (present tense).
    C. Were (past tense).

13. According to Psalm 118:17, I shall not _____ but live.

14. What shall we declare?

Remember His Goodness

1. The things which are seen.

2. The things which are not seen.

3. The things which are seen.

4. The things which are not seen.

5. Death.

6. Life and peace.

7. In perfect peace.

8. They speak of forgetting God.

9. Jesus.

10. Unto righteousness.

11. Healing.

12. C. Were (past tense).

13. Die.

14. The works of the Lord.

Remember His Goodness
LESSON 9 – SCRIPTURES

While we look not at the things which are seen, but at the things which are not seen: for the things which are seen are temporal; but the things which are not seen are eternal.

2 CORINTHIANS 4:18

For to be carnally minded is death; but to be spiritually minded is life and peace.

ROMANS 8:6

Thou wilt keep him in perfect peace, whose mind is stayed on thee: because he trusteth in thee.

ISAIAH 26:3

Our fathers understood not thy wonders in Egypt; they remembered not the multitude of thy mercies; but provoked him at the sea, even at the Red sea…They soon forgat his works; they waited not for his counsel…They forgat God their saviour, which had done great things in Egypt.

PSALM 106:7, 13, AND 21

Who his own self bare our sins in his own body on the tree, that we, being dead to sins, should live unto righteousness: by whose stripes ye were healed.

1 PETER 2:24

I shall not die, but live, and declare the works of the LORD.

PSALM 118:17

The Power of Imagination
LESSON 10

God doesn't cause His joy, peace, anointing, and healing to come and go (Rom. 11:29); we do. God isn't the variable; we are. He's not the one who moves in "waves"; it's the body of Christ who receives what Jesus has already provided in waves. The Lord is constant, but we're not. He doesn't do "this" for a while and then change His mind and do "that" instead. Everything Jesus Christ lived, died, and resurrected to provide for us has been constantly available since He sat down at the right hand of the Father!

Just like a television station constantly transmits its signal, God is always transmitting. However, whether we perceive that signal or not depends on our receivers. Is it plugged in, turned on, and tuned in? Whether we experience God's provision or not depends on whether or not we're receiving. If we aren't, the problem is with our receivers, not God's transmitter, and there are specific things we can do to fix our receivers.

The vast majority of the body of Christ begs God for things He's already given. If you pray that way, you're just going to get silence on the other end because God can't do anything that He hasn't already done for you. You just need to learn how to receive.

But after you receive, you must also maintain it. In some ways, it's more important to know how to maintain what you've received than it is to receive God's touch in the first place.

In order to maintain consistency and keep the things of God fresh and alive in your heart, you must first glorify God. This means you must value and prize Him. Many of our problems come as a result of misplaced values. We let other things compete with and occupy the place that God alone should have in our lives.

Your Spiritual Smell

The second key is to be thankful. God's Word reveals that we give off a spiritual smell. That's what the word "savour" means in these verses:

> For we are unto God a sweet savour of Christ, in them that are saved, and in them that perish: To the one we are the savour of death unto death; and to the other the savour of life unto life.
>
> 2 Corinthians 2:15-16

The praise and thanksgiving of the redeemed—like sacrifices in the Old Testament—produce a spiritual aroma that blesses God. However, just like the smell of manure attracts flies, griping and complaining attract demons. Have you wondered why bad things always seem to happen to you? It's because you're a griper and a complainer. You're drawing all the demons in the county to yourself. You need to be a God-praiser!

Praise is one of the most important things you can do. It makes you focus on what the Lord is doing. If you're the kind of person who tends toward the negative, you won't continue in praising God. If you make a decision to start praising the Lord, you'll have to start seeing the positive side of things. Why? There's nothing praiseworthy in the negative. This forces you to focus on the things of God (Phil. 4:4-8).

Counterfeits and Abuse

The third key comes from this phrase in Romans 1:21:

They "became vain in their imaginations."

If you're a leaky vessel, one of the main holes God leaks out of you is your lack of glorifying God. That leads to not being thankful. These two things combined cause your imagination to become "vain."

Vain means "idle or non-productive." It's not that your imagination isn't functioning; it's just not benefiting you.

Most Christians don't like to talk about imagination. They often think it's childish, saying, "Only kids daydream and imagine things. I'm logical and deal only in reality." They pride themselves on being "realists" instead of visionary—imaginative—people. Others see imagination as something associated with Eastern religions: "Sit down in a lotus position and visualize world peace." Just because something is abused doesn't mean we should chuck it!

Eastern religions abuse prayer, too, but that doesn't mean you should quit praying. Satan only counterfeits something that's real. The very fact that other people have counterfeited this shows it has genuine value.

It's Always Working!

Your imagination is important! It's functioning all the time. You may think *I'm not a person who sits around imagining things*, but you are—constantly. It's how you do everything. You don't have a choice as to whether your imagination works or not; you just get to choose whether it's working for or against you.

If you quit glorifying, magnifying, praising, and thanking God, your imagination will automatically gravitate toward negative things. You can't control that. Your imagination is a byproduct of your focus. If you are really valuing the things of God—praising and thanking Him—your imagination will begin to see things happening properly in your life.

Whether you realize it or not—your mind functions through imagination. You can't really do anything about it. As a matter of fact, the word *imaginations* in the Old Testament literally means "a form" and figuratively means "conception." Your imagination is the part of you where you conceive things!

If you didn't have an imagination, you would be totally non-creative. Just like an animal, you'd have to be taught and learn things by repetition. But one of the distinguishing characteristics between human beings and animals is the imagination. It's a powerful part of who you are.

Whether you recognize it or not—your imagination is the part of you that conceives everything. Before you can act anything out, you have to conceive it first in your imagination. If you can't see it with your imagination, you can't do it.

You Think in Pictures

This is why a builder uses blueprints. It's also why "a picture is worth a thousand words." Your imagination is the part of you that makes things work in your life. It's your ability to see something with your inner eyes instead of your physical eyes. Human beings think in pictures.

If I whispered the word "dog" in your ear right now, you wouldn't just see the letters "D-O-G"; you'd see a picture of a dog. It would probably be one that you've had or have personally interacted with before. However, you're not looking at an animal right now. You're looking at a book, an outline, or a teacher, but in your mind, you have a picture of a dog.

With my words, I can change your picture. You might be thinking of a poodle or a Chihuahua, but now I'm going to say, "Big dog." Instantly, your picture changes. "Big, black dog," and your image changes again. "Big, black, mean dog," and it'll change again. "Big, black, mean dog with vicious teeth." Do you get the picture? Even though I can use words to influence the image you see, you think in pictures.

What did the house look like that you grew up in? Now, you might have moved several times, and several different houses may come to mind. But if you lived primarily in one place, the picture of that house will come to mind. If I asked you "How many bathrooms were there? How many bedrooms?" you'd go look at the picture and count them. You don't have that information stored as facts, but as pictures. That's your imagination!

You can't do anything without your imagination. If I asked you "How do I get to the airport?" you'd say, "Take a right on the main road and go down to the second stoplight. Turn left and get on the highway. Get off on the third exit, and follow the signs to the airport. It'll be a mile down on your right." How would you do that? You didn't have that information just stored. You pictured it with your imagination and then described to me what you saw. But if you'd never been to the airport before, you couldn't have told me where to go. Why? You wouldn't have been able to picture it. That's how you use your imagination.

Negative Use

You use your imagination constantly. It's the conception part of you. You can't build anything without it. Dressmakers depend on a pattern. It helps them picture the dress they're making. Manufacturers give you pictures in the instructions for how to assemble something. There are words of explanation, too, but it's the picture of how this part goes together with that part and completes the final product that helps you imagine it.

Your imagination is the creative part of you. This is why it literally means "conception." There can be no creativity without using your imagination. But if you quit glorifying God and being thankful, your imagination is forced to work against you instead of for you. You'll start conceiving and seeing negative things. You'll start being fearful and operate in unbelief instead of faith. This is the negative use of imagination.

The doctor will say "You have cancer and you're going to die," and instantly your imagination causes you to see yourself in a casket. If you knew someone who suffered and died of cancer, you'll see yourself in that position. Your imagination would just go that way. The sad fact is that most people's imagination is very negative. It works against you by conceiving doubt, fear, unbelief, worry, and hatred.

Void of Speculative Imagination

One of the New Testament qualifications of an elder is to be "sober" (1 Tim. 3:2 and Titus 1:8). It's also required of a deacon's wife (1 Tim. 3:11). This isn't talking about not being drunk. *Sober* literally means "void of speculative imagination."

The Lord has really used this in my life. When you first get started in the ministry, you want people to like you. You don't want to cause problems everywhere you speak. You want to be a blessing. However, if you're not careful, you could fall into the trap of ministering for people's acceptance instead of for the Lord.

There was a particular couple that would always drive to my meetings anytime I ministered within a hundred miles of Kansas City. They were just so blessed by my ministry and had become good friends of mine. They never missed a meeting.

I went to Kansas City one time, and they were noticeably absent. I remembered how, when I was there the year before, I had given them a very specific prophecy. It wasn't a generic prophecy that could apply to anyone; it was very precise. Therefore, I'd either heard from God 100 percent or totally missed it. There was no compromise.

When I didn't see them, I started thinking, speculating, and imagining. I thought, *I bet I missed it last year, and now they're upset with me.* I saw them spreading rumors that I was a false prophet. The more I thought about it, the angrier I became. I was honestly to the point of punching them!

But the next night they showed up and said to me, "We're so sorry we missed yesterday. We just had a death in the family and couldn't get away. We never would have missed your meeting otherwise!" The Lord showed me that I was ready to take up an offense over something that didn't happen. I was speculating—imagining—what they were thinking and what was going on.

"Judge Not!"

I've been to so many churches where someone was offended and ready to quit the church just because the pastor didn't speak to them. They imagine that it's because he doesn't like them, but they never consider the fact that maybe he had somebody or something else on his mind when he passed by them in the hall. There could have been a million reasons why he didn't greet them. This is what the Bible means when it says:

> Judge not, that ye be not judged. For with what judgment ye judge, ye shall be judged: and with what measure ye mete, it shall be measured to you again. And why beholdest thou the mote that is in thy brother's eye, but considerest not the beam that is in thine own eye? Or how wilt thou say to thy brother, Let me pull out the mote out of thine eye; and, behold, a beam is in thine own eye? Thou hypocrite, first cast out the beam out of thine own eye; and then shalt thou see clearly to cast out the mote out of thy brother's eye.
>
> MATTHEW 7:1-5

Some people become confused over this because other scriptures tell us to judge. This passage simply says, "With the judgment you judge others with, so you also will be judged. Therefore, be merciful! Take the beam out of your own eye first, before you try to take the speck out of someone else's." That's the kind of judgment this passage is referring to.

However, if you found yourself in a big-city alley at night with a man dressed up like a gangster quickly coming toward you with a whip in one hand and a knife in the other—you'd better judge! There's nothing wrong with saying, "This doesn't look good. I'd better get out of here!" It's beneficial to judge this way, but it's wrong to try to figure out why he's dressed that way and doing what he's doing.

This is especially important in relationships. When someone says something that offends you, there's nothing wrong with saying, "When you said such and such, it made me feel this way." Wrong judging would say to them "What you said is wrong because…" and then you speculate about why they said what they did. You don't know why they said it. They may not have realized what they were saying. They probably had no idea they were offending you. They may have said it because someone else offended them. You don't know why people do what they do!

Why Is Not Your Business!

After the Lord showed me about being sober, I made a decision not to speculate about what's going on. I've even taught my staff this, saying, "I will not accept hints. If you're mad at me or dislike me, you're going to have to come and tell me directly." I can tell when someone isn't acting very friendly, but I refuse to speculate about why. That's their business. If they have something against me, they're going to have to tell me about it themselves. I am not going to speculate about it.

Maybe there's someone you have judged. Perhaps you've already condemned them about why they're doing what they're doing, but you don't honestly know. You don't have a clue as to why they did what they did, because you've never asked them. That's speculative imagination!

The Power of Imagination
LESSON 10 – OUTLINE

1. Everything Jesus Christ lived, died, and resurrected to provide for us has been constantly available since He sat down at the right hand of the Father (Rom. 11:29).

   A. Just like a television station constantly transmits its signal, God is always transmitting.

   B. However, whether we perceive that signal or not depends on our receivers—are they plugged in, turned on, and tuned in?

   C. You just need to learn how to receive.

   D. But after you receive, you must also maintain it.

   E. In order to maintain consistency and keep the things of God fresh and alive in your heart, you must first glorify God.

2. The second key is to be thankful.

   A. The praise and thanksgiving of the redeemed—like sacrifices in the Old Testament—produce a spiritual aroma that blesses God.

   > For we are unto God a sweet savour of Christ, in them that are saved, and in them that perish: To the one we are the savour of death unto death; and to the other the savour of life unto life.
   >
   > 2 CORINTHIANS 2:15-16

   B. However, just like the smell of manure attracts flies, griping and complaining attract demons.

   C. Praise forces you to focus on the things of God (Phil. 4:4-8).

3. The third key comes from this phrase in Romans 1:21:

   > [They] became vain in their imaginations.
   >
   > BRACKETS MINE

   A. Not glorifying God and not being thankful cause your imagination to become "vain."

   B. *Vain* means "idle or non-productive."

   C. It's not that your imagination isn't functioning; it's just not benefiting you.

4. Your imagination is important!

    A. It's functioning all the time.

    B. You don't have a choice as to whether your imagination works or not; you just get to choose whether it's working for or against you.

    C. If you quit glorifying, magnifying, praising, and thanking God, your imagination will automatically gravitate toward negative things.

    D. Your imagination is a byproduct of your focus.

    E. If you are really valuing the things of God—praising and thanking Him—your imagination will begin to see things happening properly in your life.

5. Your imagination is the part of you where you conceive things.

    A. The word *imaginations* in the Old Testament literally means "a form" and figuratively means "conception."

    B. Before you can act anything out, you have to conceive it first in your imagination.

    C. If you can't see it with your imagination, you can't do it.

    D. Human beings think in pictures.

6. One of the New Testament qualifications of an elder is to be "sober" (1 Tim. 3:2 and Titus 1:8; it's the same for a deacon's wife – 1 Tim. 3:11).

    A. *Sober* literally means "void of speculative imagination."

    > Judge not, that ye be not judged. For with what judgment ye judge, ye shall be judged: and with what measure ye mete, it shall be measured to you again. And why beholdest thou the mote that is in thy brother's eye, but considerest not the beam that is in thine own eye? Or how wilt thou say to thy brother, Let me pull out the mote out of thine eye; and, behold, a beam is in thine own eye? Thou hypocrite, first cast out the beam out of thine own eye; and then shalt thou see clearly to cast out the mote out of thy brother's eye.
    >
    > MATTHEW 7:1-5

    B. Wrong judging would say to someone "What you said is wrong because…" and then you speculate about why they said what they did.

    C. You don't know why people do what they do!

The Power of Imagination
LESSON 10 – TEACHER'S GUIDE

1.   Everything Jesus Christ lived, died, and resurrected to provide for us has been constantly available since He sat down at the right hand of the Father (Rom. 11:29). Just like a television station constantly transmits its signal, God is always transmitting. However, whether we perceive that signal or not depends on our receivers—are they plugged in, turned on, and tuned in? We just need to learn how to receive. But after we receive, we must also maintain it. In order to maintain consistency and keep the things of God fresh and alive in our hearts, we must first glorify God.

2.   The second key is to be thankful. The praise and thanksgiving of the redeemed—like sacrifices in the Old Testament—produce a spiritual aroma that blesses God (2 Cor. 2:15-16). However, just like the smell of manure attracts flies, griping and complaining attract demons. Praise forces us to focus on the things of God (Phil. 4:4-8).

3.   The third key comes from this phrase in Romans 1:21: "[They] became vain in their imaginations" (brackets mine). Not glorifying God and not being thankful cause our imagination to become "vain." Vain means "idle or non-productive." It's not that our imagination isn't functioning; it's just not benefiting us.

1. A. Read Romans 11:29. What has been constantly available since Jesus Christ sat down at the right hand of the Father? (Everything He lived, died, and resurrected to provide for us)
   B. Even though God—like a television station—is always transmitting, whether we perceive that signal or not depends on what? (Our receivers—are they plugged in, turned on, and tuned in)
2. A. Read 2 Corinthians 2:15-16. What is it that produces a spiritual aroma that blesses God? (The praise and thanksgiving of the redeemed)
   B. Read Philippians 4:4-8. What does praise do? (It forces us to focus on the things of God)
3. A. According to Romans 1:21, what does not glorifying God and not being thankful do to our imagination? (It causes it to become vain)
   B. What does vain mean? (Idle or non-productive)

4.   Our imagination is important! It's functioning all the time. We don't have a choice as to whether our imagination works or not; we just get to choose whether it's working for or against us. If we quit glorifying, magnifying, praising, and thanking God, our imagination will automatically gravitate toward negative things. Our imagination is a byproduct of our focus. If we are really valuing the things of God—praising and thanking Him—our imagination will begin to see things happening properly in our lives.

5.   Our imagination is the part of us where we conceive things. The word *imaginations* in the Old Testament literally means "a form" and figuratively means "conception." Before we can act anything out, we have to conceive it first in our imagination. If we can't see it with our imagination, we can't do it. Human beings think in pictures.

6.   One of the New Testament qualifications of an elder is to be "sober" (1 Tim. 3:2 and Titus 1:8; it's the same for a deacon's wife – 1 Tim. 3:11). *Sober* literally means "void of speculative imagination." (Matt. 7:1-5) Wrong judging would say to someone "What you said is wrong because…" and then speculating about why they said what they did. We don't know why people do what they do!

4. A. What does our imagination automatically gravitate toward if we quit glorifying, magnifying, praising, and thanking God? (Negative things)
   B. Our imagination is basically a byproduct of what? (Our focus)
5. A. What must happen before we can act anything out? (We have to conceive it first in our imagination)
   B. How do human beings think? (In pictures)
6. A. Read 1 Timothy 3:2, 11, and Titus 1:8. What does sober mean? (Void of speculative imagination)
   B. Read Matthew 7:1-5. Do we know why people do what they do? (No)

The Power of Imagination
LESSON 10 – DISCIPLESHIP QUESTIONS

1. According to Romans 11:29, _____ of God are without repentance.

2. Second Corinthians 2:15-16 says that we are what?

3. To the saved, we are the savor of _____.
   A. Death unto death.
   B. Life unto life.

4. To the perishing, we are the savor of _____.
   A. Death unto death.
   B. Life unto life.

5. According to Philippians 4:4-8, when should we rejoice in the Lord?

6. We should be full of care for what?

7. How should we make our prayer requests known to God?

8. What passes all understanding?

9. What does it keep?

10. What should we think on?
    A. Things that are true.
    B. Things that are honest.
    C. Things that are just.
    D. Things that are pure.
    E. Things that are lovely.
    F. Things that are of good report.
    G. Virtuous things.
    H. Praiseworthy things.
    I. All of the above.
    J. None of the above.

11. How does Romans 1:21 negatively express the third key to staying full of God?

12. What characteristic do 1 Timothy 3:2, Titus 1:8, and 1 Timothy 3:11 all have in common?

13. According to Matthew 7:1-5, how will we be judged?

14. What should we do before pointing to the speck in someone else's eye?

The Power of Imagination
LESSON 10 – ANSWER KEY

1. His gifts and calling.

2. A sweet savor of Christ.

3. B. Life unto life.

4. A. Death unto death.

5. Always.

6. Nothing.

7. With thanksgiving.

8. The peace of God.

9. Our hearts and minds through Christ Jesus.

10. A. Things that are true.
    B. Things that are honest.
    C. Things that are just.
    D. Things that are pure.
    E. Things that are lovely.
    F. Things that are of good report.
    G. Virtuous things.
    H. Praiseworthy things.
    I. All of the above.

11. Became vain in their imagination.

12. Sober.

13. With the same judgment we measure out to others.

14. Consider and cast out the beam in our own.

The Power of Imagination
LESSON 10 – SCRIPTURES

For the gifts and calling of God are without repentance.

ROMANS 11:29

For we are unto God a sweet savour of Christ, in them that are saved, and in them that perish: To the one we are the savour of death unto death; and to the other the savour of life unto life.

2 CORINTHIANS 2:15-16

Rejoice in the Lord alway: and again I say, Rejoice. Let your moderation be known unto all men. The Lord is at hand. Be careful for nothing; but in every thing by prayer and supplication with thanksgiving let your requests be made known unto God. And the peace of God, which passeth all understanding, shall keep your hearts and minds through Christ Jesus. Finally, brethren, whatsoever things are true, whatsoever things are honest, whatsoever things are just, whatsoever things are pure, whatsoever things are lovely, whatsoever things are of good report; if there be any virtue, and if there be any praise, think on these things.

PHILIPPIANS 4:4-8

Because that, when they knew God, they glorified him not as God, neither were thankful; but became vain in their imaginations, and their foolish heart was darkened.

ROMANS 1:21

A bishop then must be blameless, the husband of one wife, vigilant, sober, of good behaviour, given to hospitality, apt to teach.

1 TIMOTHY 3:2

But a lover of hospitality, a lover of good men, sober, just, holy, temperate.

TITUS 1:8

Even so must their wives be grave, not slanderers, sober, faithful in all things.

1 TIMOTHY 3:11

Judge not, that ye be not judged. For with what judgment ye judge, ye shall be judged: and with what measure ye mete, it shall be measured to you again. And why beholdest thou the mote that is in thy brother's eye, but considerest not the beam that is in thine own eye? Or how wilt thou say to thy brother, Let me pull out the mote out of thine eye; and, behold, a beam is in thine own eye? Thou hypocrite, first cast out the beam out of thine own eye; and then shalt thou see clearly to cast out the mote out of thy brother's eye.

MATTHEW 7:1-5

Inner Images
LESSON 11

Your imagination is a powerful force. As a matter of fact, you cannot consistently function contrary to the image you have on the inside of you.

> For as he thinketh in his heart, so is he.
>
> PROVERBS 23:7

In your heart, you have an image—a picture—of who you are and what you're like. Sadly, most people haven't let the Word of God paint that picture. Other people and experiences have shaped that image. However, we need to get a picture on the inside of us of who we are in Christ and who He is in us. We need to take God's Word like a paintbrush and change that inner image to agree with what the Word says about us. But most people are living their lives with a different image.

You may be someone who gives every time the offering bucket goes by, but you may still see yourself as poor in your heart. You may fulfill God's Word by sowing and planting lots of seed, but your image of yourself in your heart is one of poverty. You see yourself in lack, and so you are. Your imagination has locked you into this self-fulfilling prophecy. Therefore, you continue to fulfill this image that you have on the inside.

Perhaps you see yourself as an introvert. You're shy and bashful around people. This image will dominate and control you until you change it. I used to be an introvert to the max. I couldn't even look people in the face and talk to them. But through God's Word, I've totally changed the image on the inside of me. Now I'm an extrovert to the max. You can change who you are.

A Prosperous Attitude

When we lived in Segoville, Texas, we were so poor we couldn't even pay attention! We couldn't just go out and buy things. So I started praying and believing God. Even though I knew nothing about cars, I began working on them. By faith, I declared, "I can do all things through Christ who strengthens me" (Phil. 4:13). I repaired cars from problems I had no idea in the natural how to fix. I couldn't tell you why they worked, but they did.

Someone gave us a washing machine with a broken brake. I took that thing apart and looked at it, but couldn't figure it out. So I prayed over it and did something to it—and that thing worked for years after that. I just developed an attitude that I can prosper and do anything.

One time I took a job developing pictures. I told my boss, "You'll be blessed because you hired me!" His business was on the rocks, but I had this image on the inside of me. Even though I'd never developed pictures before in my life, I figured it out so well that I pulled this fellow's business out of bankruptcy within two months. I turned his business around so much, he offered me an equal partnership—no money up front—if I would just run it for him. He was going to give me 50 percent of the business! However, that's when the Lord called me to Pritchett, Colorado. So I declined his offer and left.

Through all this, I'd been changing my inner image of myself to agree with God's Word. It was my imagination I was dealing with.

Releasing the Word's Power

If you glorify and thank God, your imagination will start conceiving things differently. If you are grateful and place value on what the Lord has said and done in your life, you'll have faith for your future. Instead of being fearful and seeing negative things come to pass, you'll be hopeful and start seeing positive things come to pass.

> Thou wilt keep him in perfect peace, whose mind is stayed on thee: because he trusteth in thee.
>
> ISAIAH 26:3

The Hebrew word rendered "mind" here is the exact same word translated "imaginations" in other parts of the Old Testament. Therefore, when your imagination is stayed on the Lord, He'll keep you in perfect peace.

Your imagination is your ability to picture something on the inside. Most people don't use their imagination when it comes to relating to the Lord, but they should.

I use my imagination when I meditate on the Word. The vast majority of the revelation I receive from God doesn't come from just reading the Bible. Reading the Word is important because you can't meditate on what you haven't read. Reading the Bible is entering the data into your computer. Without this data entry, there wouldn't be anything for your computer to process. However, after I've read the Word, I sit down and meditate on it. I take the raw data and begin to process it. This is where the real revelation and power are released in Scripture.

Scripture Comes Alive

When I read about David and Goliath, I wanted to picture how tall this giant was. Since our ceilings were only eight feet high, I had to go outside the house to make this mark. Then I stood next to this nine and a half foot mark and pictured what it was really like to go up against this giant.

Why is going to the Holy Land such a life-changing experience? Why does it make the Word come alive so much? It's not that the presence of the Lord is so much greater in Israel than anywhere else in the world today; it's just that being there enables your imagination to see things in the Word more clearly.

I remember going to the Valley of Elah. I left the bus and walked down to the little stream. Then I picked up five smooth stones—exactly the way David did—to help me picture what was going on. When you can picture what the Word of God is talking about, it comes alive!

After you've read the information—data entry—sit down and let the Holy Spirit guide your imagination. Don't just let your mind think about anything. If you've been putting junk into your imagination from television or whatever, it may head in the wrong direction. But if you allow the Word of God to control your thoughts and start thinking about the scriptures you just read, you'll start seeing things in the Word—processing the data—that you can't see with your physical eyes. You must see it on the inside with your imagination.

When the Bible says you're healed, you must take this and meditate on it until you see yourself healed. Most people see themselves sick, not healed. They see the pain and hurt. They already have a clear picture of themselves deteriorating. They've been told what's going to happen and what each stage will be like. They're constantly checking themselves to see where they are in this progression. They see the end result of death or pain.

You need to say, "That's not what I see in the Word!" Then take scriptures and meditate on them until your imagination sees yourself running, jumping, sleeping through the night, living without pain, or whatever it is that you're overcoming.

Greater Works

This is how I first saw people rise from the dead. I took the Word of God and meditated on it.

> Verily, verily, I say unto you, He that believeth on me, the works that I do shall he do also; and greater works than these shall he do; because I go unto my Father.
>
> JOHN 14:12

I started speaking it and talking about it. I took all of the scriptures where people were raised from the dead—nine if you include Jesus—and meditated on them. I'd close my eyes and imagine myself in the Scripture saying, "Lazarus, come forth!" and he did. I saw myself doing all those things Jesus did. I thought about it so much that I started having dreams about raising people from the dead! Then I started actually seeing people rise from the dead.

There's a reason this happens for some people and not for others. If you can't see it on the inside, you won't see it on the outside. Why? Because your imagination is where the conception takes place. Most people just let the physical input of their eyes control their imagination. But the Word of God will paint a picture that can replace those natural things. Maybe you've never seen someone with a broken arm instantly healed. But if you meditate on it until you start seeing it on the inside, then you can see it happen on the outside. Perhaps you've never seen anyone in the situation you're in set free, but you can find it in God's Word. If you'll meditate on it, you can conceive it, begin seeing it, and it will change things.

Evil Imaginations

Although Genesis 6 records the negative use of imagination, it's still a powerful example.

> GOD saw that the wickedness of man was great in the earth, and that every imagination of the thoughts of his heart was only evil continually.
>
> GENESIS 6:5

Even though many of us have had an encounter with the Lord, been born again and baptized in the Holy Spirit, the truth is that the vast majority of our imaginations are evil. We see negative things—things contrary to God's Word. We see ourselves failing, angry, bitter, and rejected. We see ourselves in ways that are contrary to what God's Word says, and most of us just allow our imagination to run rampant. We don't honestly think there is anything wrong with imagining things, but this verse shows us that God saw the imagination of the thoughts of the people's hearts.

Before he died, David gave instructions to his son, Solomon, before he became king. He said:

> And thou, Solomon my son, know thou the God of thy father, and serve him with a perfect heart and with a willing mind: for the LORD searcheth all hearts, and understandeth all the imaginations of the thoughts: if thou seek him, he will be found of thee; but if thou forsake him, he will cast thee off for ever.
>
> 1 CHRONICLES 28:9

God sees all the imaginations of the heart. If you look through the rest of the Old Testament, you'll find at least half a dozen times where the Lord brought judgment on people for their imaginations.

Spiritual Conception

Most of us focus on our actions. We think, *I can't commit adultery. I can't do it!* But it's stupid to allow your imagination to think on and conceive that and then have to fight, resist, and try to keep from acting out what you've thought on in your heart.

That's like a woman who doesn't want to birth a child but doesn't place any restrictions whatsoever upon having physical relationships. She's constantly conceiving, but then having to abort in order to keep from having a birth. This isn't the way not to have children. If you don't want to conceive, don't have a physical relationship!

In the spiritual realm, most of us don't recognize that our imagination is where we conceive. There are very few things you can watch on television that won't give you negative imaginations. Programs constantly present sexual situations or teach you how to get angry, bitter, and fight back, but the Word says to forgive and turn the other cheek (Luke 6:29). Whether you realize it or not, those visual images are painting pictures on the inside of you. When you come into a crisis or similar temptation, you'll be tempted to act that out because it's already been conceived.

You can literally reach a place where you don't conceive things—and if you can't conceive it, you can't do it. You can actually get to a place where you don't know how to sin. "Come on, Andrew. You can't be serious." I am—and you can do it! You can literally get your mind so stayed on God that all it's doing is conceiving joy, peace, and power. If you keep your imagination stayed on Him, you'll be in perfect peace (Is. 26:3).

Rampant Thoughts

People cause themselves a tremendous amount of problems because of the way they allow their imagination to think. Very few people feel any responsibility over their imagination. Very few even know what their imagination is. They just allow their thoughts to run rampant, and they'll think on negative things.

Someone came to me once and asked, "Do you think I married the wrong person? I'm having trouble in my marriage. Do you think I missed God?" They honestly wanted me to help them decide whether they had missed God or not. I told them, "That's stupid! It doesn't matter whether you've made a mistake or not. Never—never think that stuff! There is absolutely nothing positive that could ever come of it, but there's a tremendous amount of damage that could. What are you going to do, divorce your spouse? Get another one and violate Scripture? That is not an option. You should never let your thoughts go there."

There are things that come against me that I refuse to think. I could imagine all kinds of bad things. When we first started on television, it significantly increased our expenses. I had to consider some of these things to see how much money we needed so I could make plans and communicate with our partners. I thought on some of these things, but I've never allowed myself one time to see myself fail in this endeavor. I've never allowed my mind to go there and imagine what I'd have to do if we didn't have the money and I had to back up and say, "I missed it." I've never thought it or gone there in my mind, because that's not what God told me.

I refuse to think things contrary to what God's Word says. Therefore, I don't conceive them, and I'm not tempted with them.

When God tells most people something to do, they immediately sit down and figure out every reason why it won't work. They allow their imagination to go down that road and see themselves failing. Then, after they've considered all of this junk, they say, "God, can I believe You for this?" That's like trying to swim with weights on. It's not going to work, and it's not the way God wants you to do it.

Don't Go There!

Most of us don't understand how important our imagination is. Maybe every once in a while, you get depressed and say, "I'd feel better if I just had a pity party." So you start thinking, "Nobody loves me. Everyone hates me." But you know it's not true.

When you do that, you're acting just like Elijah (1 Kin. 19): "God, I'm the only one left!" Yet Obadiah told him there were still a hundred preachers left that he had hidden in a cave and fed with bread and water (1 Kin. 18:3-4, 7, and 13). Although Elijah knew better, he started to whine, "O God, I'm the only one left." He allowed himself to get into a pity party and left this life after obeying only one of the three final instructions God gave him in 1 Kings 19:15-16, which was to anoint his replacement.

"But, Andrew, I just feel better when I gripe, complain, and throw myself a pity party." Don't go there! Don't allow your thoughts to go there. Don't see yourself failing. Don't see your prayers not being answered. You may say "Surely, you can't live this way." I say, "Yes, you can!"

Some people are so negative that all it takes is the devil whispering a word, and they will make a paragraph out of it. He can go on vacation because they're so wonderful at amplifying and magnifying the negative. They have a little pain in their chest and think it's a heart attack. Then they meditate on it until they actually are having a heart attack because of the fear. But the truth was that it was nothing to start with. People take the smallest thing and amplify it.

The imagination does that. Most people's imagination is evil. They go in the wrong direction!

Inner Images
LESSON 11 – OUTLINE

1. Your imagination is a powerful force.

    A. You cannot consistently function contrary to the image you have on the inside of you.

    For as he thinketh in his heart, so is he.

    PROVERBS 23:7

    B. We need to take God's Word like a paintbrush and change that inner image to agree with what the Word says about us.

    C. You can change who you are.

2. If you glorify and thank God, your imagination will start conceiving things differently.

    A. If you are grateful and place value on what the Lord has said and done in your life, you'll have faith for your future.

    B. Instead of being fearful and seeing negative things come to pass, you'll be hopeful and start seeing positive things come to pass.

    Thou wilt keep him in perfect peace, whose mind is stayed on thee: because he trusteth in thee.

    ISAIAH 26:3

    C. The Hebrew word rendered "mind" here is the exact same word translated "imaginations" in other parts of the Old Testament.

    D. Therefore, when your imagination is stayed on the Lord, He'll keep you in perfect peace.

3. I use my imagination when I meditate the Word.

    A. Reading the Bible is entering the data into your computer.

    B. However, after I've read the Word, I meditate on it; I take the raw data and begin to process it.

    C. This is where the real revelation and power are released in Scripture.

    D. If you allow the Word of God to control your thoughts and start thinking about the scriptures you just read, you'll start seeing things in the Word—processing the data—that you can't see with your physical eyes.

    E. You must see it on the inside with your imagination.

4. This is how I first saw people raised from the dead.

   A. I took the Word of God and meditated on it.

   > Verily, verily, I say unto you, He that believeth on me, the works that I do shall he do also; and greater works than these shall he do; because I go unto my Father.
   >
   > JOHN 14:12

   B. I took all of the scriptures where people were raised from the dead—nine if you include Jesus—and meditated on them.

   C. I saw—imagined—myself doing all those things Jesus did.

   D. Then I started actually seeing—experiencing—people rise from the dead.

   E. If you'll meditate on it, you can conceive it, begin seeing it, and it will change things.

5. God sees all the imaginations of the heart.

   A. Even though many of us have had an encounter with the Lord, been born again and baptized in the Holy Spirit, the truth is that the vast majority of our imaginations are evil.

   > GOD saw that the wickedness of man was great in the earth, and that every imagination of the thoughts of his heart was only evil continually.
   >
   > GENESIS 6:5

   B. We see negative things—things contrary to God's Word.

   C. We see ourselves in ways that are contrary to what God's Word says, and most of us just allow our imagination to run rampant.

   D. Before he died, David gave instructions to his son, Solomon, before he became king.

   > And thou, Solomon my son, know thou the God of thy father, and serve him with a perfect heart and with a willing mind: for the LORD searcheth all hearts, and understandeth all the imaginations of the thoughts: if thou seek him, he will be found of thee; but if thou forsake him, he will cast thee off for ever.
   >
   > 1 CHRONICLES 28:9

6. We cause ourselves a tremendous amount of problems because of the way we allow our imagination to think.

   A. Very few people feel any responsibility over their imagination.
   B. They just allow their thoughts to run rampant, and they think on negative things (Example of Elijah – 1 Kin. 19; 18:3-4, 7, and 13).

7. There are things that come against me that I refuse to think.

   A. I refuse to think things contrary to what God's Word says.

   B. Therefore, I don't conceive them, and I'm not tempted with them.

   C. You may say "Surely, you can't live this way," but I say, "Yes, you can!"

Inner Images
LESSON 11 – TEACHER'S GUIDE

1.   Our imagination is a powerful force. We cannot consistently function contrary to the image we have on the inside (Prov. 23:7). We need to take God's Word like a paintbrush and change that inner image to agree with what the Word says about us. We can change who we are (Phil. 4:13).

2.   If we glorify and thank God, our imagination will start conceiving things differently. If we are grateful and place value on what the Lord has said and done in our lives, we'll have faith for our future. Instead of being fearful and seeing negative things come to pass, we'll be hopeful and start seeing positive things come to pass. The Hebrew word rendered "mind" in Isaiah 26:3 is the exact same word translated "imaginations" in other parts of the Old Testament. Therefore, when our imagination is stayed on the Lord, He'll keep us in perfect peace.

3.   I use my imagination when I meditate the Word. Reading the Bible is entering the data into our computers. However, after I've read the Word, I meditate on it. I take the raw data and begin to process it. This is where the real revelation and power are released in Scripture. If we allow the Word of God to control our thoughts and if we start thinking about the scriptures we just read, we'll start seeing things in the Word—processing the data—that we can't see with our physical eyes. We must see it on the inside with our imagination.

1. A. According to Proverbs 23:7, can we consistently function contrary to the image we have on the inside? (No)
   B. Read Philippians 4:13. What should we take like a paintbrush and change our inner image to agree with?   (God's Word)
2. A. If we thank God and place value on what He has said and done in our lives, what will our imagination see? (Positive things coming to pass)
   B. According to Isaiah 26:3, what happens when we keep our imagination stayed on the Lord? (He keeps us in perfect peace)
3. A. What is reading the Bible like? (Entering data into our computers)
   B. What is meditating on the Word like? (Processing that data)
   C. What happens when we allow the Word of God to control our thoughts and we start thinking about the scriptures we've just read? (We'll start seeing things in the Word that we can't see with our physical eyes)

4.   This is how I first saw people rise from the dead. I took the Word of God and meditated on it (John 14:12). I took all of the scriptures where people were raised from the dead—nine if you include Jesus—and meditated on them. I saw—imagined—myself doing all those things Jesus did. Then I started actually seeing—experiencing—people rise from the dead. If we'll meditate on it, we can conceive it, begin seeing it, and it will change things.

5.   God sees all the imaginations of the heart. Even though many of us have had encounters with the Lord, been born again and baptized in the Holy Spirit, the truth is that the vast majority of our imaginations are evil (Gen. 6:5). We see negative things—things contrary to God's Word. We see ourselves in ways that are contrary to what God's Word says, and most of us just allow our imagination to run rampant. Before he died, David gave instructions to his son, Solomon, before he became king (1 Chr. 28:9).

6.   We cause ourselves a tremendous amount of problems because of the way we allow our imagination to think. Very few of us feel any responsibility over our imagination. We just allow our thoughts to run rampant, and we think on negative things (Example of Elijah – 1 Kin. 19; 18:3-4, 7, and 13).

7.   There are things that come against me that I refuse to think. I refuse to think things contrary to what God's Word says. Therefore, I don't conceive them, and I'm not tempted with them. Some may say "Surely, we can't live this way," but I say, "Yes, we can!"

4. A. Read John 14:12. How did Andrew first see people being raised from the dead? (He took the Word of God and meditated on it)
   B. When he meditated on the scriptures, what did he imagine? (He saw himself doing all those things that Jesus did)
   C. Then what happened? (He started seeing—experiencing—people rise from the dead)
5. A. Read Genesis 6:5 and 1 Chronicles 28:9. Even though many of us have had encounters with the Lord, been born again and baptized in the Holy Spirit, the truth is that the vast majority of our imaginations are what? (Evil, negative, contrary to God's Word)
   B. Most people just allow their imagination to what? (Run rampant)
6. Read 1 Kings 18:3-4, 7, 13; and 19. What do we cause ourselves because of the way we allow our imagination to think? (A tremendous amount of problems)
7. A. What does Andrew refuse to do? (Think things contrary to what God's Word says)
   B. What happens as a result? (Things contrary to God's Word aren't conceived, and he's not tempted by them)
   C. Can we live this way? (Yes, we can!)

Inner Images
LESSON 11 – DISCIPLESHIP QUESTIONS

1. According to Proverbs 23:7, we are as we _____ in our hearts.

2. Philippians 4:13 reveals that we can do _____ things.

3. How?

4. How does Isaiah 26:3 say that we are kept in perfect peace?

5. Who was speaking in John 14:12?

6. Whom was He speaking to?

7. Who is it that will do the works He did?

8. What else will they do?

9. Why?

10. In Genesis 6:5, what did God see that was great in the earth?

11. What was only evil continually?

12. What did David advise Solomon to do in 1 Chronicles 28:9?

13. What does the Lord search?

14. What does He understand?

15. According to Luke 6:29, what should you do when someone smites you on one cheek?

16. What should you do when someone takes away your cloak?

Inner Images
LESSON 11 – ANSWER KEY

1. Think.

2. All things.

3. Through Christ who strengthens us.

4. By keeping our minds on and trusting God.

5. Jesus.

6. His disciples, including us today.

7. Those who believe on the Lord.

8. Even greater works.

9. Because Jesus went to the Father.

10. The wickedness of man.

11. Every imagination of the thoughts of man's heart.

12. Know God and serve Him with a perfect heart and willing mind.

13. All hearts.

14. All imaginations and thoughts.

15. Offer the other.

16. Forbid not their taking away my coat also.

For as he thinketh in his heart, so is he: Eat and drink, saith he to thee; but his heart is not with thee.

PROVERBS 23:7

I can do all things through Christ which strengtheneth me.

PHILIPPIANS 4:13

Thou wilt keep him in perfect peace, whose mind is stayed on thee: because he trusteth in thee.

ISAIAH 26:3

Verily, verily, I say unto you, He that believeth on me, the works that I do shall he do also; and greater works than these shall he do; because I go unto my Father.

JOHN 14:12

And GOD saw that the wickedness of man was great in the earth, and that every imagination of the thoughts of his heart was only evil continually.

GENESIS 6:5

And thou, Solomon my son, know thou the God of thy father, and serve him with a perfect heart and with a willing mind: for the LORD searcheth all hearts, and understandeth all the imaginations of the thoughts: if thou seek him, he will be found of thee; but if thou forsake him, he will cast thee off for ever.

1 CHRONICLES 28:9

And unto him that smiteth thee on the one cheek offer also the other; and him that taketh away thy cloak forbid not to take thy coat also.

LUKE 6:29

And Ahab called Obadiah, which was the governor of his house. (Now Obadiah feared the LORD greatly: For it was so, when Jezebel cut off the prophets of the LORD, that Obadiah took an hundred prophets, and hid them by fifty in a cave, and fed them with bread and water.)…And as Obdadiah was in the way, behold, Elijah met him: and he knew him, and fell on his face, and said, Art thou that my lord Elijah?…Was it not told my lord what I did when Jezebel slew the prophets of the LORD, how I hid an hundred men of the LORD's prophets by fifty in a cave, and fed them with bread and water?

1 KINGS 18:3-4, 7, AND 13

Prepare Your Heart
LESSON 12

David gave an offering of $1.5 billion worth of gold and silver from his personal bank account (1 Chr. 29). Although he'd already given $5 billion toward the building of the temple from his government treasuries, this gift was from his own personal wealth. Not bad for a shepherd boy.

David was prosperous! When he gave, the people were so blessed they started giving too—to the amount of $3.5 billion. Altogether, it was a $5 billion spontaneous offering!

> Then the people rejoiced, for that they offered willingly, because with perfect heart they offered willingly to the LORD: and David the king also rejoiced with great joy.
>
> 1 CHRONICLES 29:9

In verse 10 David started praying. He glorified God—recognized and acknowledged Him. What had happened that day was supernatural, and he placed value on it, thanking God and saying, "Lord, all we've done is given You that which was already Yours. Everything we have, You gave to us in the first place." David started thanking God for the blessing, remembering where he came from, glorifying and thanking Him. Then in verse 18, he said:

> O LORD God of Abraham, Isaac, and of Israel, our fathers, ***keep this for ever in the imagination of the thoughts of the heart of thy people***, and prepare their heart unto thee.
>
> 1 CHRONICLES 29:18, EMPHASIS MINE

David was saying, "Lord, help us remember!"

Make Monuments

Memory is powerful! Your imagination is the part of you that remembers.

But 2 Chronicles 12:14 says,

> Rehoboam "did evil, because he prepared not his heart to seek the LORD."

Preparing your heart is vital—and remembering is one of the most important things you can do to prepare your heart.

I've prepared my heart to seek the Lord. Even though it's been almost four decades since God supernaturally intervened in my life, I've been glorifying God, thanking Him, and remembering what He's said and done.

I make monuments in my life constantly. We just drove through Arlington, Texas, so we took some time and saw our old house. I drove by the field where I received the baptism in the Holy Spirit. I also have that boulder that rolled over my hand, arm, and head where we live now to remind me of God's goodness. I'm not going to forget that Jesus saved my life, because I walk by it almost every day. Memory makes a huge difference!

"Whose Fault Is it?"

After getting married, most people start dealing with all the pressures of daily life and forget those things that really made them fall in love with their mate in the first place. They forget the good things and start focusing on the negative. Then their imagination begins to magnify those things.

Do you know what? You can't live with someone if you don't remember anything good about them.

I've actually sat down with married couples before and said, "There's something good in that person. Tell me something good about them."

And they've answered, "I can't think of anything good in my mate."

So I ask them, "Did you love them when you got married?"

"Oh, yeah. They were great!"

"Well, then, if they were okay when you got them, guess whose fault it is that they turned out this way?"

Your memory is a very important force!

"God Saved My Life!"

> But he that lacketh these things is blind, and cannot see afar off, and hath forgotten that he was purged from his old sins.
>
> 2 PETER 1:9

You can actually forget what Jesus has done for you. I've known people who were so upset that they were going to walk away from God. I reminded them of what He had done for them. Once they remember, everything changes.

Two years ago in a Chicago meeting, I said through the gifts of the Holy Spirit that someone in that meeting had tried to commit suicide or was thinking about it. When the woman came forward, she started telling me how everything in her life had gone wrong. As I prayed for her, the Holy Spirit gave me four instances where Satan had tried to kill her from the time she was a little girl. I reminded her of them, saying, "Do you remember when you were four years old and someone tried to rape and kill you? You focused on the negative side, but look what happened. The Lord says they tried to kill you, and it was a miracle you lived. Instead of magnifying the negative, you ought to say, 'God saved my life!'" Then I went through the other three things He showed me and reminded her of them. By the time she got through remembering how the Lord had delivered her, this woman—who had been contemplating suicide—was on her knees praising and thanking God for His grace and mercy.

God has done some awesome things for each and every one of us. There's no reason why you should be upset, except that you forget the goodness of God. Your memory is a vital part of your life. Your imagination is how you remember things. You must start using your imagination in a positive way.

How Great Thou Art

> Wherefore I will not be negligent to put you always in remembrance of these things.
>
> 2 PETER 1:12

Your memory needs to be stirred up. You need to remember things over and over and over again.

> Moreover I will endeavour that ye may be able after my decease to have these things always in remembrance.
>
> 2 PETER 1:15

> This second epistle, beloved, I now write unto you; in both which I stir up your pure minds by way of remembrance.
>
> 2 PETER 3:1

You can stir yourself up through memory. Almost ten years ago I was in a service in Lima, Ohio. There were 600 people, and we had seen so many good things happen during our time together. There were actually people standing outside the building and listening through the open windows. We started singing "How Great Thou Art," and I had a flashback to my father's funeral. That had been my dad's favorite song. I remembered sitting there as a twelve-year-old boy thinking, *God, this doesn't compute. My dad just died and we're singing about how great You are.* I remembered praying, "If You really are great, reveal Yourself to me and give me a purpose for my life." I was overwhelmed with God's faithfulness as that memory brought me to my knees. A memory can stir you powerfully!

Disconnected

Very few take time to remember. It takes effort to remember. You have to be still, turn off the television, shut off the radio, and spend time reflecting. You ought to spend some quiet time each and every day just remembering. If you did, it would transform your life. It's your imagination that does this. Go back through your mind and picture things.

My mother and I were recently in Marietta, Texas, talking to people who knew our relatives, and remembering things in our lives. Every time I get a chance, I go to these places that have been really significant in my life. I just sit and remember. Those are some of the most powerful times I have, and it really makes a difference in my life.

Our whole society is moving away from this. How much do we know about our grandparents? What about our great-grandparents? As a whole, we are a society that lives life only in the moment, and we are so occupied with ourselves that we don't know these things.

While in England recently, I preached in a church. Afterward the pastor took us to his home for lunch. His family had lived in the exact same house since the 1400s. He took me into the house and said, "Right here is where my great, great, great, great, great-grandfather was born, and here is where they were married." He knew this!

As he was sharing, I was thinking, *Man, the history this guy lives with! How would that impact his life and his actions? How would knowing what his grandparents had done in this house and how they conducted themselves enter into his reasoning and the things he does today?* Most of us are so disconnected from anything like that. We don't even like to think about it.

Memory is a powerful force. That's the reason the Lord told us to erect monuments and not tear down our neighbors' landmarks.

"Don't You Remember?"

You need to rehearse your victories! When the Lord rebuked David for his sin with Bathsheba, He said, "David, don't you remember that I took you from following the sheep? Don't you remember that your name wasn't even put in the hat when Samuel came? You were out keeping the sheep. They didn't even esteem you enough to think you had a chance of becoming king. Don't you remember what I did—how I overcame your enemies? Don't you remember how I gave you all of these things? If that wasn't enough, I would have given you more!" God referred him back to memory (2 Sam. 12:7-8).

In order for you to do some of the stuff you do, you have to forget the goodness and faithfulness of God. I'm not encouraging anyone to try this, but what would happen if right before you jumped into bed with a prostitute, you said, "Let's just pray and dedicate this to the Lord. Let's just take a moment and thank God for His goodness"? I bet it would ruin the whole thing! That's what remembering the goodness of God will do to you—it'll ruin sin in your life.

All of the keys to staying full of God are interrelated: glorify God, be thankful, and remember. If you were doing these on a consistent basis, it would create such an atmosphere of God's goodness and faithfulness in your life. It would prevent you from doing some of the things that you do. Your imagination would start focusing on positive things. Instead of seeing yourself fail, you'd see God's goodness and your circumstances working out.

A worrywart is just someone with a vivid imagination in the negative realm. If you're anxious about things, your imagination is functioning in the wrong direction. But the good news is that you can turn that around. Just start using your imagination in the right way!

Prepare Your Heart
LESSON 12 – OUTLINE

1. David was prosperous!

   A. When he gave, the people were so blessed that they started giving spontaneously, too—to the amount of $3.5 billion.

   Then the people rejoiced, for that they offered willingly, because with perfect heart they offered willingly to the LORD: and David the king also rejoiced with great joy.

   1 CHRONICLES 29:9

   B. David started thanking God for the blessing, remembering where he came from, glorifying and thanking Him.

   O LORD God of Abraham, Isaac, and of Israel, our fathers, *keep this for ever in the imagination of the thoughts of the heart of thy people*, and prepare their heart unto thee.

   1 CHRONICLES 29:18, EMPHASIS MINE

   C. David was saying, "Lord, help us remember!"

2. Memory is powerful!

   A. Your imagination is the part of you that remembers.

   B. Preparing your heart is vital—and remembering is one of the most important things you can do to prepare your heart.

   [Rehoboam] did evil, because he prepared not his heart to seek the LORD.

   2 CHRONICLES 12:14, BRACKETS MINE

   C. Memory makes a huge difference.

   D. You can't live with someone if you don't remember anything good about them.

   E. Your memory is a very important force.

3. You can actually forget what Jesus has done for you.

   But he that lacketh these things is blind, and cannot see afar off, and hath forgotten that he was purged from his old sins.

   2 PETER 1:9

A. God has done some awesome things for each and every one of us.

B. Your memory needs to be stirred up so you can remember things over and over and over again.

Wherefore I will not be negligent to put you always in remembrance of these things.

2 PETER 1:12

Moreover I will endeavour that ye may be able after my decease to have these things always in remembrance.

2 PETER 1:15

This second epistle, beloved, I now write unto you; in both which I stir up your pure minds by way of remembrance.

2 PETER 3:1

C. A memory can stir you powerfully!

4. It takes effort to remember.

A. You have to be still, turn off the television, shut off the radio, and spend time reflecting.

B. You ought to spend some quiet time each and every day just remembering.

C. If you did, it would transform your life.

5. You need to rehearse your victories!

A. When the Lord rebuked David for his sin with Bathsheba, He referred him back to memory (2 Sam. 12:7-8).

B. In order for you to do some of the stuff you do, you have to forget the goodness and faithfulness of God.

C. Remembering the goodness of God will ruin sin in your life.

6. All of the keys to staying full of God are interrelated.

A. Glorify God, be thankful, and remember.

B. If you were doing these things on a consistent basis, it would create such an atmosphere of God's goodness and faithfulness in your life.

C. It would prevent you from doing some of the things that you do.

D. Your imagination would start focusing on positive things.

E. Instead of seeing yourself fail, you'd see God's goodness and your circumstances working out.

Prepare Your Heart
LESSON 12 – TEACHER'S GUIDE

1. David was prosperous! When he gave, the people were so blessed that they started giving spontaneously too—to the amount of $3.5 billion (1 Chr. 29:9). David started thanking God for the blessing, remembering where he came from, glorifying and thanking Him (1 Chr. 29:10-18). David was saying, "Lord, help us remember!" (1 Chr. 29:18).

2. Memory is powerful! Our imagination is the part of us that remembers. Preparing our hearts is vital—and remembering is one of the most important things we can do to prepare our hearts (2 Chr. 12:14). Memory makes a huge difference. We can't live with someone if we don't remember anything good about them. Our memory is a very important force.

3. We can actually forget what Jesus has done for us (2 Pet. 1:9). God has done some awesome things for each and every one of us. Our memory needs to be stirred up so we can remember things over and over and over again (2 Pet. 1:12-13, 15, and 3:1). A memory can stir us powerfully!

1. A. Read 1 Chronicles 29:9-18. What happened when David gave? (The people were so blessed that they started giving spontaneously too)
   B. In this passage, what was David doing? (He was thanking God for the blessing, remembering where he came from, and glorifying the Lord)
2. A. What is the part of us that remembers? (Our imagination)
   B. Read 2 Chronicles 12:14. What is one of the most important things we can do to prepare our hearts? (Remember)
3. A. According to 2 Peter 1:9, is it possible to forget what Jesus has done for us? (Yes)
   B. Read 2 Peter 1:12-13, 15; and 3:1. Our memory needs to be _____ so we can remember things over and over and over again. (Stirred up)

4.   It takes effort to remember. We have to be still, turn off the television, shut off the radio, and spend time reflecting. We ought to spend some quiet time each and every day just remembering. If we did, it would transform our lives.

5.   We need to rehearse our victories! When the Lord rebuked David for his sin with Bathsheba, He referred him back to memory (2 Sam. 12:7-8). In order for us to do some of the stuff we do, we have to forget the goodness and faithfulness of God. Remembering the goodness of God will ruin sin in our lives.

6.   All of the keys to staying full of God are interrelated: glorify God, be thankful, and remember. If we were doing these things on a consistent basis, it would create such an atmosphere of God's goodness and faithfulness in our lives, it would prevent us from doing some of the things we do. Our imagination would start focusing on positive things. Instead of seeing ourselves fail, we'd see God's goodness and our circumstances working out.

4. A. What does it take to remember? (Effort, stillness, quiet, and time)
   B. What would happen if we spent some quiet time each and every day just remembering? (It would transform our lives)
5. A. Read 2 Samuel 12:7-8. When the Lord rebuked David for his sin with Bathsheba, He referred him back to what? (Memory)
   B. What does remembering the goodness of God do? (It ruins sin in our lives)
6. A. How do we create an atmosphere of God's goodness and faithfulness in our lives? (Glorify God, be thankful, and remember—all on a consistent basis)
   B. What happens to our imagination when we do this? (It focuses on the positive, and instead of seeing ourselves fail, we see God's goodness and our circumstances working out)

Prepare Your Heart
LESSON 12 – ADDITIONAL INFORMATION

My teaching entitled *How to Prepare Your Heart* expands and enlarges upon the concepts mentioned in **Lesson 12**. I was only able to briefly touch on them here.

Prepare Your Heart
LESSON 12 – DISCIPLESHIP QUESTIONS

1. According to 1 Chronicles 29:9, what did the people do as they gave their offering willingly?

2. With what kind of heart did they willingly give this offering to the Lord?

3. What did King David do?

4. In 1 Chronicles 29:18, what did David ask?

5. According to 2 Chronicles 12:14, why did Rehoboam do evil?

6. What does 2 Peter 1:9 say about the person who lacks these things?

7. What have they forgotten?

8. What is the common theme across 2 Peter 1:12, 15; and 3:1?

9. How do we stir up our pure minds?

10. When David sinned, what did the Lord remind him of in 2 Samuel 12:7-8?
    A. I anointed you king over Israel.
    B. I delivered you out of the hand of Saul.
    C. I gave you your master's house and your master's wives into your bosom.
    D. I gave you the house of Israel and of Judah.
    E. All of the above.
    F. None of the above.

Prepare Your Heart
LESSON 12 – ANSWER KEY

1. They rejoiced.

2. A perfect heart.

3. He also rejoiced with great joy.

4. Lord, please help us remember and prepare our hearts unto You.

5. He didn't prepare his heart to seek the Lord.

6. They're blind and cannot see afar off.

7. That they were purged from their sins.

8. To remember.

9. By way of remembrance.

10. A. I anointed you king over Israel.
    B. I delivered you out of the hand of Saul.
    C. I gave you your master's house and your master's wives into your bosom.
    D. I gave you the house of Israel and of Judah.
    E. All of the above.

Prepare Your Heart
LESSON 12 – SCRIPTURES

Then the people rejoiced, for that they offered willingly, because with perfect heart they offered willingly to the LORD: and David the king also rejoiced with great joy. Wherefore David blessed the LORD before all the congregation: and David said, Blessed be thou, LORD God of Israel our father, for ever and ever.

1 CHRONICLES 29:9-10

O LORD God of Abraham, Isaac, and of Israel, our fathers, keep this for ever in the imagination of the thoughts of the heart of thy people, and prepare their heart unto thee.

1 CHRONICLES 29:18

And he did evil, because he prepared not his heart to seek the LORD.

2 CHRONICLES 12:14

But he that lacketh these things is blind, and cannot see afar off, and hath forgotten that he was purged from his old sins.

2 PETER 1:9

Wherefore I will not be negligent to put you always in remembrance of these things, though ye know them, and be established in the present truth.

2 PETER 1:12

Moreover I will endeavour that ye may be able after my decease to have these things always in remembrance.

2 PETER 1:15

This second epistle, beloved, I now write unto you; in both which I stir up your pure minds by way of remembrance.

2 PETER 3:1

And Nathan said to David, Thou art the man. Thus saith the LORD God of Israel, I anointed thee king over Israel, and I delivered thee out of the hand of Saul; And I gave thee thy master's house, and thy master's wives into thy bosom, and gave thee the house of Israel and Judah; and if that had been too little, I would moreover have given unto thee such and such things.

2 SAMUEL 12:7-8

What Do You See?
LESSON 13

And when the day was now far spent, his disciples came unto him, and said,
This is a desert place, and now the time is far passed: Send them away, that they
may go into the country round about, and into the villages, and buy themselves
bread: for they have nothing to eat. He answered and said unto them, Give ye
them to eat.

MARK 6:35-37

The disciples saw the need, but they didn't see themselves as having the ability to meet it. They wanted to send the people somewhere else.

The church is doing this today. We're sending people to psychologists, bankers, doctors, and lawyers, when in reality we're the ones who have the answer. They don't have to depart. We could meet their needs, but most of the body of Christ doesn't see that. We don't see ourselves as being able to heal the sick, cleanse the lepers, or raise the dead, so we send them somewhere else. The Lord said, "They don't need to depart. You give them something to eat." Most of us think, *But that's unreasonable!* Jesus wouldn't have asked them—or us—to do something they couldn't have done. They could have fed these people. They had the ability to do it. But they couldn't see themselves feeding five thousand people.

And they say unto him, Shall we go and buy two hundred pennyworth of
bread, and give them to eat?

MARK 6:37

They pulled their wallets out of their pockets and peeked inside. They looked at their natural resources instead of their spiritual resources.

Receive Spiritual Sight

He saith unto them, How many loaves have ye? go and see. And when they
knew, they say, Five, and two fishes. And he commanded them to make all
sit down by companies upon the green grass. And they sat down in ranks, by
hundreds, and by fifties. And when he had taken the five loaves and the two fishes,
he looked up to heaven, and blessed, and brake the loaves, and gave them to his
disciples to set before them; and the two fishes divided he among them all.

MARK 6:38-41, EMPHASIS MINE

When Jesus looked up to heaven, He did more than just lift His head. This Greek word—
anablepo—is a combination of *blepo* and *ana*. *Blepo* means "to see," and *ana*—when used in a
compound like this—means "again." Jesus literally saw twice, or saw again.

This same word is translated "receive sight" fifteen times in the Bible. When Bartimaeus received his sight—anablepo. When others' blind eyes opened—anablepo. It's this same word!

So when Jesus looked up, He saw twice. He saw differently than His disciples. Do you know what He did? He saw on the inside. He saw in the spirit realm instead of seeing with His physical eyes. The disciples were looking at their physical resources and were limited to what they could see, taste, hear, smell, and feel. Jesus could see past the physical and into the spiritual realm. That's what this is talking about. When He looked up, He didn't just lift up His head; He perceived the situation with His spiritual eyes. In other words, it's talking about His imagination. He had a pure mind that was able to see things by faith. He wasn't limited to what He physically saw with His eyes. He could see whatever God's Word said.

Jesus saw with His spiritual eyes that these five loaves and two fish were enough. The disciples looked at them and at the crowd and saw that it wasn't enough. Most of us look at the little bit we have and at the need and say, "O God, it's not enough. I'll never make it!" We curse what we have. Jesus blessed it instead. We say, "O God, I could never do what You've called me to do. I can't preach!" But Jesus blessed.

See by Faith

He fed five thousand men—and that's not including the women and children. He fed over ten thousand people with five loaves and two fish, and the fragments left over after everyone's seconds and thirds added up to much more than what they started with.

Think of the logistics! If Jesus had broken the bread and multiplied it all in His hands, and then gave it to the disciples to run back and forth distributing to all these groups of people, this would have taken at least seven hours. However, it's much more likely that the Lord broke the bread once and gave it to the disciples. Then they went out with one little fish and one piece of bread, which they started breaking, giving, and seeing multiply in their hands.

Jesus, in effect, blessed this food and gave it to His disciples. Then they had to have a lot of faith to walk toward each group of fifty hungry people, with just this little bit of food and start passing it out. Some of them could have said, "But, Jesus, I need more!" They didn't need more. They had enough. That one little loaf and that one little fish was more than enough for thousands of people when it was blessed. But they had to see it spiritually.

Whatever you have is more than enough if you could renew your imagination so you don't see with your physical eyes. If you saw your true potential, you could start seeing with your heart what God has really given you. Take God's Word and let it paint a picture on the inside of you. Let it show you that you have the same power that raised Christ from the dead living on the inside of you. You don't need to plead with God to give you something more; you just need to look up, receive sight, and see what you already have. If you would do that, you could go to the masses and see people saved, healed, and delivered. You'd have words to say, and you could flow in the gifts of the Holy Spirit. Anything you'd need would function.

But the problem is we aren't looking up. We aren't receiving spiritual sight. We aren't seeing with our inner man. We aren't using our imagination to see ourselves like God sees us. We're looking in the mirror instead. We're listening to what everybody else thinks about us. We're looking at other churches and thinking, *Well, do other people do this?* We're making comparisons and letting other people paint the image inside us. You need to go to God's Word and find out what He says about you. That's who you are and that's what you can do. You need to see yourself that way.

How Do You See Yourself?

Most Christians have never seen their real self. If I asked someone what they looked like, they would describe to me their outward man, but they probably wouldn't know who they are in Christ. Due to this, they live like beggars—poor, depressed, and defeated. God has already given them everything, but they just haven't seen it.

Jesus prayed for a blind man and made him—anablepo—look up (Mark 8:25). He received his sight and his eyes were opened. You need to get the eyes of your heart opened, and the way you do this is to glorify God. Start putting value on and magnifying Him. Take Scripture and say, "Jesus, You are above every name. Cancer has a name. Poverty has a name. If I can name this thing, then You're above it!" Make God bigger in your own eyes than this situation. Then start thanking Him for all the things He's already done. Use your memory to rehearse your victories. If you did all that, your imagination would start seeing good things happen instead of bad. You'd start seeing yourself succeed instead of fail. Your imagination would start functioning *for* you instead of *against* you. Then your imagination wouldn't be vain (Rom. 1:21).

But if you don't glorify God, be thankful, and remember His goodness, then you're going to be a negative person. One little whisper from the devil and your imagination will run wild with it and see him destroying your life. That's where most people are today.

Your imagination is important! You don't get to choose whether or not it functions; you just get to choose which direction it goes—for you or against you.

If your imagination is vain, then your foolish heart will be darkened (Rom. 1:21). You cannot function contrary to your heart. Your heart is the most important aspect.

Ignorant, Lazy, or a Doer?

This is so simple, you have to have somebody help you misunderstand it. I haven't talked about a single hard thing yet. Everything I've shared has been super simple.

People would rather go to great effort than renew their minds. They'd rather organize a million people to pray for God to pour out His Spirit and move and make them victorious without glorifying God and being thankful. "Just pour out the Holy Spirit so I can go back to my television and watch my soap operas and talk shows. I don't want to have to spend effort focusing my attention and using my mind." People try every way possible to circumvent this and put it back on God. "Bring in an evangelist. Let them do it!"

If you would consistently glorify God, be thankful, and use your imagination in a positive way, it would be impossible for you to fail. That doesn't mean you won't have problems. They'll come, but you'll succeed. The inner pressure of God in your life would overcome the outward pressure of the world, circumstances, and the devil. It's just that simple.

Ignorance and laziness are the only two reasons why people don't latch on to this. Either they haven't seen it, or they just don't want to put forth any effort toward it. They want someone else to wave their hand over them and make it happen. Well, you can't claim ignorance anymore. Are you going to be a doer of the Word or not? It really is that simple. This will change your life!

What Do You See?
LESSON 13 – OUTLINE

1. The disciples saw the need, but they didn't see themselves as having the ability to meet it.

   > And when the day was now far spent, his disciples came unto him, and said, This is a desert place, and now the time is far passed: Send them away, that they may go into the country round about, and into the villages, and buy themselves bread: for they have nothing to eat. He answered and said unto them, Give ye them to eat.
   >
   > MARK 6:35-37

   A. The disciples wanted to send them all somewhere else.

   B. They looked at their natural resources instead of their spiritual resources.

2. When Jesus looked up to heaven, He did more than just lift His head.

   > He saith unto them, How many loaves have ye? go and see. And when they knew, they say, Five, and two fishes. And he commanded them to make all sit down by companies upon the green grass. And they sat down in ranks, by hundreds, and by fifties. And when he had taken the five loaves and the two fishes, **he looked up to heaven**, and blessed, and brake the loaves, and gave them to his disciples to set before them; and the two fishes divided he among them all.
   >
   > MARK 6:38-41, EMPHASIS MINE

   A. Jesus literally saw twice, or saw again.

   B. This same word is translated "receive sight" fourteen times in the Bible.

   C. He saw in the spirit realm instead of seeing with His physical eyes.

   D. He wasn't limited to what He physically saw with His eyes; He could see whatever God's Word said.

3. He fed over ten thousand people with five loaves and two fish, and the fragments left over after everyone's seconds and thirds added up to much more than what they started with.

   A. Jesus, in effect, blessed this food and gave it to His disciples.

   B. They had to have a lot of faith to walk toward each group of fifty hungry people with just this little bit of food and pass it out.

   C. That one little loaf and that one little fish was more than enough for thousands of people when it was blessed—but they had to see it spiritually.

4. Whatever you have is more than enough if you renew your imagination so you don't see with your physical eyes.

   A. Take God's Word and let it paint a picture on the inside of you.

   B. You just need to look up, receive sight, and see what you already have.

   C. If you would do that, you could go to the masses and see people saved, healed, and delivered.

   D. God has already given us everything, but we just haven't seen it.

5. Your imagination is important!

   A. You don't get to choose whether or not it functions; you just get to choose which direction it goes—for you or against you.

   B. If your imagination is vain, then your foolish heart will be darkened (Rom. 1:21).

   C. You cannot function contrary to your heart.

6. If you would consistently glorify God, be thankful, and use your imagination in a positive way, it would be impossible for you to fail.

   A. Problems will come, but you'll succeed.

   B. The inner pressure of God in your life would overcome the outward pressure of the world, circumstances, and the devil.

   C. Are you going to be a doer of the Word or not?

What Do You See?
LESSON 13 – TEACHER'S GUIDE

1.   The disciples saw the need, but they didn't see themselves as having the ability to meet it (Mark 6:35-37). They wanted to send them all somewhere else. They looked at their natural resources instead of their spiritual resources.

2.   When Jesus looked up to heaven, He did more than just lift His head (Mark 6:38-41); He literally saw twice, or saw again. This same word is translated "receive sight" fourteen times in the Bible. He saw in the spirit realm instead of seeing with His physical eyes. He wasn't limited to what He physically saw with His eyes; He could see whatever God's Word said.

3.   He fed over ten thousand people with five loaves and two fish, and the fragments left over after everyone's seconds and thirds added up to much more than what they started with. Jesus, in effect, blessed this food and gave it to His disciples. Then they had to have a lot of faith to walk toward each group of fifty hungry people, with just this little bit of food and pass it out. That one little loaf and that one little fish was more than enough for thousands of people when it was blessed—but they had to see it spiritually.

1. A. Read Mark 6:35-37. What did the disciples see? (The need)
   B. What didn't they see? (Themselves as having the ability to meet the need)
   C. Why? (They were looking at their natural resources instead of their spiritual resources)
2. A. Read Mark 6:38-41. When Jesus looked up to heaven, what did He see? (He saw in the spirit realm)
   B. Was Jesus limited only to what He physically saw with His eyes? (No, He could see whatever God's Word said)
3. A. When Jesus blessed this food and gave it to His disciples, what did they have to do? (They had to step out in faith and walk toward each group of fifty hungry people, with just this little bit of food and pass it out)
   B. That one little loaf and that one little fish was more than enough for thousands of people when it was blessed—but they had to what? (See it spiritually)

4.   Whatever we have is more than enough if we could renew our imagination so we don't see with our physical eyes. We need to take God's Word and let it paint a picture on the inside of us. We just need to look up, receive sight, and see what we already have. If we would do that, we could go to the masses and see people saved, healed, and delivered. God has already given us everything, but we just haven't seen it.

5.   Our imagination is important! We don't get to choose whether or not it functions; we just get to choose which direction it goes—for us or against us. If our imagination is vain, then our foolish hearts will be darkened (Rom. 1:21). We cannot function contrary to our hearts.

6.   If we would consistently glorify God, be thankful, and use our imagination in a positive way, it would be impossible for us to fail. Problems will come, but we'll succeed. The inner pressure of God in our lives would overcome the outward pressure of the world, circumstances, and the devil. Are we going to be doers of the Word or not?

4. A. What must we do in order to be able to go to the masses and see people saved, healed, and delivered? (We need to look up, receive sight, and see what we already have)
   B. What has God already given us? (Everything)
5. A. According to Romans 1:21, what happens when our imagination is vain? (Our foolish hearts are darkened)
   B. Can we function contrary to our hearts? (No)
6. A. What will happen if we consistently glorify God, be thankful, and use our imagination in a positive way? (We'll succeed—it would be impossible for us to fail)
   B. What is it that overcomes the outward pressure of the world, circumstances, and the devil? (The inner pressure of God in our lives)

What Do You See?
LESSON 13 – ADDITIONAL INFORMATION

For a detailed explanation on the logistics of feeding that multitude, please see the footnote for Luke 9:16 on page 177 of my *Life for Today:* the Gospels Edition. This Bible commentary is also available free online at our website (www.awmi.net).

What Do You See?
LESSON 13 – DISCIPLESHIP QUESTIONS

1. Read Mark 6:35-37. What time of day was it?

2. What kind of environment were they in?

3. What did the disciples suggest Jesus do?

4. How did Jesus answer them?

5. Read Mark 6:38-41. How much food did they start out with?

6. What did Jesus command the people to do?

7. After Jesus took the five loaves and two fish, what did He do?
    A. He looked up into heaven and blessed.
    B. He broke the loaves and divided the fish.
    C. He gave them to the disciples to distribute.
    D. All of the above.
    E. None of the above.

8. What happened, according to Mark 6:42?

9. What did Jesus do to the blind man in Mark 8:25?

10. What was the result?

11. According to Romans 1:21, what happens when our imagination is vain?

What Do You See?
LESSON 13 – ANSWER KEY

1. Evening.

2. A desert place.

3. Send the people away to buy themselves bread.

4. He told them to give the people something to eat.

5. Five loaves of bread and two fish.

6. Sit down in groups.

7. D. All of the above.

8. They all ate and were filled.

9. He put His hands upon his eyes again and made him look up.

10. He was restored and saw every man clearly.

11. Our foolish hearts become darkened.

What Do You See?
LESSON 13 – SCRIPTURES

And when the day was now far spent, his disciples came unto him, and said, This is a desert place, and now the time is far passed: Send them away, that they may go into the country round about, and into the villages, and buy themselves bread: for they have nothing to eat. He answered and said unto them, Give ye them to eat. And they say unto him, Shall we go and buy two hundred pennyworth of bread, and give them to eat? He saith unto them, How many loaves have ye? go and see. And when they knew, they say, Five, and two fishes. And he commanded them to make all sit down by companies upon the green grass. And they sat down in ranks, by hundreds, and by fifties. And when he had taken the five loaves and the two fishes, he looked up to heaven, and blessed, and brake the loaves, and gave them to his disciples to set before them; and the two fishes divided he among them all.

MARK 6:35-41

After that he put his hands again upon his eyes, and made him look up: and he was restored, and saw every man clearly.

MARK 8:25

Because that, when they knew God, they glorified him not as God, neither were thankful; but became vain in their imaginations, and their foolish heart was darkened.

ROMANS 1:21

Warfare and the Heart
LESSON 14

Some people have trouble mixing grace and faith together. They tend to lean toward one or the other.

Grace-oriented people say, "God does everything by grace, so we have absolutely nothing to do with it." Well, that's not exactly true. God is God, and He does love you independent of your performance. He does have a perfect plan for every single person, and His grace toward you is totally unmerited. There is nothing you can do to make God's grace abound in you anymore than what He's already done. But consider what 1 Corinthians 15:10 says:

> But by the grace of God I am what I am: and his grace which was bestowed upon me was not in vain; ***but I laboured more abundantly than they all: yet not I, but the grace of God which was with me***.
>
> EMPHASIS MINE

God's grace is toward you. He has a perfect plan for your life. God has already healed every person. He's already provided abundantly. He's commanded a financial blessing on you. There is no need for you to ever have financial problems. God has already blessed you with financial prosperity and given you perfect health. The same power that raised Christ from the dead is on the inside of every born-again believer. You already have love, joy, and peace. There's never a moment in your born-again life that you don't have these things just flooding in your spirit.

But there are things you can do to release what God has done in the spirit realm and make it manifest in the natural. You can either experience the eternal life of God that resides within your born-again spirit or just keep it dammed up in there.

What you do doesn't affect God's heart toward you, but it will affect your heart toward Him. If you aren't seeking God, He'll love you exactly the same, but you won't love Him the same. You'll be hardened in your heart toward God. There is a balance between grace and faith!

Unclog Your Pipe

Faith is your positive response to what God has already given you by grace. Many people don't understand this. When they feel empty, depressed, and discouraged, they're asking God to do something. The Lord has already commanded His blessing upon you. You never have to ask Him to bless you, heal you, give you joy, or love you. God has already given all those things to you. If you aren't experiencing them, it's your pipe that's clogged—not God's.

Since God's transmitter is always transmitting, we need to check our receivers to see whether or not we're receiving. We need to work on ourselves and on our receiving. This is what we've been talking about.

Romans 1:21 reveals four progressive things we do to block the flow of God in our lives. But if we turn them around and use them positively instead, they become four keys to staying full of God.

The first key to maintaining the flow of God in your life is to glorify Him. This means to value, prize, honor, and esteem God properly. It also means to magnify—make bigger. You can magnify God and make Him bigger in your life. As you focus on the Lord and place value on what He's said and done, He'll become bigger to you than your circumstances and problems. But first you must esteem Him as more valuable than anything else in your life. This is where most people miss it. They don't properly recognize and value what the Lord has done in their lives.

The second key is being thankful. We live in a thankless generation. Unthankfulness is unholy (2 Tim. 3:2). It's a sin. However, most people see being thankful as a byproduct of things going well. "If my life were going well, I'd be thankful!" The truth is we should be thankful for what we have right now. If we're waiting until everything in our lives is perfect before we're thankful, we'll never be thankful.

Captive and Obedient

The third key is to understand the power of your imagination.

> For though we walk in the flesh, we do not war after the flesh: (For the weapons of our warfare are not carnal, but mighty through God to the pulling down of strong holds;) Casting down imaginations, and every high thing that exalteth itself against the knowledge of God, and bringing into captivity every thought to the obedience of Christ.
>
> 2 CORINTHIANS 10:3-5

In case you haven't figured it out yet, there is warfare in the Christian life. If you really commit yourself to the Lord once you're born again, it's as if you have a big target painted on you. The devil is definitely going to come against you. Some people reason, "Well, then, I don't want to commit myself to the Lord." But I'm not saying you lose. You can win. In fact, I'm more victorious now than I've ever been, but it isn't because I don't have fights. In fact, I have more fights now than I've ever had, but I'm winning. I'm not preaching defeat; I'm just saying there is warfare.

It takes effort to walk in victory. This scripture says the weapons of our warfare tear down strongholds, imaginations, and high things that exalt themselves against the knowledge of God. These weapons bring all these thoughts into the captivity and obedience of Christ.

A Diversion

Most of what we hear about "spiritual warfare" floating around the body of Christ today is absolutely wrong. It's a diversionary tactic. One of the things an enemy tries to do in battle is make us think the attack is in a certain place. Then, as we marshal all our forces over to that spot, they attack our flank. This is what the devil has been doing.

Satan has been encouraging a lot of this spiritual warfare stuff. Many of us are busy binding this and fighting that. We're trying to do "warfare" with demonic powers over cities and countries, but that's not where the battle is. Scripture says the true battle is in our thoughts and imagination (2 Cor. 10:3-5). Spiritual warfare is right between our ears!

People try to "bind" the devil out of a service. In the conservative denominational church I grew up in, we used to "plead the blood" over all the doors and windows. We thought that if the devil could get through the blood, he'd have to be a saved devil. It doesn't work that way.

Satan was present at the Last Supper. The Word says he immediately entered into Judas (John 13:26-27). This means he had to be right there in the room. If Jesus couldn't keep the devil out of the Last Supper, then you can't keep him out of your meetings. If we could bind the devil and keep him out of our meetings, very few people would come!

The Battle and the Link

It's not what's going on externally that's the issue; the battle is internal—right between your ears. You're fighting thoughts and imaginations. Can you see how important your imagination is?

Most people don't recognize the positive side of imagination—dreams, hopes, goals, and aspirations. But they do recognize the negative side—fear, worry, and dread. How you see things on the inside is actually a driving force in your life.

Your imagination is where you conceive things. If your imagination isn't working for you, then it's working against you—making you creatively sterile. If it's working against you, all you'll be able to do is bring negative things to pass. This is super important.

Romans 1:21 reveals the link between glorifying God, being thankful, and your imagination working properly. They're all interrelated and connected. You can't just work on your imagination without glorifying God and being thankful. It's the opposite. If you esteem God above everyone and everything else and really begin to praise Him, your imagination will automatically move toward the positive. If you'll place the proper value on the Lord and begin expressing your gratefulness to Him for all He's said and done, your imagination will start functioning in a positive way. But if you don't glorify God, aren't thankful, and your imagination becomes vain, then the last step is that your foolish heart becomes darkened (Rom. 1:21).

Tearing Yourself Apart?

Your heart is a major topic in the Bible. There is a huge amount of material in the Word to help you understand your heart.

Jesus said:

> Out of the abundance of the heart the mouth speaketh.
>
> MATTHEW 12:34

Your heart controls what you say and do. It's the essence of who you are.

> As he thinketh in his heart, so is he.
>
> PROVERBS 23:7

Most people don't understand this. They're into what's called "behavior modification." They are trying to change their actions without changing their hearts.

People don't realize that their value system is what causes them to act a certain way in the first place. They get drunk or high on dope. They have a car wreck and lose their job. Finally, they realize that their actions are destroying their lives and endangering other people. It's causing problems and putting them in big trouble.

So they try to change their actions without changing their hearts. What are they actually doing? They're tearing themselves apart! God's Word calls this "hypocrisy."

Hypocrisy

People in the church—to a large degree—put all of the emphasis on actions. They preach, "Don't dip or cuss or chew or go with those that do! Praise God, you have to do this and this and this, and not do that and that and that." The emphasis is placed on actions but not on changing the heart. Therefore, it's actually creating hypocrisy in people.

Many Christians don't give financially because they understand it properly and have a giving heart; they do so out of a fear of punishment. They give—act—but not with the right motive and attitude. Due to this, they aren't able to receive the full benefit of their actions.

> And though I bestow all my goods to feed the poor, and though I give my body
> to be burned, and have not charity [God's kind of love], it profiteth me nothing.
>
> 1 CORINTHIANS 13:3, BRACKETS MINE

It doesn't matter what you do; God's Word plainly reveals that your heart attitude is more important than your actions.

Jesus told the Pharisees:

> Woe unto you, scribes and Pharisees, hypocrites! for ye make clean the outside
> of the cup and of the platter, but within they are full of extortion and excess.
> Thou blind Pharisee, *cleanse first that which is within the cup and platter, that
> the outside of them may be clean also*. Woe unto you, scribes and Pharisees,

hypocrites! for ye are like unto whited sepulchres, which indeed appear beautiful outward, but are within full of dead men's bones, and of all uncleanness.

MATTHEW 23:25-27, EMPHASIS MINE

The Lord is more concerned about your heart than your actions. If your heart is right, your actions will be too.

God Is after Your Heart

This sounds good on the surface, but religious people hate to apply it. They're more into the form and outward action than truly dealing with the heart. Some folks are all hung up about external things.

If someone came to your church with a heart to know God but violated your dress code, would you judge them? If they clapped when they shouldn't clap and shouted praises out loud in your quiet church, would you judge them?

Man looketh on the outward appearance, but the LORD looketh on the heart.

1 SAMUEL 16:7

If you give your heart to God, your actions will eventually change. There's an important relationship here, but people tend to look only on the outward appearance.

Most of religion is human operated. It's according to man's ideas, so they put all of the emphasis on outward appearance. They don't care if a person's heart is in it or not, as long as they see them cleaned up and looking and acting like them. All that matters is for people to come to church dressed the right way, doing the right things, and putting their money in the plate, because it doesn't matter to them what their heart is like.

But it does matter to God. He's into changing your heart. Even in your own individual life, it's amazing how much emphasis you put on your actions and ignoring the status of your heart. You need to realize that God is after your heart. That's what pleases Him!

Warfare and the Heart
LESSON 14 – OUTLINE

1. Some people have trouble mixing grace and faith together—they tend to lean toward one or the other.

   > But by the grace of God I am what I am: and his grace which was bestowed upon me was not in vain; *but I laboured more abundantly than they all: yet not I, but the grace of God which was with me*.
   >
   > 1 CORINTHIANS 15:10, EMPHASIS MINE

   A. There are things you can do to release what God has done in the spirit realm and make it manifest in the natural.

   B. You can either experience the eternal life of God that resides within your born-again spirit or just keep it dammed up in there.

   C. There is a balance between grace and faith!

2. Faith is your positive response to what God has already given you by grace.

   A. Since God's transmitter is always transmitting, we need to check our receivers to see whether or not we're receiving.

   B. We need to work on ourselves and on our receiving.

3. Romans 1:21 reveals four progressive things we do to block the flow of God in our lives.

   A. But if we turn them around and use them positively instead, they become four keys to staying full of God.

   B. The first key to maintaining the flow of God in your life is to glorify Him.

   C. The second key is to be thankful.

   D. The third key is to understand the power of your imagination.

   E. The final key is that our heart will become sensitive to God.

4. In case you haven't figured it out yet, there is warfare in the Christian life.

   > For though we walk in the flesh, we do not war after the flesh: (For the weapons of our warfare are not carnal, but mighty through God to the pulling down of strong holds;) Casting down imaginations, and every high thing that

exalteth itself against the knowledge of God, and bringing into captivity every thought to the obedience of Christ.

2 CORINTHIANS 10:3-5

A. It takes effort to walk in victory.

B. These weapons bring all these thoughts into the captivity and obedience of Christ.

C. Most of what we hear about "spiritual warfare" floating around the body of Christ today is absolutely wrong.

D. Scripture says the true battle is in your thoughts and imagination (2 Cor. 10:3-5).

E. Most people don't recognize the positive side of imagination—dreams, hopes, goals, and aspirations.

5. Romans 1:21 reveals the link between glorifying God, being thankful, and your imagination working properly.

A. If you'll place the proper value on the Lord and begin expressing your gratefulness to Him for all He's said and done, your imagination will start functioning in a positive way.

B. But if you don't glorify God, aren't thankful, and your imagination becomes vain, then the last step is your foolish heart becomes darkened (Rom. 1:21).

6. Your heart controls what you say and do—it's the essence of who you are.

Out of the abundance of the heart the mouth speaketh.

MATTHEW 12:34

As he thinketh in his heart, so is he.

PROVERBS 23:7

A. Most people are trying to change their actions without changing their hearts.

i. They don't realize that their value system is what caused them to act that way in the first place.

ii. They try to change their actions without changing their hearts (tearing themselves apart).

iii. God's Word calls this "hypocrisy."

B. People in the church—to a large degree—put all of the emphasis on actions.

C. It doesn't matter what you do, God's Word plainly reveals that your heart attitude is more important than your actions.

And though I bestow all my goods to feed the poor, and though I give my body to be burned, and have not charity [God's kind of love], it profiteth me nothing.

1 CORINTHIANS 13:3, BRACKETS MINE

7. The Lord is more concerned about your heart than your actions.

Woe unto you, scribes and Pharisees, hypocrites! for ye make clean the outside of the cup and of the platter, but within they are full of extortion and excess. Thou blind Pharisee, *cleanse first that which is within the cup and platter, that the outside of them may be clean also*. Woe unto you, scribes and Pharisees, hypocrites! for ye are like unto whited sepulchers, which indeed appear beautiful outward, but are within full of dead men's bones, and of all uncleanness.

MATTHEW 23:25-27, EMPHASIS MINE

Man looketh on the outward appearance, but the LORD looketh on the heart.

1 SAMUEL 16:7

A. If your heart is right, your actions will be too.

B. If you give your heart to God, your actions will eventually change.

C. God is into changing your heart.

Warfare and the Heart
LESSON 14 – TEACHER'S GUIDE

1. Some people have trouble mixing grace and faith together—they tend to lean toward one or the other (1 Cor. 15:10). There are things we can do to release what God has done in the spirit realm and make it manifest in the natural. We can either experience the eternal life of God that resides within our born-again spirits or just keep it dammed up in there. There is a balance between grace and faith!

2. Faith is our positive response to what God has already given us by grace. Since God's transmitter is always transmitting, we need to check our receivers to see whether or not we're receiving. We need to work on ourselves and on our receiving.

3. Romans 1:21 reveals four progressive things we do to block the flow of God in our lives. But if we turn them around and use them positively instead, they become four keys to staying full of God. The first key to maintaining the flow of God in our lives is to glorify Him. The second key is to be thankful. The third key is to understand the power of our imagination. The final key is that your heart will become sensitive to God.

4. There is warfare in the Christian life. It takes effort to walk in victory. These weapons bring all your thoughts into the captivity and obedience of Christ. Most of what we hear about "spiritual warfare" floating around the body of Christ today is absolutely wrong. Scripture says the true battle is in our thoughts and imagination (2 Cor. 10:3-5). Most people don't recognize the positive side of imagination—dreams, hopes, goals, and aspirations.

1. A. Read 1 Corinthians 15:10. What do some people have trouble with? (Mixing grace and faith together)
    B. Are there things we can do to release what God has done in the spirit realm and make it manifest in the natural? (Yes)
    C. Where does the eternal life of God reside? (Within our born-again spirits)
2. A. What is faith? (Faith is our positive response to what God has already given us by grace)
    B. Since God is always transmitting, what do we need to work on? (Ourselves and our receiving)
3. A. What happens when we, as born-again believers, do the negative things Romans 1:21 speaks about? (We block the flow of God in our lives)
    B. What are the three keys to staying full of God that we've studied thus far? (Glorify God, be thankful, and understand the power of our imagination)
4. A. According to 2 Corinthians 10:3-5, where is the warfare and true battle in the Christian life? (In our thoughts and imagination)
    B. What is the positive side of imagination? (Dreams, hopes, goals, and aspirations)

5. Romans 1:21 reveals the link between glorifying God, being thankful, and our imagination working properly. If we'll place the proper value on the Lord and begin expressing our gratefulness to Him for all He's said and done, our imagination will start functioning in a positive way. But if we don't glorify God, aren't thankful, and our imagination becomes vain, then the last step is our foolish hearts become darkened (Rom. 1:21).

6. Our hearts control what we say and do—it's the essence of who we are (Matt. 12:34 and Prov. 23:7). Most people are trying to change their actions without changing their hearts. They don't realize that their value system is what caused them to act that way in the first place. They try to change their actions without changing their hearts, which is tearing them apart. God's Word calls this "hypocrisy." People in the church—to a large degree—put all of the emphasis on actions. But it doesn't matter what we do; God's Word plainly reveals that our heart attitude is more important than our actions (1 Cor. 13:3).

7. The Lord is more concerned about our hearts than our actions (Matt. 23:25-27 and 1 Sam. 16:7). If our hearts are right, then our actions will be too. If we give our hearts to God, our actions will eventually change. God is into changing our hearts.

5. A. What happens when we place the proper value on the Lord and begin expressing our gratefulness to Him for all He's said and done? (Our imagination starts functioning in a positive way)
    B. According to Romans 1:21, what happens if we don't glorify God, aren't thankful, and our imagination becomes vain? (Our foolish hearts become darkened)
6. A. Read Matthew 12:34 and Proverbs 23:7. What do most people try to change without changing their hearts? (Their actions)
    B. What does God's Word call this? (Hypocrisy)
    C. According to 1 Corinthians 13:3, what does God's Word plainly reveal as more important than our actions? (Our heart attitude)
7. A. Read Matthew 23:25-27 and 1 Samuel 16:7. The Lord is more concerned about our hearts than our what? (Actions)
    B. In order to see our actions change, what must we do? (Give our hearts to God)

Warfare and the Heart
LESSON 14 – ADDITIONAL INFORMATION

There is a balance between grace and faith. My teachings entitled "Living in the Balance of Grace and Faith"; *Spirit, Soul & Body*; and *You've Already Got It!* all go into much greater detail about this important subject. I highly recommend them to you!

Also, there's a huge amount of material in the Word to help you understand your heart. My teachings *Hardness of Heart* and *How to Prepare Your Heart* go much further in depth than this **Lesson**.

And finally, God's Word plainly reveals that your heart attitude is more important than your actions. For more about how this applies to your giving, please refer to my teachings entitled *Financial Stewardship*, "The Grace of Giving," and "Grace and Faith in Giving."

Warfare and the Heart
LESSON 14 – DISCIPLESHIP QUESTIONS

1. According to 1 Corinthians 15:10, how did Paul become what he was?

2. Why was the grace of God that was bestowed upon Paul not in vain?

3. What are the four progressive things we do to block the flow of God in our lives, according to Romans 1:21?

4. Expressed positively, what are these four keys to staying full of God?

5. According to 2 Corinthians 10:3-5, do we war after the flesh?

6. Since the weapons of our warfare are not carnal, what are they?
   A. Weak through God to the pulling down of strongholds.
   B. Mighty through God to the reinforcing of strongholds.
   C. Mighty through God to the pulling down of strongholds.
   D. All of the above.
   E. None of the above.

7. What do these weapons do to imaginations and every high thing that exalts itself against the knowledge of God?

8. What is brought into captivity to the obedience of Christ?

9. According to this passage, where does the battle—spiritual warfare—take place?
   A. In the heavenlies.
   B. Over cities and nations.
   C. In our minds—thoughts and imagination.

10. According to John 13:26-27, Jesus dipped the piece of bread and gave it to whom?

11. What happened next?

12. What, then, did Jesus say?

13. According to Matthew 12:34, can an evil person speak good things?

14. Why?

15. According to Proverbs 23:7, as we think in our hearts, so _____ we.

16. According to 1 Corinthians 13:3, is it possible to give all of our goods to feed the poor, even our bodies to be burned, and it profit us nothing?

17. Why?

18. In Matthew 23:25-27, what did Jesus call the scribes and Pharisees?

19. What did He compare them to?

20. First Samuel 16:7 reveals that man looks on what?

21. What does the Lord look upon?

Warfare and the Heart
LESSON 14 – ANSWER KEY

1. By the grace of God.

2. Because he labored more abundantly—cooperating by faith with that grace.

3. They glorified Him not as God, neither were thankful, became vain in their imaginations, and their foolish hearts were darkened.

4. Glorify God, be thankful, recognize the power of our imagination, and have a good heart.

5. No.

6. C. Mighty through God to the pulling down of strongholds.

7. They cast them down.

8. Every thought.

9. C. In our minds—thoughts and imagination.

10. Judas Iscariot.

11. Satan entered into him.

12. What you do, do quickly.

13. No.

14. Out of the abundance of the heart, the mouth speaks.

15. Are.

16. Yes.

17. In order for it to profit us, what we do must be motivated by God's kind of love—charity.

18. Hypocrites.

19. Cups, dishes, and whitewashed tombs—clean and beautiful on the outside but dirty and full of death within.

20. The outward appearance.

21. Our hearts.

Warfare and the Heart
LESSON 14 – SCRIPTURES

But by the grace of God I am what I am: and his grace which was bestowed upon me was not in vain; but I laboured more abundantly than they all: yet not I, but the grace of God which was with me.

1 CORINTHIANS 15:10

Because that, when they knew God, they glorified him not as God, neither were thankful; but became vain in their imaginations, and their foolish heart was darkened.

ROMANS 1:21

For men shall be lovers of their own selves, covetous, boasters, proud, blasphemers, disobedient to parents, unthankful, unholy.

2 TIMOTHY 3:2

For though we walk in the flesh, we do not war after the flesh: (For the weapons of our warfare are not carnal, but mighty through God to the pulling down of strong holds;) Casting down imaginations, and every high thing that exalteth itself against the knowledge of God, and bringing into captivity every thought to the obedience of Christ.

2 CORINTHIANS 10:3-5

Jesus answered, He it is, to whom I shall give a sop, when I have dipped it. And when he had dipped the sop, he gave it to Judas Iscariot, the son of Simon. And after the sop Satan entered into him. Then said Jesus unto him, That thou doest, do quickly.

JOHN 13:26-27

O generation of vipers, how can ye, being evil, speak good things? for out of the abundance of the heart the mouth speaketh.

MATTHEW 12:34

For as he thinketh in his heart, so is he: Eat and drink, saith he to thee; but his heart is not with thee.

PROVERBS 23:7

And though I bestow all my goods to feed the poor, and though I give my body to be burned, and have not charity, it profiteth me nothing.

1 CORINTHIANS 13:3

Woe unto you, scribes and Pharisees, hypocrites! for ye make clean the outside of the cup and of the platter, but within they are full of extortion and excess. Thou blind Pharisee, cleanse first that which is within the cup and platter, that the outside of them may be clean also. Woe unto you, scribes and Pharisees, hypocrites! for ye are like unto whited sepulchres, which indeed appear beautiful outward, but are within full of dead men's bones, and of all uncleanness.

MATTHEW 23:25-27

But the LORD said unto Samuel, Look not on his countenance, or on the height of his stature; because I have refused him: for the LORD seeth not as man seeth; for man looketh on the outward appearance, but the LORD looketh on the heart.

1 SAMUEL 16:7

Live from Your Heart
LESSON 15

While ministering in Phoenix, I noticed a lady who was literally bouncing up and down on the front row. She was excited because she had just been born again two months before. One night I asked her to come up and share her testimony.

She stood up and said, "Oh, this is the best blankety-blank…" and every third word was profanity. People gasped and some laughed. She looked at me and asked, "Did I do something wrong?"

I answered, "No, you didn't do anything wrong. Just keep going."

She continued sharing her testimony and cussing up a storm for ten minutes. After the service, people said to me, "I can't believe you let her say that in church. I would never do that!" They criticized her vocabulary—judging her outward man and totally missing her heart.

I told them, "Do you know what? God was more pleased with her testimony than He's been with yours in the last twenty years. Some of you are straight as a gun barrel and twice as empty. You have the mannerisms and behaviors, but your heart isn't on fire for God. You'd never cuss except when you smash your thumb or when something goes wrong. You've just learned how to control yourself in church. This woman loves God with all her heart. Her brain just hasn't caught up yet!"

When I returned a year later, she came to me and apologized, saying, "I'm sorry! I didn't know Christians don't talk like that. I'd been out in the world. I was a prostitute and thought everybody talked like that. I didn't know I was doing anything wrong." I just gave her some time, and it worked out.

"She'll Learn!"

We led a certain lady to the Lord in Childress, Texas. She and her husband had lived in a nudist colony for the past three years. Although this woman was born again, all she had when she first came to church were short shorts—shorts so short she could hardly sit on them! She also had a halter-top—and this was a well-endowed lady. We used to sit in a semicircle in this little church. Since we only had about fifty people, it was impossible not to be in front of her and watch. When we started dancing and praising God, her attire left nothing to your imagination!

The religious people in this church criticized me and demanded, "Aren't you going to do something about this?"

I responded, "Did we have to throw a sheet over her in the park before we witnessed to her and told her how much Jesus loved her? Give her time; she'll learn." I think it took her about six weeks, but it wasn't very long.

One day she was in a women's Bible study that my wife was leading. She said, "You know, I've never owned a dress in my life. I'd really like to have one and start dressing like the rest of you. Would you all pray that we would get enough money to buy a dress?" By two o'clock that afternoon, she had a dozen dresses! They were all up to her neck and all the way down to the floor. Praise God! She came to church wearing her dress so proudly. Never once did anyone have to tell her, "God is upset and doesn't love you if you don't dress a certain way."

I believe you should dress in a way that keeps other people from lusting after you. You shouldn't encourage it. But that's something that comes with growth. God looks at your heart. This woman was seeking Him with all her heart. I believe the Lord would have been displeased if we had come up to her, taken her attention off of Him, and put it on all these externals. In my heart, I knew the Lord would show her these things, and He did.

Actions Are Byproducts

Most religious people just can't handle that. They are so focused on getting others to act right that it causes hypocrisy. They put the emphasis on conforming to a certain standard whether the individual really wants to or not. So they give in just to be accepted. This breeds hypocrisy. We just catch the fish. It's the Lord's job to clean them. Be tolerant and loving—and let God work on their hearts.

The condition of your heart dictates how you act. Some people try to change their actions without changing their hearts. That's not the way it's supposed to be. God wants to change your heart, and then your actions will change as a byproduct. Actions aren't the driving force—they follow. Right actions are a byproduct of an intimate relationship with God.

I'm not telling you not to act godly. I'm just saying that it needs to come from your heart, or it doesn't please God. It may please your religion and may score points with certain people, but God looks on your heart.

It doesn't matter that you're doing the right things. You could give all you have to feed the poor and even die a martyr's death, but if you're not motivated by God's kind of love, it'll profit you nothing (1 Cor. 13:3). You must do things from a pure heart of love.

A Darkened Understanding

When Romans 1:21 speaks of your heart becoming "darkened," it's talking about becoming insensitive to God. You are no longer responsive. You aren't hearing the voice of God. It's talking about a hardened heart.

> This I say therefore, and testify in the Lord, that ye henceforth walk not as other Gentiles walk, in the vanity of their mind, Having the ***understanding*** darkened.
>
> EPHESIANS 4:17-18, EMPHASIS MINE

"Understanding" is the same Greek word as "imagination." It's your imagination that enables you to understand. Therefore, imagination = understanding.

> Being alienated from the life of God through the ignorance that is in them, because of *the blindness of their heart*.
>
> EPHESIANS 4:18, EMPHASIS MINE

The phrase "their foolish heart was darkened" in Romans 1:21 means the same thing as having your heart blinded in Ephesians 4:18. It's talking about your heart not being able to see, perceive, listen to, and hear from God.

Original Intent

God didn't originally create us to live the way the vast majority of us do. Most of us live from our mental, emotional, and physical parts (soul and body). We feed ourselves external information. We educate ourselves and teach ourselves how to do things. Our natural minds are the driving force in most of us. We make decisions based on all of this external, natural information we gather through our five senses. God didn't create human beings to live this way!

He did give you the capacity to process natural information. That's important when you're driving a car. If the light turns red, you need to be able to react to it and stop. But God never intended your natural man to be your driving force.

Mankind was originally created in fellowship with God. He spoke to us in our spirits because our hearts—spirits—were in constant communion with Him. We were totally led by the spirit. Our hearts dictated what we thought, felt, and did. When man sinned against God, that communion was broken and our spirits died. They didn't cease to exist and function; they just became separated from God. That's what the word "death" means in Scripture.

There is no such thing as "ceasing to exist" in the Bible. When someone dies, their body turns to dust, but they don't cease to exist. They separate from their body. When the Word talks about us being dead in trespasses and sin, we're still functioning—but we're separated from God (Eph. 2:1).

Once that happened, we were separated from God until He provided the way back into communion. Instead of hearing the Lord and following Him, people just started ruling their own lives based on this external information. However, as born-again believers, we have the ability once again to let our hearts dictate and dominate our lives instead of our carnal minds and external circumstances (2 Cor. 5:7). But very few of us are doing that.

Things to Come

Jesus told us that when the Holy Spirit has come, He'll teach us all things, lead us into all truth, bring all things to our remembrance, and show us things to come (John 14:26 and 16:13). We simply haven't drawn on our spiritual man's potential like we can.

As I was meditating on that scripture fifteen years ago, the Lord spoke to me and said, "You haven't really been listening to Me and letting Me show you things to come." So I started praying about it and spending time being quiet in God's presence, letting Him speak to and influence me.

At the time, I had kept my four horses on a friend's property for two or three years. Every Sunday at church, he would come to me and say, "Oh, I'm so glad you have those horses there. I don't have to mow my property anymore. I just love having your horses on my property." He'd feed them and play with them. Everything was going well.

As I began to ask the Lord to show me things to come, one of the first things He told me was, "You need to find a new place to put those horses." At first I thought, *But this is free, and he loves having them!* It didn't make sense to me, so I waited a week.

Finally, I started asking around and found a place where I could put my horses. I'd have to pay for it, but I found something. I made the deal on Saturday and told the man, "I'm not sure when it'll be, but I know I'm going to have to move those horses."

On Sunday, this good friend of mine who owned the property my horses were on came to me and said, "I can't stand it anymore. Those horses have to be gone by Tuesday. I will not have them anymore!" That was the first negative word he had ever spoken to me. I had no indication it was coming, except that God had prepared me. I already had the place lined up the day before he spoke to me. This was the first of many things the Lord showed me that eventually led us to where we live today.

The Lord told me eighteen months before we actually started on television that it was coming. Then two people came and prophesied it over me. This confirmed it. These are just small examples, but that's where we have to start. If you can't hear the Lord speak to you in small matters, you won't hear Him in the bigger things. Most of us wait until something external tells us, but God wants to speak to us in our hearts.

Spiritually Minded

Did you know that you have two minds?

> That ye put off concerning the former conversation the old man, which is corrupt according to the deceitful lusts; And be renewed in the spirit of your mind.
>
> EPHESIANS 4:22-23

You have a natural mind and a spirit mind. Your spirit mind is the mind of Christ in your born-again spirit (1 Cor. 2:16). Again, understanding spirit, soul, and body will really help you with this.

God will speak things to you, and you can make decisions based on your spiritual mind instead of your physical mind. To most people, this sounds like I'm from another planet. They've never thought about the fact that they have two minds before. But the reason the Bible tells you not to be double minded is because you have two minds (James 4:8). You don't want to just be going back and forth between the two. You need to be spiritually minded—where your spirit mind is the master control and it just uses your natural mind as a processor. You can take natural information in, but let your spiritual mind—your heart—make the decisions. Your heart has the ability to see, hear, think, and make decisions. You should be living from your heart—not your head!

This is so hard for people to get a hold of—especially in our society where education is so exalted and esteemed. The people in charge of the news media are influencing people to be carnal. *Carnal* simply means "of the five senses." It's what you can see, taste, hear, smell, and feel. "That's what truly matters," so we are told. When you say "chili con carne," you're saying chili with meat. That's because the word *carne* means "meat." It's where we get the English word *carnal* from. Therefore, when you're carnal, you're a meathead! You're living out of your old physical brain.

I know this sounds pretty radical to most believers, but God intended for you to live from your heart!

Live from Your Heart
LESSON 15 – OUTLINE

1. Most religious people are so focused on getting others to act right that it causes hypocrisy.

    A. We just catch the fish—it's the Lord's job to clean them.

    B. Be tolerant and loving—and let God work on their hearts.

    C. God wants to change your heart, and then your actions will change as a byproduct.

        i. Right actions are a byproduct of an intimate relationship with God.

        ii. You must do things from a pure heart of love.

2. When Romans 1:21 speaks of your heart becoming "darkened," it's talking about becoming insensitive to God.

    > This I say therefore, and testify in the Lord, that ye henceforth walk not as other Gentiles walk, in the vanity of their mind, Having the ***understanding*** darkened.
    >
    > EPHESIANS 4:17-18, EMPHASIS MINE

    A. "Understanding" is the same Greek word as "imagination."

    B. It's your imagination that enables you to understand.

    > Being alienated from the life of God through the ignorance that is in them, because of ***the blindness of their heart***.
    >
    > EPHESIANS 4:18, EMPHASIS MINE

    C. The phrase "their foolish heart was darkened" in Romans 1:21 is the same thing as having your heart blinded that's talked about in Ephesians 4:18.

    D. It's talking about your heart not being able to see, perceive, listen, and hear from God.

3. God didn't originally create us to live the way the vast majority of us do.

    A. Most of us live from our mental, emotional, and physical parts (soul and body).

    B. Mankind was originally created in fellowship with God.

        i. He spoke to us in our spirits because our hearts—spirits—were in constant communion with Him.

ii. Our hearts dictated what we thought, felt, and did.

iii. When man sinned against God, that communion was broken and our spirits died.

C. When the Word talks about us being dead in trespasses and sin, we're still functioning—but we're separated from God (Eph. 2:1).

D. As born-again believers, we have the ability once again to let our hearts dictate and dominate our lives instead of our carnal minds and external circumstances (2 Cor. 5:7).

4. Jesus told us that when the Holy Spirit has come, He'll teach us all things, lead us into all truth, bring all things to our remembrance, and show us things to come (John 14:26 and 16:13).

A. We simply haven't drawn on our spiritual man's potential like we can.

B. If you can't hear the Lord speak to you in small matters, you won't hear Him in the bigger things.

C. Most of us wait until something external tells us, but God wants to speak to our hearts.

5. You have a natural mind and a spirit mind.

That ye put off concerning the former conversation the old man, which is corrupt according to the deceitful lusts; And be renewed in the spirit of your mind.
EPHESIANS 4:22-23

A. Your spirit mind is the mind of Christ in your born-again spirit (1 Cor. 2:16).

B. The reason the Bible tells you not to be double minded is because you have two minds (James 4:8).

C. You need to be spiritually minded—where your spirit mind is the master control, and it just uses your natural mind as a processor.

i. You can take natural information in, but let your spiritual mind—your heart—make the decisions.

ii. Your heart has the ability to see, hear, think, and make decisions.

D. You should be living from your heart—not your head!

Live from Your Heart
LESSON 15 – TEACHER'S GUIDE

1.   Most religious people are so focused on getting others to act right that it causes hypocrisy. We just catch the fish—it's the Lord's job to clean them. Be tolerant and loving—and let God work on their hearts.

      God wants to change our hearts, and then our actions will change as a byproduct. Right actions are a byproduct of an intimate relationship with God. We must do things from a pure heart of love (1 Cor. 13:3).

2.   When Romans 1:21 speaks of our hearts becoming "darkened," it's talking about becoming insensitive to God. "Understanding" in Ephesians 4:17-18 is the same Greek word as "imagination." It's our imagination that enables us to understand. "Their foolish heart was darkened" in Romans 1:21 is saying the same thing as having our heart blinded in Ephesians 4:18. It's talking about our hearts not being able to see, perceive, listen to, and hear from God.

3.   God didn't originally create us to live the way the vast majority of us do. Most of us live from our mental, emotional, and physical parts (soul and body). Mankind was originally created in fellowship with God. He spoke to us in our spirits because our hearts—spirits—were in constant communion with Him. Our hearts dictated what we thought, felt, and did. When man sinned against God, that communion was broken and our spirits died. When the Word talks about us being dead in trespasses and sin, we're still functioning—but we're separated from God (Eph. 2:1). However, as born-again believers, we have access once again to letting our hearts dictate and dominate our lives instead of our carnal minds and external circumstances (2 Cor. 5:7).

1. A. What are most religious people focused on? (Getting others to act right)
   B. Right actions are a byproduct of what? (An intimate relationship with God)
   C. According to 1 Corinthians 13:3, what must we do things from? (A pure heart of love)
2. A. The word "darkened" in Romans 1:21 speaks of what? (Our hearts becoming insensitive to God)
   B. What is it that enables us to understand? (Our imagination)
   C. What does Ephesians 4:18 mean when it says our hearts are blinded? (It's talking about our hearts not being able to see, perceive, listen to, and hear from God)
3. A. What do most people live from? (Their mental, emotional, and physical parts—soul and body)
   B. Read Ephesians 2:1. What happened when Adam and Eve sinned against God? (Their communion with Him was broken and their spirits died)
   C. Read 2 Corinthians 5:7. What do we, as born-again believers have access to once again? (Letting our hearts dictate and dominate our lives instead of our carnal minds and external circumstances)

4.   Jesus told us that when the Holy Spirit has come, He'll teach us all things, lead us into all truth, bring all things to our remembrance, and show us things to come (John 14:26 and 16:13). We simply haven't drawn on our spiritual man's potential like we can. If we can't hear the Lord speak to us in small matters, we won't hear Him in the bigger things. Most of us wait until something external tells us, but God wants to speak to our hearts.

5.   We have a natural mind and a spirit mind (Eph. 4:22-23). Our spirit minds are the mind of Christ in our born-again spirits (1 Cor. 2:16). The reason the Bible tells us not to be double minded is because we have two minds (James 4:8). We need to be spiritually minded—where our spirit minds are the master control, and our natural minds are just a processor. We can take natural information in but let our spiritual mind—our heart—make the decisions. Our hearts have the ability to see, hear, think, and make decisions. We should be living from our hearts—not our heads!

4. A. According to John 14:26 and 16:13, what does the Holy Spirit want to do in our lives? (Teach us all things, lead us into all truth, bring all things to our remembrance, and show us things to come)
   B. Most of us wait until something external tells us, but how does God want to speak to us? (In our hearts)
5. A. Read Ephesians 4:22-23 and 1 Corinthians 2:16. What is the spirit mind that we have? (The mind of Christ in our born-again spirits)
   B. Read James 4:8. Why does the Bible tell us not to be double minded? (Because we have two minds—our natural mind and our spirit mind)
   C. What does it mean to be spiritually minded? (Our spirit minds are the master control and they just use our natural minds as a processor)
   D. What should we be living from instead of our heads? (Our hearts)

Live from Your Heart

1. According to 1 Corinthians 13:3, what is necessary for our actions to profit us?

2. What word does Romans 1:21 use to speak of our hearts becoming hardened and insensitive to God?

3. According to Ephesians 4:17-18, believers should not walk as whom?

4. How is it that they walk?

5. Because of the ignorance that is in them and the blindness of their hearts, they are alienated from what?

6. According to Ephesians 2:1, what were we before we were quickened?

7. How does 2 Corinthians 5:7 reveal that believers should walk?

8. Who does John 14:26 reveal is the Comforter?

9. What does He do?
   A. Teach us all things.
   B. Condemn us over our sin.
   C. Bring to our remembrance everything Jesus has told us.
   D. All of the above.
   E. None of the above.

10. How does Jesus describe the Holy Spirit in John 16:13?

11. What does He do?
   A. Guide us into all truth.
   B. Listens and speaks to us what Jesus says.
   C. Shows us things to come.
   D. All of the above.
   E. None of the above.

12. What should we put off, according to Ephesians 4:22-23?

13. What should be renewed?

14. What does 1 Corinthians 2:16 reveal that we have?

15. According to James 4:8, what does God do when we draw nigh to Him?

16. What does this verse instruct sinners to do?

17. What does this verse tell double-minded people to do?

Live from Your Heart
LESSON 15 – ANSWER KEY

1. We must have the right motive—love.

2. Darkened.

3. Other Gentiles—meaning unbelievers.

4. In the vanity of their minds, having the understanding darkened.

5. The life of God.

6. Dead in trespasses and sins.

7. By faith, not by sight.

8. The Holy Spirit.

9. A. Teach us all things.
   C. Bring to our remembrance everything Jesus has told us.

10. The Spirit of truth.

11. A. Guide us into all truth.
    B. Listens and speaks to us what Jesus says.
    C. Shows us things to come.
    D. All of the above.

12. The old man.

13. The spirit of our minds—meaning our attitude.

14. The mind of Christ.

15. He draws nigh to us.

16. Cleanse their hands.

17. Purify their hearts—meaning become single minded, which is when our natural minds are renewed to the Word and agree with the mind of Christ in our born-again spirits.

Live from Your Heart
LESSON 15 – SCRIPTURES

And though I bestow all my goods to feed the poor, and though I give my body to be burned, and have not charity, it profiteth me nothing.

1 Corinthians 13:3

This I say therefore, and testify in the Lord, that ye henceforth walk not as other Gentiles walk, in the vanity of their mind, Having the understanding darkened, being alienated from the life of God through the ignorance that is in them, because of the blindness of their heart.

Ephesians 4:17-18

Because that, when they knew God, they glorified him not as God, neither were thankful; but became vain in their imaginations, and their foolish heart was darkened.

Romans 1:21

And you hath he quickened, who were dead in trespasses and sins.

Ephesians 2:1

For we walk by faith, not by sight.

2 Corinthians 5:7

But the Comforter, which is the Holy Ghost, whom the Father will send in my name, he shall teach you all things, and bring all things to your remembrance, whatsoever I have said unto you.

John 14:26

Howbeit when he, the Spirit of truth, is come, he will guide you into all truth: for he shall not speak of himself; but whatsoever he shall hear, that shall he speak: and he will shew you things to come.

John 16:13

That ye put off concerning the former conversation the old man, which is corrupt according to the deceitful lusts; And be renewed in the spirit of your mind.

Ephesians 4:22-23

For who hath known the mind of the Lord, that he may instruct him? But we have the mind of Christ.

1 Corinthians 2:16

Draw nigh to God, and he will draw nigh to you. Cleanse your hands, ye sinners; and purify your hearts, ye double minded.

James 4:8

Sensitive to God
LESSON 16

This I say therefore, and testify in the Lord, that ye henceforth walk not as other Gentiles walk, in the vanity of their mind.

EPHESIANS 4:17

"Gentile" here is talking about someone who was a non-Jew. It was someone outside of God's covenants—like any person today who has yet to commit their life to the Lord Jesus Christ. "Therefore, don't be like a lost person who just lives from their brain and not their heart." It's out of your heart that the issues of life flow (Prov. 4:23). You need to learn to listen to your heart. You should be directed by your heart—not your brain.

Most Christians are living like people who don't know God and wonder why they're getting the same results. If you think like a lost person, you'll get lost-person results (Prov. 23:7). If you start thinking like a new creation in Christ, you'll get spiritual results (Rom. 8:6 and 12:1-2).

But if you do walk in the vanity of your mind, it darkens your understanding/imagination (Eph. 4:18). Again, all of these things are interrelated. If you are living from your natural mind—what you can see, taste, hear, smell, and feel—and your ability to process that information in your little peanut brain in your head, you're going to severely limit what God can do!

When your heart becomes hardened—cold, insensitive, unfeeling, and unyielding to God—it still functions, but it automatically becomes sensitive toward physical, flesh-oriented things. This is where most of us live. Our hearts are conditioned to be sensitive to, dominated by, and controlled by our physical senses.

What's Your Focus?

Worry, fear, unbelief, and anger all come out of the heart.

> For out of the heart proceed evil thoughts, murders, adulteries, fornications, thefts, false witness, blasphemies.
>
> MATTHEW 15:19

> For from within, out of the heart of men, proceed evil thoughts, adulteries, fornications, murders, Thefts, covetousness, wickedness, deceit, lasciviousness, an evil eye, blasphemy, pride, foolishness.
>
> MARK 7:21-22

These are products of your heart. The reason your heart responds this way is because you let it be dominated by external, physical things. Your understanding is darkened, so you become insensitive to God. He's transmitting and speaking to you, but you don't hear, because your heart is insensitive.

Your heart becomes sensitive to whatever you focus your attention on, and your heart becomes hardened to whatever you neglect. If you would glorify, magnify, and value God, then you would put a greater priority upon the Lord and His Word. He would occupy more of your focus and attention than other things. If you start being thankful, you'll humble yourself and direct your attention away from negative things and put it on positive things. This places all of your attention on God—and you become sensitive to whatever you focus your attention upon. If you glorify and thank God, your imagination will start seeing godly things instead of the negative. The end result is that your heart becomes sensitive to God. This isn't hard—it's easy!

But if you're neglecting the things of God and listening to the doubt, unbelief, fear, anger, criticism, and negativity of the world, there's no way your heart will be sensitive to Him. You can still retain knowledge, but it isn't dominating you anymore. You're insensitive because of the condition of your heart.

Refuse to Empower

How do you keep your heart sensitive to the Lord? Glorify God. Put more value on Him than anything else. This also means you have to put more attention on Him than anything else and become thankful. Constantly rehearse your victories, remember what He's done in your life, and force your imagination in a positive direction. Recognize that your imagination is where things are conceived. If you don't want something birthed in you, don't think it.

Your imagination is where thoughts take on power. You can't keep thoughts from coming to you, but you can refuse to empower them. Someone spit in my face once while I was witnessing to them. It was a big wad of stuff. Do you know what? I had a thought—but it was a fleeting thought. I just kept witnessing to them and never missed a beat with what I was saying. I refused to empower it.

Thoughts will come at times, but when you let them enter into your imagination and you start seeing them is when they become empowered. Stop those thoughts before they ever become imagination. You can't allow your imagination to follow a train of thought that is contrary to God's Word. This is an important truth!

If you'll do these things, you'll find it will sensitize your heart toward the Lord.

Let Peace Rule

Once you really experience God's kind of love, what the world calls "love" is just cheap in comparison. I walk in love. I don't get angry with people. If I find myself operating in unforgiveness or criticizing someone, I immediately go to the Lord about it and say, "Father, something is wrong because this isn't the way Your kind of love is." At the first sign of something like this, I'll separate myself and spend time in the Word seeking God. I'll get myself back into that position of feeling God's kind of love—even for people who hate me.

Let the peace of God rule in your hearts.

COLOSSIANS 3:15

I use Colossians 3:15 constantly. I don't allow myself to become stressed out in traffic trying to get somewhere in a hurry. I'll even pull over on the side of the road if I have to, because I am not going to get out of peace. I don't get anxious either. I see other people running to catch a plane in airports. I'll just walk—and if I miss it, I miss it. It doesn't matter to me. But I refuse to get out of peace over things. I highly value peace. If anything starts making me anxious and upset, I change whatever is going on in my life in a hurry.

"Well, Andrew, you wouldn't last ten minutes in the life I live." That's your fault! I wouldn't work a job that took my peace away.

There are two ways to approach this. If you don't know how to walk in peace, you'll be stressed out no matter what the situation is. But if you truly are in a bad situation that's stealing your peace, you need to change that situation. That's not healthy for you—physically or spiritually.

I just don't live in a manner that takes my peace away. I don't do things like that. This is why I don't go certain places to minister. I make a lot of decisions based on peace.

"I'm Not Coming"

In 1980 I was planning on going to Central America. I had been there before and saw awesome results. I'd already bought the tickets and everything was set up, but I lost my peace about it. At the time, I was moving my mother from Texas to Colorado. I prayed about this Central American trip while driving the U-Haul truck for seventeen hours. The more I prayed in tongues, the more I didn't like it and didn't want to go. I just didn't have any peace about it.

First of all, I checked to see if I was truly meditating on the Lord. Well, after seventeen hours of praying in tongues, I knew I was meditating on the Lord. But I still didn't have any peace. The more I prayed about it, the less peace I had. Finally, I just called the people involved and said, "I don't know what the situation is, but I'm not coming." I canceled that trip because I didn't have any peace about it. Later on, I found out the plane I was scheduled to be on had taken off from Mexico City, crashed, and killed all 169 people on impact. I was preserved because I listened to my heart and kept my peace.

God speaks to you through your heart! You need to let your heart begin to dominate you. However, if you aren't glorifying God, being thankful, and your imagination has become vain, then your foolish heart will be darkened (Rom. 1:21). In other words, it's blind. You're alienated from the life of God within you because of the hardness and dullness of your heart (Eph. 4:18). This is where most Christians are because they haven't been seeking God, putting value on Him, praising His name, and using their imagination properly. They're so dull and insensitive to God that they can't hear Him speaking to them constantly.

"Pull Over and Park"

John G. Lake was driving up a mountain road. As he went around a sharp left-hand curve with a thousand-foot drop off, the Lord said, "Pull into the left lane and park." That doesn't make sense! If you pulled into the left lane on a mountain road during a sharp left hand curve, anybody coming down the other way would run right into you. I hear the voice of God, but I'm not quite that sensitive yet. I probably would have wanted three visions and a confirmation, and been two miles up the road before I responded. But Lake just instantly pulled over and parked. Within seconds, a log truck came barreling out of control down the mountain. It couldn't handle the curve and was over in the outside lane. If Lake hadn't been parked where he was on the inside, he would have collided with that log truck and both of them would have gone off the mountain.

God is no respecter of persons. He speaks to every one of us whenever anything is about to go wrong in our lives. He speaks, but if our hearts are darkened, we're alienated from that life—that voice of God—because of the hardness of our hearts.

Many people wondered why God "allowed" Keith Green, a Christian singer and songwriter, to die. He took off in a small airplane and hit some high wires. When the plane crashed, the pilot, Keith, and two of his children were killed. Keith's wife had a dream that the plane was going to crash. She begged Keith not to fly. The pilot even told him the plane was over the weight limit and they shouldn't fly, but Keith prevailed.

God speaks to us all the time. I've heard testimonies of people whom God told not to get on the freeway and then something major happened. It's not God who is unfaithful; it's us who don't hear His voice because we aren't letting our hearts dominate and lead us. Instead, we're just going along in the ignorance and blindness of our minds.

Perfect Wisdom

Your mind doesn't have near the capacity for understanding and processing things that your heart does. Your heart is where the real wisdom lies. As a born-again believer, you "have the mind of Christ" (1 Cor. 2:16). Colossians 3:10 says to:

> Put on the new man [your spirit man], which is renewed in knowledge after
> the image of him that created him.
>
> BRACKETS MINE

Even in the natural realm, experts say we only use 10 percent of our brains. I believe if you were using 100 percent of your brain, it still couldn't compete with just 10 percent of your spiritual mind. Your spiritual mind has the mind of Christ in it.

> But ye have an unction from the Holy One, and ye know all things.
>
> 1 JOHN 2:20

That's not talking about your natural mind. Your last test score proves that. It's your spirit—not your brain—that knows all things. In your born-again spirit, you have the perfect wisdom and mind of Christ. You know all things in your spirit. But if you allow your heart to become darkened, what good is God speaking to you and all of this wisdom if you can't perceive it? God speaks to you through your heart.

Head or Heart?

We have this tremendous presence of God in our hearts, but most of us aren't listening. He speaks to us in a still small voice, but we're listening to all these external things instead, and our little natural minds are trying to figure out how to make our lives work.

If you don't get to the place where you honestly trust your heart more than your head, you're never going to become a successful Christian.

> My son, attend to my words; incline thine ear unto my sayings. Let them not depart from thine eyes; keep them in the midst of thine heart.
>
> PROVERBS 4:20-21

Where do you keep God's Word? In the midst of your heart.

> Thy word have I hid in mine heart, that I might not sin against thee.
>
> PSALM 119:11

> For they [God's words] are life unto those that find them, and health to all their flesh. Keep thy heart with all diligence; for out of it are the issues of life.
>
> PROVERBS 4:22-23, BRACKETS MINE

Life comes from your heart—not your mind or external things. You need to keep your heart with all diligence. This means putting a priority on your heart and making sure it's the most important thing.

We educate our brains. We even have laws that say if we don't go to school, we're truant and they'll prosecute us. So we get up, drag ourselves out of bed, and make ourselves go to school. We make ourselves do things. But when it comes to our spiritual lives, we'd like to study the Word more, fellowship with God more, and pray in the Spirit more, but that's only if everything else isn't too pressing and we have enough time. We attend church if we feel like it.

Most of us haven't put the priority on seeking the wisdom that's already in our spirits and drawing on that life. We haven't put God first place in our hearts—and we wonder why we aren't receiving better results. Our lifestyle simply isn't conducive to really walking with God.

Sit and Soak

Sadhu Sundar Singh was a Hindu holy man in India. He had a vision and was converted to the Lord. He went to Bombay once (called Mumbai today) and saw something like fifteen or twenty people raised from the dead in one day. This guy saw hundreds of people raised from the

213

dead! He had half a million people at his meetings in India and finally had to quit praying for the sick, because there were so many people to pray for that he never had an opportunity to preach the Gospel. So he quit praying for the sick because he felt that preaching the Gospel was more important. Great things happened. When I went to India, everyone knew about Sadhu Sundar Singh. He's a legend over there. He died in about 1929.

Around 1920, he came over to the United States. It took a month or two for him to get here by boat. He got off the ship in New York City, spent thirty minutes walking around, got back on the boat, canceled all of his appointments, and said, "These people will never listen to the Gospel. They're too busy." That was 1920! Can you imagine what he would think of our lifestyle today?

Be still, and know that I am God.

PSALM 46:10

It takes time to meditate and give all diligence to your heart. You can't say, "I give quality time. It's only five minutes a day, but it's quality." You have to have some quantity time too. You need to sit and soak in the presence of God.

That's the reason for extended meetings. If you went to a meeting sometime that just went for a whole month, by the end of that time you'd see things happen that you would never see in a three-day or four-day meeting. Why? You just sat and soaked. If you could commit that much time to sit under the Word and soak in God's awesome presence, it would transform the way you receive.

You have to start spending time in God's presence listening to your heart and paying attention to the Lord speaking to you. God doesn't work like a microwave. You can't microwave your miracle. You need to spend time sitting in the presence of the Lord. There's just no shortcut to it!

Sensitive to God
LESSON 16 – OUTLINE

1. You should be directed by your heart—not your brain.

> This I say therefore, and testify in the Lord, that ye henceforth walk not as other Gentiles walk, in the vanity of their mind.
>
> EPHESIANS 4:17

   A. "Gentile" here is talking about someone who was a non-Jew, someone outside of God's covenants—like any person today who has yet to commit their life to the Lord Jesus Christ.

   B. It's out of your heart that the issues of life flow (Prov. 4:23).

   C. Most Christians are living like people who don't know God and wonder why they're getting the same results.

      i. If you think like a lost person, you'll get lost-person results (Prov. 23:7).

      ii. If you start thinking like a new creation in Christ, you'll get spiritual results (Rom. 8:6 and 12:1-2).

      iii. But if you do walk in the vanity of your mind, it darkens your understanding/imagination (Eph. 4:18).

   D. If you are living from your natural mind—what you can see, taste, hear, smell, and feel—and how you process that information in your little peanut brain in your head, you're going to severely limit what God can do!

2. When your heart becomes hardened—cold, insensitive, unfeeling, and unyielding to God—it still functions, but it automatically becomes sensitive toward physical, natural, flesh-oriented types of things.

   A. Worry, fear, unbelief, and anger all come out of the heart.

> For out of the heart proceed evil thoughts, murders, adulteries, fornications, Thefts, false witness, blasphemies.
>
> MATTHEW 15:19

> For from within, out of the heart of men, proceed evil thoughts, adulteries, fornications, murders, thefts, covetousness, wickedness, deceit, lasciviousness, an evil eye, blasphemy, pride, foolishness.
>
> MARK 7:21-22

B. God is transmitting and speaking to you, but you don't hear, because your heart is insensitive.

3. Your heart becomes sensitive to whatever you focus your attention on, and your heart becomes hardened to whatever you neglect.

    A. If you glorify and thank God, your imagination will start seeing godly things instead of the negative.

    B. If you don't want something birthed in you, don't think it.

    C. You can't allow your imagination to follow a train of thought that is contrary to God's Word.

    D. If you'll do these things, you'll find it will sensitize your heart toward the Lord.

4. I value peace highly.

    Let the peace of God rule in your hearts.

                               COLOSSIANS 3:15

    A. If anything starts making me anxious and upset, I change whatever is going on in my life in a hurry.

    B. If you don't know how to walk in peace, you'll be stressed out no matter what the situation is.

    C. If you truly are in a bad situation that's stealing your peace, you need to change that situation.

5. As a born-again believer, you "have the mind of Christ" (1 Cor. 2:16).

    Put on the new man [your spirit man], which is renewed in knowledge after the image of him that created him.

                    COLOSSIANS 3:10, BRACKETS MINE

    A. It's your spirit—not your brain—that knows all things.

    But ye have an unction from the Holy One, and ye know all things.

                             1 JOHN 2:20

    B. We have this tremendous presence of God in our hearts, but most of us aren't listening.

6. If you don't get to the place where you honestly trust your heart more than your head, you're never going to become a successful Christian.

My son, attend to my words; incline thine ear unto my sayings. Let them not depart from thine eyes; keep them in the midst of thine heart.

PROVERBS 4:20-21

Thy word have I hid in mine heart, that I might not sin against thee.

PSALM 119:11

For they [God's words] are life unto those that find them, and health to all their flesh. Keep thy heart with all diligence; for out of it are the issues of life.

PROVERBS 4:22-23, BRACKETS MINE

A. Life comes from your heart—not your mind or external things.

B. It takes time to meditate and give all diligence to your heart.

Be still, and know that I am God.

PSALM 46:10

C. You have to start spending time in God's presence listening to your heart and paying attention to the Lord speaking to you.

D. There's just no shortcut to it!

Sensitive to God
LESSON 16 – TEACHER'S GUIDE

1.   We should be directed by our hearts—not our brains. "Gentile" in Ephesians 4:17 is talking about someone who was a non-Jew, someone outside of God's covenants—like any person today who has yet to commit their life to the Lord Jesus Christ. It's out of our hearts that the issues of life flow (Prov. 4:23). Most of us are living like people who don't know God and wonder why we're getting the same results. If we think like a lost person, we'll get lost-person results (Prov. 23:7). If we start thinking like a new creation in Christ, we'll get spiritual results (Rom. 8:6 and 12:1-2). But if we do walk in the vanity of our minds, it darkens our understanding/imagination (Eph. 4:18). If we are living from our natural minds—what we can see, taste, hear, smell, and feel—and our ability to process that information in our little peanut brain in our head, we're going to severely limit what God can do!

2.   When our hearts becomes hardened—cold, insensitive, unfeeling, and unyielding to God—they still function, but they automatically become sensitive toward physical, natural, flesh-oriented things. Worry, fear, unbelief, and anger all come out of the heart (Matt. 15:19 and Mark 7:21-22). God is transmitting and speaking to us, but we don't hear, because our hearts are insensitive.

3.   Our hearts becomes sensitive to whatever we focus our attention on, and our hearts become hardened to whatever we neglect. If we glorify and thank God, our imagination will start seeing godly things instead of the negative. If we don't want something birthed in us, we don't think it. We can't allow our imagination to follow a train of thought that is contrary to God's Word. If we'll do these things, we'll find it will sensitize our hearts toward the Lord.

1. A. Read Ephesians 4:17-18; Proverbs 4:23, and 23:7. What happens when we, as Christians, think like a lost person? (We get lost-person results)
    B. Read Romans 8:6 and 12:1-2. If we start thinking like a new creation in Christ, what will we get? (Spiritual results)
    C. How is it that we severely limit what God can do in our lives? (By living from our natural minds—what we can see, taste, hear, smell, and feel)
2. A. What are the characteristics of a hard heart? (Cold, insensitive, unfeeling, and unyielding to God, but sensitive toward physical, natural, flesh-oriented things)
    B. Read Matthew 15:19 and Mark 7:21-22. Why don't we receive and hear what God is transmitting and speaking to us? (Because our hearts are insensitive)
3. A. What do our hearts become sensitive to? (Whatever we focus our attention on)
    B. What do our hearts become hardened to? (Whatever we neglect)
    C. How do we avoid something being birthed in us? (Don't think it)

4.   I highly value peace (Col. 3:15). If anything starts making me anxious and upset, I change whatever is going on in my life in a hurry.

If we don't know how to walk in peace, we'll be stressed out no matter what the situation is. But if we truly are in a bad situation that's stealing our peace, we need to change that situation.

5.   As born-again believers, we "have the mind of Christ" (1 Cor. 2:16 and Col. 3:10). It's our spirits—not our brains—that know all things (1 John 2:20). We have this tremendous presence of God in our hearts, but most of us aren't listening.

6.   If we don't get to the place where we honestly trust our hearts more than our heads, we're never going to become successful Christians (Prov. 4:20-23 and Ps. 119:11). Life comes from our hearts—not our minds or external things. It takes time to meditate and give all diligence to our hearts (Ps. 46:10). We must spend time in God's presence, listening to our hearts and paying attention to the Lord speaking to us. There's just no shortcut to it!

4. A. Read Colossians 3:15. What happens to people who don't know how to walk in peace? (They're stressed out no matter what the situation is)
   B. What should we do if we're truly in a bad situation that is stealing our peace? (Change that situation)
5. Read 1 Corinthians 2:16, Colossians 3:10, and 1 John 2:20. Where is it that we know all things? (The mind of Christ in our born-again spirits)
6. A. Read Proverbs 4:20-23 and Psalm 119:11. Where does life come from? (Our hearts)
   B. Read Psalm 46:10. We need to start spending time in God's presence doing what? (Listening to our hearts and paying attention to the Lord speaking to us)

Sensitive to God
LESSON 16 – DISCIPLESHIP QUESTIONS

1. According to Ephesians 4:17, how do other Gentiles—unbelievers—walk?

2. Should believers in Christ walk this way?

3. Proverbs 4:23 says that life issues come from what?

4. In light of this truth, what should we do?

5. Proverbs 23:7 reveals that we are as we _____.

6. According to Romans 8:6, what does carnal-mindedness bring?

7. What does spiritual-mindedness bring?

8. According to Romans 12:1-2, what is our reasonable service?

9. What should we not be conformed to?

10. How are we transformed?

11. When that happens, what will we prove—make manifest to our physical senses?

12. When believers do walk in the vanity of their natural, un-renewed minds, what does Ephesians 4:18 say this does to their understanding/imagination?

13. According to Matthew 15:19 and Mark 7:21-22, what proceeds from the heart of man?
    A. Evil thoughts and murders.
    B. Adulteries and fornications.
    C. Thefts, covetousness, and wickedness.
    D. All of the above.
    E. None of the above.

14. What does Colossians 3:15 say should rule our hearts?

15. According to 1 Corinthians 2:16, what do born-again believers have?

16. According to Colossians 3:10, what should we do?

17. Our spirit man is renewed in knowledge after the image of whom?

18. First John 2:20 reveals that we have an unction from whom?

19. In our born-again spirits, what do we know?

20. According to Proverbs 4:20-23, where should we keep God's Word?
    A. In our ears.
    B. In our eyes.
    C. In our hearts.
    D. All of the above.
    E. None of the above.

21. What are God's words to those who find them?

22. What should we keep with all diligence?

23. Why?

24. According to Psalm 119:11, what is an important reason for hiding God's Word in our hearts?

25. What does Psalm 46:10 reveal as the first step to knowing God?

Sensitive to God
LESSON 16 – ANSWER KEY

1. In the vanity of their minds.

2. No.

3. Our hearts.

4. Keep our hearts with all diligence.

5. Think in our hearts.

6. Death.

7. Life and peace.

8. To present our bodies as living sacrifices, holy and acceptable to the Lord.

9. This world.

10. By the renewing of our minds.

11. God's good, acceptable, and perfect will.

12. It darkens it.

13. A. Evil thoughts and murders.
    B. Adulteries and fornications.
    C. Thefts, covetousness, and wickedness.
    D. All of the above.

14. The peace of God.

15. The mind of Christ.

16. Put on our new man—our spirit man.

17. Him who created him.

18. The Holy One.

19. All things.

20. A. In our ears.
    B. In our eyes.
    C. In our hearts.
    D. All of the above.

21. Life and health to all their flesh.

22. Our hearts.

23. Because out of it flow the issues of life.

24. That we would not sin against God.

25. Be still.

Sensitive to God

LESSON 16 – SCRIPTURES

This I say therefore, and testify in the Lord, that ye henceforth walk not as other Gentiles walk, in the vanity of their mind, Having the understanding darkened, being alienated from the life of God through the ignorance that is in them, because of the blindness of their heart.

EPHESIANS 4:17-18

For as he thinketh in his heart, so is he: Eat and drink, saith he to thee; but his heart is not with thee.

PROVERBS 23:7

For to be carnally minded is death; but to be spiritually minded is life and peace.

ROMANS 8:6

I beseech you therefore, brethren, by the mercies of God, that ye present your bodies a living sacrifice, holy, acceptable unto God, which is your reasonable service. And be not conformed to this world: but be ye transformed by the renewing of your mind, that ye may prove what is that good, and acceptable, and perfect, will of God.

ROMANS 12:1-2

For out of the heart proceed evil thoughts, murders, adulteries, fornications, thefts, false witness, blasphemies.

MATTHEW 15:19

For from within, out of the heart of men, proceed evil thoughts, adulteries, fornications, murders, Thefts, covetousness, wickedness, deceit, lasciviousness, an evil eye, blasphemy, pride, foolishness.

MARK 7:21-22

And let the peace of God rule in your hearts, to the which also ye are called in one body; and be ye thankful.

COLOSSIANS 3:15

Because that, when they knew God, they glorified him not as God, neither were thankful; but became vain in their imaginations, and their foolish heart was darkened.

ROMANS 1:21

For who hath known the mind of the Lord, that he may instruct him? But we have the mind of Christ.

1 CORINTHIANS 2:16

Put on the new man, which is renewed in knowledge after the image of him that created him.

COLOSSIANS 3:10

But ye have an unction from the Holy One, and ye know all things.

1 JOHN 2:20

My son, attend to my words; incline thine ear unto my sayings. Let them not depart from thine eyes; keep them in the midst of thine heart. For they are life unto those that find them, and health to all their flesh. Keep thy heart with all diligence; for out of it are the issues of life.

PROVERBS 4:20-23

Thy word have I hid in mine heart, that I might not sin against thee.

PSALM 119:11

Be still, and know that I am God: I will be exalted among the heathen, I will be exalted in the earth.

PSALM 46:10

Meditate the Word
LESSON 17

God's Word tells us how to get understanding and train our hearts so they can listen and see.

> I have more understanding than all my teachers: for thy testimonies are my meditation.
>
> PSALM 119:99

What is meditation? It's reading the Word, then closing your physical eyes to think about what you've read until you can see it with the spiritual eyes of your heart—your imagination.

Inside First, Then Outside

John 14:12 is a powerful verse, but you need to see it in your heart before you can experience it for yourself.

> Verily, verily, I say unto you, He that believeth on me, the works that I do shall he do also; and greater works than these shall he do; because I go unto my Father.
>
> JOHN 14:12

Don't just read it and move on—stop and think about it. Sit down, close your Bible, and pray, "Lord, this says that as a believer in You, I will do the same works You did—and even greater." Think about doing the works Jesus did. With your mind, start seeing yourself healing the sick, cleansing the lepers, and expelling demons. See yourself laying hands on someone who's dead—and then see them come back to life! See the blind receiving sight and the deaf hearing. Then say, "That's what Jesus told me to do. Since I'm a believer, I'm going to see these things come to pass!"

If you would meditate on that, you'd have more understanding than all of your teachers. Your spirit would begin to open up, and you'd start seeing things with your heart. You'd hear God speaking to you in your heart and leading you to do certain things. This is how it works.

However, until you see it on the inside, you can't see it on the outside.

"What Am I Preaching?"

I used John 14:12 to preach a message in a Wednesday night service once in Corpus Christi, Texas. I left the next day, but the pastor had listened and meditated on that verse the rest of the week. On Sunday morning, he stood up and preached on John 14:12 again, saying, "We're going to see the dead raised! I've been meditating on this, and I've conceived something on the inside. I just know it's going to happen!"

While he was preaching this, a man stood up on the side, walked forward, grabbed his heart, and fell over dead. They had a nurse in the audience. She checked his vital signs, and said, "He's dead. There's no pulse." They tried CPR. They called the fire station, which—by the way—was just across the street. Normally, the emergency personnel would have been there almost instantaneously. But this time it took them twenty-five minutes!

Since they had already tried CPR and the man didn't revive, the service was ruined, and the pastor didn't know what to do. With this dead man laying at the front of the church, he finally said, "Let's pray." As they started to pray, he exclaimed, "What am I preaching? We're going to see the dead raised. This guy is dead." So he walked over and spoke to him, and this guy rose up from the dead—right as the paramedics walked in!

After taking him to the hospital and examining him, they declared him totally healthy and let him go. This guy had to catch a taxi back to the church. He made the pastor pay the fare, saying, "I didn't want to go to the hospital in the first place. You made me go!" So they saw this man raised from the dead.

How did that happen? First of all, the pastor started meditating on that Word.

Exercise Your Mind

I'm not trying to scold anyone. I just want to make it clear that God isn't our problem. We're our problem. Very few believers meditate on the Word day and night like Joshua 1:8 tells us to do. "Come on, Andrew, not everyone is a preacher like you. Somebody has to work! I can't meditate on the Word day and night." Yes, you can.

The same part of you that worries also meditates. Worry is nothing but meditation on something bad. You can meditate on the things of God and still work at your job. In fact, you'll do it even better. You can keep your mind stayed on God. You can bring every thought into captivity and under obedience to Christ. You don't have to be a minister to meditate on the Word day and night.

Most preachers are on-call twenty-four hours a day, and they have so many things coming at them. It's hard to spend time meditating on the Word when you're a minister. There are so many other things that need to be done. So don't tell me, "It doesn't work for everyone else." The Bible says you can bring every thought into captivity and under obedience. God wouldn't have commanded you to meditate on the Word day and night if you couldn't do it. You can do it!

Our minds are like a muscle that hasn't been exercised. In some of us, they're nearly atrophied. We sit down in front of a television and turn it on and let it do the thinking for us so we won't have to put forth any effort. Reading the newspaper is too much effort for some folks. We just want to sit down and have someone give it to us intravenously. It takes time and effort to exercise your mind. But you can get to a place where it'll respond to you and do what you want it to. You can exercise your mind!

Read with Your Heart

Through thy precepts I get understanding: therefore I hate every false way.

PSALM 119:104

God's Word gives you understanding. It opens up your heart.

The entrance of thy words giveth light; it giveth understanding unto the simple.

PSALM 119:130

God's Word touches your heart. Some people struggle with the Word because they're trying to understand it with their brains. But God's Word is written to your heart. If you'll read it with your heart, you'll have understanding. If you just try to pick it apart with your brain, you'll mess up and miss things. God's Word is written on your heart. If you'll listen, the entrance of His Word will give you light. It gives understanding to the simple.

The purpose of the book of Proverbs is:

To know wisdom and instruction; to perceive the words of understanding; To receive instruction of wisdom, justice, and judgment, and equity; To give subtilty to the simple, to the young man knowledge and discretion. A wise man will hear, and will increase learning; and a man of understanding shall attain unto wise counsels: To understand a proverb, and the interpretation; the words of the wise, and their dark sayings.

PROVERBS 1:2-6

The book of Proverbs was written to give you God's wisdom and understanding. If you don't have it, take Proverbs and read it. Put your finger on a particular verse or passage and say, "Lord, You said You'd give me wisdom and understanding. I open my heart to Your Word." Then meditate on it, and it'll give you more understanding than all of your teachers.

The Principal Thing

My son, if thou wilt receive my words, and hide my commandments with thee; So that thou incline thine ear unto wisdom, and apply thine heart to understanding; Yea, if thou criest after knowledge, and liftest up thy voice for understanding; If thou seekest her as silver and searchest for her as for hid treasures.

PROVERBS 2:1-4

Sometimes we spiritualize things and miss them, but this means that you ought to desire God's Word more than seeing your business prosper. When you get to the point where you want wisdom more than you want money, you'll get it!

If thou seekest her as silver, and searchest for her as for hid treasures; Then shalt thou understand the fear of the LORD, and find the knowledge of God. For the LORD giveth wisdom: out of his mouth cometh knowledge and understanding.

PROVERBS 2:4-6

Out of His mouth is the Word of God.

Discretion shall preserve thee, understanding shall keep thee.

PROVERBS 2:11

Wisdom is the principal thing; therefore get wisdom: and with all thy getting get understanding.

PROVERBS 4:7

This isn't just talking about carnal knowledge, but an attitude of the heart. Understanding is a function of the heart.

Adulterers and Animals

But whoso committeth adultery with a woman lacketh understanding: he that doeth it destroyeth his own soul.

PROVERBS 6:32

Be ye not as the horse, or as the mule, which have no understanding: whose mouth must be held in with bit and bridle, lest they come near unto thee.

PSALM 32:9

Don't act like an animal that has no understanding. An animal has to have something in its mouth causing it pain in order to restrain it. All it responds to is something physical. You need to be able to listen to your heart, have understanding, and not have to be punished physically.

I'm amazed how many people don't follow this. Don't wait to listen to your spirit until things are going wrong, your marriage falls apart, and everything in the natural is crashing and burning. If you make that a habit, you'll be someone who is constantly going from pit to pit instead of glory to glory. You need to listen to your heart!

If you're committing adultery, you lack understanding. You aren't listening to your heart. You're just like a horse—letting your hormones drive you.

Horses aren't stupid, but they can't reason and understand—especially when a stallion's hormones start flowing. There is simply no reasoning to it whatsoever. I know. I've had one before. Once that stallion's hormones started raging, he always made a beeline straight to the nearest mare no matter who or what stood in his way! He was totally insensitive to anything other than his hormones and that mare.

Access to Change

A person who commits adultery is just like that. They're brain dead! They aren't listening to God or to their heart. They aren't sensitive to that inner witness. They've fallen out of communion with God.

If you were to get to a place where your heart ruled, it would be impossible for you to commit adultery. You have to literally shut off your heart before you can do something like that. You can't be in communion with God and act that way. This isn't just true of adultery; it's true of a thousand things. If you were in communion with God, you couldn't be so selfish, angry, mean, or depressed. You couldn't be a lot of things that you are, if you'd just stay in communion with God.

The four keys I've shared in this study are progressive steps that lead to an established heart. First, we value God and what He has said and done in our lives. Second, we are thankful, which involves remembering. Third, we use our imagination in a positive way. If we've done all of these things, our hearts will naturally become sensitive to God. But failure to do the first three things makes it impossible for our hearts to be sensitive toward the Lord.

Again, most of us are trying to change our behavior without first changing our hearts. Our hearts are filled with all kinds of junk. We're thinking on the wrong things. We're cold and insensitive toward God. This is how our hearts are, but we want different results. However, "behavior modification" is the wrong way to fix this problem.

What I'm sharing may not be the easiest, but it's how God designed us. Most people would like to come forward, have somebody lay hands on them, and cast out their desire to commit adultery, their depression, or whatever. We want instantaneous results, and we don't want to have to do something that takes effort. Although it takes more time and effort to change your heart and get it established, once it's changed, it also takes time to get out of it. Once you start acting right from the heart, you won't find yourself falling into sin. Once your heart is established, it'll direct you.

You can't change your heart for the good without glorifying God, being thankful, and using your imagination in a positive way. This is how you access your heart. This is how you begin to change. These are the four keys to staying full of God!

Meditate the Word
LESSON 17 – OUTLINE

1. God's Word tells us how to get understanding and train our hearts so they can listen and see.

   > I have more understanding than all my teachers: for thy testimonies are my meditation.
   >
   > PSALM 119:99

   A. Meditation is reading the Word, then closing your physical eyes to think about what you've read until you can see it with the spiritual eyes of your heart—your imagination.

   B. John 14:12 is a powerful verse, but you need to see it in your heart before you can experience it for yourself.

   > Verily, verily, I say unto you, He that believeth on me, the works that I do shall he do also; and greater works than these shall he do; because I go unto my Father.
   >
   > JOHN 14:12

   C. Until you see it on the inside, you can't see it on the outside.

2. Very few believers meditate on the Word day and night like Joshua 1:8 tells us to do.

   A. You can meditate on the things of God and still work at your job.

   B. You don't have to be a minister to meditate on the Word day and night.

   C. God wouldn't have commanded you to meditate on the Word day and night if you couldn't do it—you can do it!

3. God's Word gives you understanding and opens up your heart.

   > Through thy precepts I get understanding: therefore I hate every false way.
   >
   > PSALM 119:104

   A. God's Word touches your heart—it's written to your heart.

      i. If you'll read it with your heart, you'll have understanding.

      ii. If you just try to pick it apart with your brain, you'll mess up and miss things.

   B. If you'll listen, the entrance of His Word will give you light.

The entrance of thy words giveth light; it giveth understanding unto the simple.

PSALM 119:130

4. The book of Proverbs was written to give you God's wisdom and understanding.

To know wisdom and instruction; to perceive the words of understanding; To receive instruction of wisdom, justice, and judgment, and equity; To give subtilty to the simple, to the young man knowledge and discretion. A wise man will hear, and will increase learning; and a man of understanding shall attain unto wise counsels: To understand a proverb, and the interpretation; the words of the wise, and their dark sayings.

PROVERBS 1:2-6

My son, if thou wilt receive my words, and hide my commandments with thee; So that thou incline thine ear unto wisdom, and apply thine heart to understanding; Yea, if thou criest after knowledge, and liftest up thy voice for understanding; If thou seekest her as silver, and searchest for her as for hid treasures; Then shalt thou understand the fear of the LORD, and find the knowledge of God. For the LORD giveth wisdom: out of his mouth cometh knowledge and understanding…Discretion shall preserve thee, understanding shall keep thee.

PROVERBS 2:1-6 AND 11

Wisdom is the principal thing; therefore get wisdom: and with all thy getting get understanding.

PROVERBS 4:7

But whoso commiteth adultery with a woman lacketh understanding: he that doeth it destroyeth his own soul.

PROVERBS 6:32

Be ye not as the horse, or as the mule, which have no understanding: whose mouth must be held in with bit and bridle, lest they come near unto thee.

PSALM 32:9

5. The four keys I've shared in this study are progressive steps that lead to an established heart.

   A. First, we value God and what He has said and done in our lives.

   B. Second, we are thankful, which involves remembering.

   C. Third, we use our imagination in a positive way.

   D. If we've done all of these things, our hearts will naturally become sensitive to God.

6. You can't change your heart for the good without glorifying God, being thankful, and using your imagination in a positive way.

   A. This is how you access your heart.

   B. This is how you begin to change.

   C. These are the four keys to staying full of God!

Meditate the Word
LESSON 17 – TEACHER'S GUIDE

1.   God's Word tells us how to get understanding and train our hearts so they can listen and see (Ps. 119:99). Meditation is reading the Word, then closing our physical eyes to think about what we've read until we can see it with the spiritual eyes of our hearts—our imagination. John 14:12 is a powerful verse, but we need to see it in our hearts before we can experience it for ourselves. Until we see it on the inside, we can't see it on the outside.

2.   Very few believers meditate on the Word day and night like it says to in Joshua 1:8. We can meditate on the things of God and still work at our jobs. We don't have to be ministers to meditate on the Word day and night. God wouldn't have commanded us to meditate on the Word day and night if we couldn't do it—we can do it!

3.   God's Word gives us understanding and opens up our hearts (Ps. 119:104). God's Word touches our hearts—it's written to our hearts. If we'll read it with our hearts, we'll have understanding. If we just try to pick it apart with our brains, we'll mess up and miss things. If we'll listen, the entrance of His Word will give us light (Ps. 119:130).

1. A. Read Psalm 119:99 and John 14:12. What is meditation? (It's reading the Word, then closing our physical eyes to think about what we've read until we can see it with the spiritual eyes of our hearts—our imagination)
   B. Before we see something on the outside, where must we see it first? (On the inside)
2. A. Read Joshua 1:8. Can we meditate on the things of God and still do our jobs? (Yes)
   B. What has God commanded us to do? (Meditate on His Word day and night)
3. A. Read Psalm 119:104 and 130. What happens when we read God's Word with our hearts? (We get understanding)
   B. What happens when we try to pick it apart with our brains? (We mess up and miss things)

4.   The book of Proverbs was written to give us God's wisdom and understanding (Prov. 1:2-6, 2:1-6, 11, 4:7, 6:32; and Ps. 32:9).

5.   The four keys I've shared in this study are progressive steps that lead to an established heart. First, we value God and what He has said and done in our lives. Second, we are thankful, which involves remembering. Third, we use our imagination in a positive way. If we've done all of these things, our hearts will naturally become sensitive to God.

6.   We can't change our hearts for the good without glorifying God, being thankful, and using our imagination in a positive way. This is how we access our hearts. This is how we begin to change. These are the four keys to staying full of God!

4. Read Proverbs 1:2-6, 2:1-6, 11, 4:7, 6:32; and Psalm 32:9. Why was the book of Proverbs written? (To give us God's wisdom and understanding)
5. A. The four keys to staying full of God are progressive steps that lead to what? (An established heart)
   B. What happens when we've done all those things? (Our hearts just naturally become sensitive to God)
6. A. Can we change our hearts for the good without glorifying God, being thankful, and using our imagination in a positive way? (No)
   B. How do we access our hearts, begin to change, and stay full of God? (We glorify God, are thankful, use our imagination in a positive way, and live from our hearts)

Meditate the Word
LESSON 17 — ADDITIONAL INFORMATION

My teachings entitled "Revelation Knowledge," "Remembering Scripture," and "Meditate the Word" all deal with the subject of meditating God's Word in greater depth and detail. And remember, all of my CD products are available as free MP3 downloads on my website.

Meditate the Word
LESSON 17 – DISCIPLESHIP QUESTIONS

1. According to Psalm 119:99, how do we gain more understanding than all of our teachers?

2. What did the Lord promise in John 14:12?

3. According to Joshua 1:8, when should we meditate God's Word?

4. What would be the result of this?
   A. We would observe to do according to all that is written.
   B. We would make our way prosperous.
   C. We would have good success.
   D. All of the above.
   E. None of the above.

5. What does Psalm 119:104 say we get from God's Word?

6. What does this produce?

7. According to Psalm 119:130, what does the entrance of God's Word give?

8. To whom does it give understanding?

9. According to Proverbs 1:2-6, what is the purpose of the book of Proverbs?
   A. To give knowledge and discretion to young people.
   B. To perceive words of understanding and receive instruction of wisdom.
   C. To give subtlety to the simple.
   D. All of the above.
   E. None of the above.

10. Read Proverbs 2:1-6. What does the Lord give?

11. Out of His mouth come what?

12. According to Proverbs 2:11, what do discretion and understanding do?

13. What does Proverbs 4:7 reveal as the principal thing?

14. In all our getting, what should we get?

15. According to Proverbs 6:32, what does an adulterer lack?

16. What do those who commit adultery destroy?

17. Psalm 32:9 exhorts us to not be like what?

18. Why?

19. How are their mouths held in?

20. What scripture reveals the four keys to staying full of God?

21. What are the four keys?

Meditate the Word
LESSON 17 – ANSWER KEY

1. Meditate God's Word.

2. Those who believe on Him shall do the works He did, and greater works.

3. Day and night.

4. A. We would observe to do according to all that is written.
   B. We would make our way prosperous.
   C. We would have good success.
   D. All of the above.

5. Understanding.

6. It causes us to hate every false way.

7. Light.

8. The simple.

9. A. To give knowledge and discretion to young people.
   B. To perceive words of understanding and receive instruction of wisdom.
   C. To give subtlety to the simple.
   D. All of the above.

10. Wisdom.

11. Knowledge and understanding.

12. They preserve and keep us.

13. Wisdom.

14. Understanding.

15. Understanding.

16. Their own souls.

17. A horse or mule.

18. They have no understanding.

19. With bit and bridle.

20. Romans 1:21.

21. Glorify God, be thankful, recognize the power of our imagination, and have a good heart.

Meditate the Word
LESSON 17 – SCRIPTURES

I have more understanding than all my teachers: for thy testimonies are my meditation.

PSALM 119:99

Verily, verily, I say unto you, He that believeth on me, the works that I do shall he do also; and greater works than these shall he do; because I go unto my Father.

JOHN 14:12

This book of the law shall not depart out of thy mouth; but thou shalt meditate therein day and night, that thou mayest observe to do according to all that is written therein: for then thou shalt make thy way prosperous, and then thou shalt have good success.

JOSHUA 1:8

Through thy precepts I get understanding: therefore I hate every false way.

PSALM 119:104

The entrance of thy words giveth light; it giveth understanding unto the simple.

PSALM 119:130

My son, if thou wilt receive my words, and hide my commandments with thee; So that thou incline thine ear unto wisdom, and apply thine heart to understanding; Yea, if thou criest after knowledge, and liftest up thy voice for understanding; If thou seekest her as silver, and searchest for her as for hid treasures; Then shalt thou understand the fear of the LORD, and find the knowledge of God. For the LORD giveth wisdom: out of his mouth cometh knowledge and understanding.

PROVERBS 2:1-6

To know wisdom and instruction; to perceive the words of understanding; To receive instruction of wisdom, justice, and judgment, and equity; To give subtilty to the simple, to the young man knowledge and discretion. A wise man will hear, and will increase learning; and a man of understanding shall attain unto wise counsels: To understand a proverb, and the interpretation; the words of the wise, and their dark sayings.

PROVERBS 1:2-6

Discretion shall preserve thee, understanding shall keep thee.

PROVERBS 2:11

Wisdom is the principal thing; therefore get wisdom: and with all thy getting get understanding.

PROVERBS 4:7

But whoso committeth adultery with a woman lacketh understanding: he that doeth it destroyeth his own soul.

PROVERBS 6:32

Be ye not as the horse, or as the mule, which have no understanding: whose mouth must be held in with bit and bridle, lest they come near unto thee.

PSALM 32:9

Conclusion

This process revealed in Romans 1:21 doesn't work backwards. You must start from the beginning.

Make a conscious decision to glorify God. Place more value on the Lord, what He's said, and what He's done in your life than anything or anyone else. Don't let them even compete!

You can't desire the acclaim of people. You can't be codependent on your spouse, children, or job. You have to get to the place where your love for and commitment to God stands alone. Even if everything else in your life fell apart, you'd still esteem, honor, and place more importance on Him. You can stand on God's Word alone.

Magnify the Lord and make Him bigger. Praise Him, thank Him, and rehearse your victories. Make a conscious effort to minimize the negative, despise the shame, set joy before you, and fix your eyes on the good things God has done. If you'll do this, your imagination will start seeing positive things, and your heart will become sensitized to God. These are the steps you must take. There is no other way to get there. It really is that simple.

This is how God made your heart. It's how He designed you to function. You may not like it. You might want a different way of doing it. But according to His Word, this is how the Lord made you. It's how He set it up.

If you give priority to these things, it'll save your life. If you listen to and follow your heart, you'll walk in supernatural wisdom and peace. God will speak to you about these things, but you must practice what you've learned.

Listen to Your Heart

We have our annual Andrew Wommack Ministries board meeting every January. While I was packing for it last year, I asked the Lord if I had forgotten anything. You might think, "Come on, Andrew, that's why God gave you a brain!" Well, I don't believe it bothers the Lord. I just ask Him to remind me of things.

Personally, I don't use an alarm clock. I just ask the Lord to wake me up. I'm not saying it's wrong for you to use one. I just choose not to because it keeps me listening to God. I make myself live in such a way that I have to be dependent on God. I've gone to bed with only two hours to sleep and had to get up in order to catch an international flight I couldn't miss. I just asked Him to wake me up on time, and He did. You don't have to do this. There are different ways to accomplish the same thing. This is just how I've chosen to do it. But I listen to my heart, and the Lord always wakes me up. I've never missed a flight!

In getting ready for that board meeting, I asked the Lord if there was something else I needed to take. My eyes fell upon a Denver Broncos Super Bowl Champion hat that someone had given to me. I thought to myself, *I bet one of my board members would like that hat.* Believing that was the Lord, I packed it without saying anything to anyone.

After the board meeting, we were all getting ready to leave. I was at my car saying goodbye, when one of my board members who lives in Oregon asked, "Do you know where I can get one of those Broncos hats? I've been wanting one and have tried two or three different places, but I just can't find one."

I replied "Well, I just happen to have one right here" and gave it to him. This just encouraged me, that the Holy Spirit will show us things if we'll listen to our hearts.

I actually believe that's a part of me operating in the gifts of the Spirit. If I can't hear things like that, how am I going to hear God say "There's someone here who's been contemplating suicide" and things like that? Don't just listen to God during your devotions and operate in the flesh the rest of the day. It's not right to compartmentalize your life that way.

What Are You Going to Do?

God will help you do whatever it is you do! He'll make you a better accountant. He'll show you where the errors are and make things work. God will make you a better truck driver. He'll show you when there are obstacles in your path. There isn't anything you can do that you can't do better by being sensitive and listening to God.

We've really messed it up by operating entire parts of our lives carnally. God didn't make us to function that way!

As you start listening to your heart, you'll be amazed by what God will do through you. This isn't the easiest way, but it's the best. You need to get your heart established. It really is that simple!

If you receive these four keys to staying full of God and start implementing them in your daily life, you'll experience a radical transformation. This could change your life forever, but it all depends on what you do with it. What value will you place on what you've learned? Only you can decide!

Receive Jesus as Your Savior

Choosing to receive Jesus Christ as your Lord and Savior is the most important decision you'll ever make!

God's Word promises,

> That if thou shalt confess with thy mouth the Lord Jesus, and shalt believe in thine heart that God hath raised him from the dead, thou shalt be saved.   For with the heart man believeth unto righteousness; and with the mouth confession is made unto salvation.
>
> ROMANS 10:9–10

And,

> For whosoever shall call upon the name of the Lord shall be saved.
>
> ROMANS 10:13

By His grace, God has already done everything to provide salvation. Your part is simply to believe and receive.

Pray out loud, *"Jesus, I confess that You are my Lord and Savior. I believe in my heart that God raised You from the dead. By faith in Your Word, I receive salvation now. Thank You for saving me!"*

The very moment you commit your life to Jesus Christ, the truth of His Word instantly comes to pass in your spirit. Now that you're born again, there's a brand-new you!

Receive the Holy Spirit

As His child, your loving heavenly Father wants to give you the supernatural power you need to live this new life.

>For every one that asketh receiveth; and he that seeketh findeth; and to him that knocketh it shall be opened...If ye...know how to give good gifts unto your children: how much more shall your heavenly Father give the Holy   Spirit to them that ask him?

LUKE 11:10 AND 13

All you have to do is ask, believe, and receive!

Pray, *"Father, I recognize my need for Your power to live this new life. Please fill me with Your Holy Spirit. By faith, I receive it right now! Thank You for baptizing me. Holy Spirit, You are welcome in my life."*

Congratulations! Now you're filled with God's supernatural power. Some syllables from a language you don't recognize will rise up from your heart to your mouth (1 Cor. 14:14). As you speak them out loud by faith, you're releasing God's power from within and building yourself up in the spirit. (1 Cor. 14:4.) You can do this whenever and wherever you like.

It doesn't really matter whether you felt anything or not when you prayed to receive the Lord and His Spirit. If you believed in your heart that you received, then God's Word promises you did. "Therefore I say unto you, What things soever ye desire, when ye pray, believe that ye receive them, and ye shall have them" (Mark 11:24). God always honors His Word; believe it!

Please contact me and let me know that you've prayed to receive Jesus as your Savior or to be filled with the Holy Spirit. I would like to rejoice with you and help you understand more fully what has taken place in your life. I'll send you a free gift that will help you understand and grow in your new relationship with the Lord. Welcome to your new life!

Other Teachings by Andrew Wommack

Spirit, Soul & Body

Understanding the relationship of your spirit, soul, and body is foundational to your Christian life. You will never truly know how much God loves you or believe what His Word says about you until you do. In this series, learn how they're related and how that knowledge will release the life of your spirit into your body and soul. It may even explain why many things are not working the way you had hoped.

Item Code: 1027-C CD album
Item Code: 1027-D DVD album (as recorded from television)
Item Code: 318 Paperback
Item Code: 418 Companion Study Guide

The True Nature of God

Are you confused about the nature of God? Is He the God of judgment found in the Old Testament or the God of mercy and grace found in the New Testament? Andrew's revelation on this subject will set you free and give you a confidence in your relationship with God like never before. This is truly nearly-too-good-to-be-true news.

Item Code: 1002-C CD album
Item Code: 308 Paperback

Living in the Balance of Grace and Faith

This book explains one of the biggest controversies in the church today. Is it grace or faith that releases the power of God? Does God save people in His sovereignty, or does your faith move Him? You may be surprised by the answers as Andrew reveals what the Bible has to say concerning these important questions and more. This will help you receive from God in a greater way and will change the way you relate to Him.

Item Code: 1064-C CD album
Item Code: 1064-D DVD album (as recorded from television)
Item Code: 3208-D DVD album (recorded live)
Item Code: 328 Paperback
Item Code: 428 Companion Study Guide

The Believer's Authority

Like it or not, every one of us is in a spiritual war. You can't be discharged from service, and ignorance of the battlefield only aids the enemy. In war, God is always for us, and the devil is against us; whichever one we cooperate with will win. And there's only one way the enemy can get your cooperation—that's through deception. In this teaching, Andrew exposes this war and the enemy for what he is.

Item Code: 1045-C CD album
Item Code: 1045-D DVD album (as recorded from television)
Item Code: 3205-D DVD album (recorded live)
Item Code: 327 Paperback
Item Code: 427 Companion Study Guide

The Effects of Praise

Every Christian wants a stronger walk with the Lord. But how do you get there? Many don't know the true power of praise. It's essential. Listen as Andrew teaches biblical truths that will not only spark understanding but will help promote spiritual growth so you will experience victory.

Item Code: 1004-C CD album
Item Code: 309 Paperback

God Wants You Well

Health is something everyone wants. Billions of dollars are spent each year trying to retain or restore health. So why does religion tell us that God uses sickness to teach us something? It even tries to make us believe that sickness is a blessing. That's just not true. God wants you well!

Item Code: 1036-C CD album
Item Code: 1036-D DVD album (as recorded from television)
Item Code: 330 Paperback
Item Code: 430 Companion Study Guide

About the Author

For over three decades, Andrew Wommack has traveled America and the world teaching the truth of the Gospel. His profound revelation of the Word of God is taught with clarity and simplicity, emphasizing God's unconditional love and the balance between grace and faith. He reaches millions of people through the daily *Gospel Truth* radio and television programs, broadcast both domestically and internationally. He founded Charis Bible College in 1994 and has since established CBC extension schools in other major cities of America and around the world. Andrew has produced a library of teaching materials, available in print, audio, and visual formats. And, as it has been from the beginning, his ministry continues to distribute free audio materials to those who cannot afford them.